The Rain and the Night

Wilton Sankawulo

MACMILLAN

First published 1979

Published by
Macmillan Education Ltd.
London and Basingstoke
Companies and representatives throughout the world

Published for
Mr. Wilton Sankawulo
Ministry of Information, Cultural Affairs and Tourism
Monrovia
Liberia

ISBN 0 333 25960 2 (Hardback)
    0 333 25961 0 (Paperback)

Printed in Hong Kong

To
Professor Andrew Jolly

He leaped out of the house into the cold, drizzling night and wended his way among cows, goats and sheep that lay on their bellies in the village square, absently chewing the cud. Now he stumbled against a cow, now against a goat or a sheep, and each animal would prance up, blocking his way with its invisible body. Kortuma would bump into the beast, curse under his breath, and push it forcefully aside; then he would continue his journey, simply to run into another one. Normally, he did not fear goats and sheep but cows. To him, the long, pointed horns of a cow meant instant death, and so he never ventured beyond a safe distance from one. But this night, he fearlessly pushed all the animals out of his way alike. It was extremely cold and windy. The sleeveless shirt and the short pants which he wore did nothing to relieve the biting cold. The wind blew him fiercely and rustled the thatched roofs of houses and the foliage of kola trees on the outskirts, presaging doom. His skin grew taut and his movements became stiff.

But Kortuma was scarcely aware of all these things, for he was dumb and disconcerted as he walked in the sloshing mud that was strewn with animal dung, instinctively heading to his own house which stood on a high foundation of packed earth on the eastern edge of the village. He clambered up the dirt stairs. On entering the porch, a group of goats scrambled up in a disorderly fashion, the sound of their clattering hoofs jarring his mind and body. As they jumped into the yard by turns, one of them butted his legs; its sharp, pointed horns cut his left leg slightly. He felt no pain, but the effrontery of the animals piqued him. "You nasty, stinking beasts!" he said, heaving a malevolent sigh. In the confusion of the day, none of his wives had remembered to push the sticks through the gate at the porch entrance in order to ward off animals. Kortuma wrung his hands in frustration, pushed the creaking, scabrous door gently and entered the house. His three wives and daughter who sat on low stools around the fire gazed at him with wide-open eyes.

1

Impulsively, they poked the dying fire with saplings, and blew on it until a saffron blaze danced with animation under the sooty bamboo dryer that hung over the fireplace.

Kortuma latched the door and walked silently into his bedroom. As he was about to sit on the bamboo bed with a mattress made from banana leaves wrapped in several sheets of country cloth and a blanket, severe and alarming knocks on the door which he had just latched assaulted the household most brutally. The knocks came in rapid succession and were animated like the explosion of talking drums in a deep forest. Stepping into pots and pans, kicking firewood about, Kortuma's wives and daughter huddled frantically in the extreme right corner of the central room where the large white, drinking pan sat on a low bamboo bench, a blue cup floating in it. Kortuma rushed to the door, but halted for a moment near the fireplace when a terrified and piercing voice cried out:

"I have remained alone! I have remained alone! Oh, my people, I have remained alone! Gbolokai, why? Why, why have you deceived me? What wrong have I done?"

Glancing at his family over his shoulder as he walked to the door, Kortuma said, "Stand where you are and don't move." The pounding and the wailing subsided. He opened the door and a fat, short woman fell into his arms, clutching his coarse and wet country cloth shirt, her body shuddering with sobs. Warm tears welled up profusely in her eyes and poured on his arms. He stroked the small of her back, saying soothingly, "You are not alone. Kortuma is alive. Lorpu, come to Gwator," he called to his headwife.

Lorpu was already beside him, staring at Gwator with pity. Grabbing her by the shoulders, and pulling her with increasing force, she said:

"Keep quiet. From where will you get money to pay a fine?" She spoke in a sober voice, strongly emphasising each word.

Kortuma pushed Gwator gently until they disengaged. She stopped crying and wiped her face dry with the tip of her lapa. Leaving her with Lorpu, he turned to Korlu, his second wife, and said:

"Call the Master."

"I'll call him," Gwator volunteered and left.

Lorpu returned to the central room and joined the other women who were putting things in order as Kortuma walked into his bedroom, his head bowed in solemn reflection.

He sat on the bed, cupped his chin in his hand, and trained his eyes on a hurricane lantern which was perched on a small wooden

2

table that stood against the wall. The flickering flame in the lantern popped repeatedly. Withdrawn into himself, he was not aware of it. He felt relieved, for the burden had finally descended from his shoulders, though, somehow, the irreparable loss was most unbearable. True, it was a great and personal loss — a part of him was dead — but he felt relieved because the long suspense had ended. Never had he rested for a moment during the long illness of the Chief, an illness which frequently verged on death. At one moment, the Chief would be cheery, full of life, and would saunter to the bank of the Deyn River nearby to exercise his legs and breathe some fresh air. At the next, he would lie prostrate in bed like a corpse. Only his slow, irregular breathing would indicate that he was still alive. He was virtually wasting away! Kortuma could not bear this. He felt that his father should either live or die, for the old Chief was a good man who had no malice against anyone and, therefore, did not deserve such a cruel fate.

Kortuma did not remember making any mistake in serving the river gods, and so he believed that they could not possibly punish his father on that account. He had many years of experience in ministering to the gods and was even considered by some as a Minister, though he was simply deputising for his father. His only concern had been that a blood sacrifice be made for the ailing Chief, for only blood can save blood. He had personally bought an unspotted, white ram for the sacrifice. But the dying Chief had preferred a peace offering so that the gods might receive his spirit with grace. Whatever enemy might have dealt with him so unkindly would reap his just reward.

"Henceforth you are a full Minister of the gods," the Chief had told him on one of his good days. "They stood behind me in the day and in the night. There is nothing bad in my heart against anyone. I want to make peace with them at the end of my life. It has been a good and happy life. May they bless you in the difficult days ahead."

Kortuma had bent forward in his seat, clasped both hands, his forearms resting on his thighs, and stared gravely at his father in the face.

"We want you to live," he had said grimly. "And we want your enemies to die. Let's make a blood sacrifice. If you let your enemies go free, they'll kill all your offspring and relatives. In the mouth of a witch blood is very delicious."

But the Chief had disposed of the rejoinder with the command, "Do as I said, son."

With that, Kortuma had concluded that there was no more hope, for the gods might have revealed to the old Chief the end of his journey. It was not unusual for a dying man to see his own end, while members of his family blindly tried to save his life. Therefore, Kortuma had obediently placed a peace offering of white rice powder on the Deyn River bank, opposite Luen, the home of the gods.

Rising slowly, Kortuma took off his country cloth shirt, wiped the sweat off his body with it and flung it on the bed. He pulled his medical shirt out of a wooden box at the head of the bed, flapped it in the air, and put it on. A baggy country cloth gown, yellow and white striped and bedecked with cowries, it emitted a stale odour. Yet its power was great. Prayers on his lips, Kortuma watched it with satisfaction and brushed it with his hands. It hung to his knees. Opening the door with a little more force than he intended, he went to the central room where his wives and daughter sat around the fire, nonplussed. He looked around the room in a preoccupied fashion, then walked to the door and held it tentatively by the wooden latch. "Stay here and keep the door closed until you hear the Crier," he told them and stepped out carefully, closing the door.

It no longer drizzled, though it was still dark. His mind in utter disarray, Kortuma paced up and down in the yárd, waiting for the Master. He breathed the cold, moist air, the coarse fabric of the medical shirt scratching his unfeeling skin. The air pained his nostrils and constricted his throat. He kept rubbing his nose with his fingers and swallowing in an effort to combat the pain. Squinting his eyes in the dark, he saw some blurred figures approaching him. When the figures came to a close range, he recognised Gwator and the Master. The Master held Gwator by the arms as they staggered towards him. Kortuma surmised that she had broken down again.

"Was she crying?" he asked harshly.

"No," the Master lied. Gwator cast a beseeching look at Kortuma.

"Leave her!" he ordered the Master. "You told the girls about it?" he asked Gwator.

Composing herself and standing erect, Gwator said in a clear voice, "No. I left them sleeping."

"Go and tell them to leave the house at once. The Master and I will soon be there."

Kortuma turned to the Master. Their eyes met briefly. Then, clasping their hands behind them, they stared into space.

"A Master is not God," Kortuma broke the painful silence, bowing his head in distress and taking a few uncertain steps. The Master also bowed his head as if trying to appraise the encouraging remark. "You did your best. Death has no cure," Kortuma added.

Speechless, the Master sighed with resignation, and stamped the muddy soil with one foot. He fastened his stare on the cloudy, black sky and once again on the ground.

"Everyone must answer the Ancestors' call at his appointed time," Kortuma continued in a voice that was becoming unsteady. He cleared his throat. "Everybody knows that you are a great Zoe." He could not determine what effect his words had on the Master. In fact, his voice became so unsteady that he stopped talking altogether.

The Master had performed every known ritual, administered every known herb to the Chief with persistence to the very end. But any keen observer could tell all along that he was fighting a losing battle.

As Kortuma spoke to him, he tinkered with a ram horn that was attached to a leather strap which hung on his left shoulder. Knowing that whatever he told him would only add to his disappointment, Kortuna changed the subject.

"Let's go there and see," he told him. "The girls should be out by now".

As they approached the Chief's house, an outburst of rain suddenly besieged the village and the surrounding forest. The storm blew with a mighty force. It broke boughs and rustled thatched roofs. Loose thatch and leaves flew everywhere. The rain poured in torrents. Lightning flashed repeatedly. At each flash, the village would be bright as day, the thunder would blast, then darkness. Bleating and mooing with alarm, goats, sheep and cows scrambled about in a frenzy, managing to squeeze themselves under the eaves of houses for refuge. But the rainstorm lashed them constantly. As if they had become resigned to their fate, they stopped crying. The rain washed the village, coursing down to the northern outskirts into a swamp cluttered with bamboo bushes.

Dawn came like a sudden explosion of light. A rainbow appeared perilously on the eastern outskirts. Kortuma and the Master spied it now and then as they fought their way through the melee. All this proved to them, beyond doubt, that the Chief had gone. Battered and thoroughly drenched, but paying no attention to their plight, the two men stood before the Chief's house and bowed their heads in reverence. Then with calculated steps, they entered the open door into the dark and stifled central room. Kortuma bent over the fireplace and stirred the ashes with a piece of bamboo splinter until he found several live charcoals. Feeding them with bark he broke off the firewood and with pieces of sapling, he blew on the fire vigorously. First, a large column of smoke filled the room. His eyes watered. Then all of a sudden a blaze of fire shot out and lit the entire room. A mouse bolted out of the bedroom which was opposite the fireplace and got lost in a heap of pots and pans stacked in the extreme left corner of the room. Kortuma stood up and watched the fire awhile as if to make sure it wouldn't go out again.

Meanwhile, the Master planted 'the horn of vengeance' at the front door, though it was no longer needed. It was an antelope horn plaited with black thread, a cowrie fastened to the mouth. Whenever he visited the ailing Chief, he never forgot to plant it somewhere in the house, most often at the front door. The habit had grown on him. With a sudden awareness, he remarked, "What is the use?" and put the horn back into the breast pocket of his medical shirt.

The two men entered the bedroom where they found the Chief lying on his back in a plank bed with a palliasse wrapped in blankets. He was covered with a large sheet of stripy country cloth, his head poking from the bedclothes and resting peacefully on a bunch of clothes. His soft, silvery hair glittered in the light of a white hurricane lantern that sat on a wooden table near the head of the bed, below an open window. His face was pallid and distorted, his eyes closed. Their dripping medical shirts sticking to their skins, Kortuma and the Master observed the Chief carefully. The Master stroked the entire length of the body of the Chief with the back of his right hand, listened to his chest with his left ear, stood up on an impulse and shook his head in disappointment, looking at Kortuma who wore a baffled stare on his face, his arms akimbo; and then looked at the Chief again.

Kortuma ceremoniously raised both arms in the air, threw his head backwards, and spoke in a frenzy:

"You, Gbolokai, were my father. We lived together, toiled together, shared every secret, and . . . and . . . and now you are before the river. May you cross it in peace . . ."

"Wait!" exclaimed the Master. "He shook!" Falling on his knees by the bed, the Master drew the bedclothes down to the Chief's breast. The Chief opened his eyes and turned his head to Kortuma who was now on his knees by the Master and gazing at him with puzzled eyes.

"Is that my son?" Chief Gbolokai asked weakly.

"Yes, " Kortuma said, holding the bedclothes, his hand shaking. The Master was busy adjusting the bedclothes over the Chief's legs.

"Gwator told you that I was dead?" the Chief asked, heaving a sigh, and feebly twitching his wan figure.

"Yes. She said so," Kortuma admitted.

"I knew she would . . . is that the Master?" The Chief watched the Master who was still busy wrapping his legs with the bedclothes.

"Yes," answered the Master.

"Leave us." To Kortuma: "Take a chair." He drew his trembling right hand out of the bedclothes and pointed at a sagging rattan chair that sat in the right corner of the room opposite the head of the bed.

Kortuma drew the creaking chair near the bed, sat down and clasped his hands on his lap, his eyes trained on the Chief. Lying on his right side, the Chief turned to him. He propped his head with his right hand, cleared his throat and spat out a lump of phlegm. The Master walked to the door, paused and looked at the Chief over his shoulder as if awaiting instructions, and then stepped out.

"I must answer the Ancestors' call," Chief Gbolokai began. A cough. "Be strong. Save . . . save the land."

His lips went on moving, forming no words. At length they closed. Then they twitched violently and gasped for breath. It had ceased to rain. Like a search-light, a beam of the morning sun flashed into the room through the open window and landed directly on the Chief's face. Rooted in his seat like a statue, Kortuma fearfully watched the wrinkled face. Pepper birds chirped with glee and fluttered their wings in the kola trees behind the house. Kortuma could not bear the agonising distortion of the old Chief's face, the painful writhing, and the final bout of effort that forced his pallid eyes open. The Chief forcefully gasped again as if the last vestige of breath was suddenly snapped from him. Then his eyes closed in peaceful repose. With a sudden jerk, he lay quietly in the bed. Chief Gbolokai's long and arduous journey had ended.

Kortuma watched the gaunt, stiff body which looked like a figure carved from wood. Unexpectedly, the Chief opened his eyes once again, eyes that were filled with a great light like the last brilliant flare of a dying sun. Then they closed and did not open again.

As the rainstorm had raged all night, the Crier believed that at least one of his traps should have caught a deer. For, during a rainstorm, animals, in a bid to find refuge, run at random in the bush, dodging boughs that fall from giant trees. Consequently, they are liable to be trapped. Like many a trapper, the Crier usually prayed for rain when he set his traps. As the rain pelted down on the crisp, black thatch all through the night, he had lain awake and restless, anxiously watching for the first sign of daylight through holes in the thatched roof which was roughly tied with rattan ropes to lolo rafters.

On hearing pepper birds and wrens squeak and chirp in the briery bushes behind the house, the Crier quickly rose from bed, donned his tattered hunting clothes, took his hunting knife and bag, and shook his wife briefly.

"I'm going to the bush," he said. But the woman only stretched and groaned. Meanwhile, a rooster crowed. It became clear to him that day had broken. Giving up further attempts to wake his sleeping wife, he hung his hunting bag on his left shoulder, and departed for the bush.

The village was strewn with squelching mud, puddles, clusters of foliage and thatch which the rainstorm had left in its wake. Pale, blue smoke shot out of the roofs of houses, indicating that housewives were preparing hot baths for themselves and their families. The kola trees around the village looked battered, the storm having ripped off many of their branches; yet they swayed gently in the soft morning breeze like heroes who, having lost the war, remained undefeated. Floating hawks decked the foggy horizon, bathing in the tender sunshine that began to appear.

The Crier made for the river, beyond which he had set more than a dozen powerful deer traps. As he approached the outskirts, he took a last look at the village. Women and children were now in the square. The women carried empty zinc buckets in the crooks of their left arms and hurriedly retied their lapa around their waists, greeting each other cheerfully. The children hauled clusters of foliage and thatch towards the outskirts, shouting, giggling, and running.

Much to his surprise, the Crier saw Kortuma going to his house. The son of the Chief was dressed in medical clothes, his head bowed, his hands clasped behind his back. Growing suspicious, the Crier went to him at a trot.

"What has happened?" he enquired, gazing at Kortuma with concern.

"The Chief has died," Kortuma blurted out the tragic news.

The Crier's jaws fell, his leathery, creased face grew long. Crestfallen, he went back into his house. His wife who had woken and was on her knees by the fireplace, hitching firewood together and blowing on it frantically, was surprised to see him back so soon.

"Why," she said, "have you decided to stay?"

Without saying a word, the Crier went into the stuffy, dark bedroom, laid his hunting knife and bag on a small wooden table that stood near the head of the bed, and went out, his hands clasped behind him; stooping, he walked slowly and declared in a sonorous voice:

"Prick up your ears! Chief Gbolokai has gone to look for herbs!" There was a tremor in his voice despite his effort to sound natural. He stopped before each house and repeatedly declared his solemn, dismal message for everyone to get it with the utmost clarity.

Wailing broke out in the village. Struck with stupefaction and grief, men, women and children ran out of their houses in disarray, crying. Kortuma, still numb and perplexed, stared about absently as if what was happening did not concern him. He listened to the Crier awhile and then went to the Master's house that was located on the southern outskirts.

The porch of the Master's house was stockaded with sticks to ward off goats and sheep. In spite of the stockade, goat and sheep dung was found all over the porch. Kortuma could not understand the unruly and disturbing attitudes of animals. He pushed the sticks to one side and knocked on the door, calling out his own name.

"Who's that?" cried the Master's wife in a high-pitched voice. From the sharp and harsh tone of her voice, Kortuma realised that she was frightened.

"I'm no ghost," he said aloud. "Open the door!"

"Oh, Kortuma!" Yata exclaimed with reassurance, opening the door. Bending double, she held her lapa which was tied loosely on her waist, her bare breasts dangling. "Come in," she said, spying the frenzied crowd in the square. She started shaking all over, her eyes bulging out in alarm. Tying her lapa firmly, she returned to the fireplace and resumed building the fire. "It's dark in here," she apologised, trying to sound normal; yet her voice broke, betraying her agitation. "Let me make the fire — Gayflor is in the bedroom." She pointed at the bedroom door. Kortuma judged that she resented the intrusion, even though she spoke like one who was resigned to the fate of a Master's wife. After she struggled briefly with the fire, it blazed and lighted the central room. Kortuma glanced around, seeing nothing except a bamboo bed that was placed on four forked posts behind the fireplace, on which the Master's daughter, a girl of five or six, slept peacefully.

Knocking on the bedroom door four times, Kortuma stood still and listened. He heard murmurs, groans, and whispers in the bedroom. Then a long silence. Heavy breathing. Hissing sounds. Finger snaps. Silence. Another knock, and the Master opened the door.

"Oh, Kortuma!" he exclaimed. "Come in! How is he?" All the Master wore was a pair of black short pants. He looked withdrawn.

The rancid odour of the room blew in Kortuma's face. It had made him retch the first time he had entered there, but now he wasn't aware of it. He watched a red hurricane lantern with a high flame on a wooden box near the head of the bed; it emitted a column of thick, black smoke which streaked the wall with soot. The Master's medicines were scattered all over the floor: horns plaited with black and white thread; chunks of medicines that looked like black soap bars plastered with cowries; tiny gourds; pieces of iron; red kola nuts; a small porcelain plate with white powder; assorted feathers tied in a bunch; several strips of black and red cloth; a piece of carving that depicted the distorted face of some unusual creature; and a piece of rod. These gave the room an ominous atmosphere that could frighten the non-initiate. Kortuma sat in a rattan chair at the foot of the bed, looked aside as the Master gazed at him grimly, and said:

"The Chief has gone to look for herbs."

The Master grew calm and sober. He carefully put his medicines back in a raffia bag which he pulled from under the bed, put on a shirt, and walked silently out of the house, Kortuma following him.

"I ordered the Crier to announce it," he said behind the Master's back. Apparently the Master did not hear him or care to hear him, for he continued walking with slow, determined steps to the square.

Kortuma paused on the porch and looked at the Master's wife over his shoulder. He opened his mouth and closed it almost at once without saying a word. Yata stood in the doorway, waiting for him to say the word that would break the suspense. But it was the Crier who broke it. Presently he walked past the house, declaring his sad message. Desperate and extremely shocked, the woman beat her breast and lap and was about to cry out with alarm, but Kortuma looked at her with disapproval. Thereupon, she suppressed the wail, calmed down, and began putting more wood onto the fire that was already blazing. Then she packed her pots and pans in a corner of the room, and adjusted the bedclothes over her daughter, trembling all the while. The girl stretched and woke up when several tears fell on her face. Sitting up, she grasped her mother's hands, and stared fearfully into her face.

Kortuma went to the Chief's house where he met the Master

standing among women and children who were crying and reeling in the muddy yard, smearing themselves with mud, beating their breasts, slapping their thighs, stamping their feet, and tearing their hair. Some raised their hands to the sky in supplication to the Supreme Being, Kunuunamui, Allah, the Saviour, who had power over life and death. Some pressed their hands on their heads — fingers interlocked — and twisted their bodies sideways in anger and resentment. A group of men stood at a distance and watched the wailing crowd with solemn faces. Kortuma hushed the wailers and told them to leave. He ordered the men who gathered around him to clear the bush behind the Chief's house.

He and the Master entered the house. Cooking utensils and fire-wood were scattered about the dark central room as if a fight had occurred there. They bravely entered the bedroom which was still full of light — the birds still sang in the kola trees behind the house.

Kortuma stood about a yard from the deathbed while the Master examined the corpse, whispering incantations. At length he removed the bedclothes from the Chief's pale face and scrutinised the tired, sunken eyes, the broad forehead, and the soft, white hair. Soon he abandoned the effort, stood up and said:

"He wasn't that old," heaving a sigh.

"No," Kortuma agreed, "but the Ancestors wanted him to rest from his earthly toils."

"We must honour him right away."

"Sure, we must."

Walking to the bed, Kortuma bent down and took a close look at the corpse. The Master drew the bedclothes over the Chief's face after Kortuma's brief inspection. The two men then went behind the house to inspect the clearing of the bush.

"Make haste!" the Master ordered the men who were clearing the bush. "We have to honour him right away!" Kortuma left the Master with the men and went to his house.

He met his family paralysed with grief. They assaulted him with sobs when he stepped on the threshold. But he hushed them and went into his bedroom.

Judging that only his highest, prized possession would render justice to the fallen leader, he decided to bury his father in the "Shirt of Honour", the highest military prize in the land. Chief Gbolokai had conferred it upon him after he had led a successful campaign in a war with the Zorkwelle, the most elusive and dangerous warriors he had ever fought. Kortuma pulled the Shirt from a raffia rope behind the bed. Stained yellow, plastered with cowries, and made of coarse fabric, it resembled a medical shirt. He grasped it fondly and pressed it to his chest like a lover he had met again after years of separation. Then he shook it in the air to get rid of as much dust as possible. He had last worn it five years ago during a celebration marking the end of a session of the Poro Society. Because it was forbidden to wash it, since this would diminish its power, it had gathered dust and mildew.

Kortuma took the Shirt and a sheet of new white country cloth to the men behind the Chief's house. They had cleared a large, circular area, enclosed it in a blind of palm fronds, and brought in the body of the Chief. Chief Gbolokai lay on a newly made bamboo bed. Four Elders, who were prominent leaders of the Poro Society, and the Master were bathing him with herb water. The other men stood and watched. Kortuma gave the Shirt and the country cloth to one of them.

Soon the men completed their job. Well dressed in the Shirt of Honour, lying on another new bamboo bed and covered with the white country cloth, Chief Gbolokai was prepared for his last journey that would take him to the palaver house and then to the cemetery on the river bank.

Kortuma and the Master hurried to the palaver house where the Chief would lie in state. The sun was growing dim, black clouds gathered in the sky — the wind blew, the lightning flashed. It began to drizzle again.

Looking up in the sky, the Master said, "It'll rain for a while. Your father was a great Chief. Even the weather is mourning his loss."

"Since last night the weather has been mourning him," Kortuma agreed. "He loved the land. Only love makes one great. His last words to me were all about the land: 'Save the land,' he said — those were his last words."

"He was also a great warrior," the Master continued. "Only old age and sickness made the Gola take advantage of him."

"I'm sure he was thinking about them when he instructed me to save the land. The Gola are no threat. They know how to sing and dance but they don't know how to fight. I don't know why he worried about them when we are perfectly safe."

"As he came to the end of his journey, he became more and more convinced that war does not solve problems. Whether you win or lose, you are defeated anyway. That's why he became so compromising towards the end."

They walked into the palaver house. It was swept clean, several

12

rattan chairs placed in it. The wind blew in the drizzle which was gradually turning to rain. "I'm sure the rain will not be that heavy," Kortuma said. As if in contempt of his statement, it began to rain in earnest.

"It'll soon stop," said the Master, looking at the rain and adjusting his shirt.

They drew two chairs close together and sat down. Surprisingly, a goat jumped into the palaver house and stood right before the two men. As if shocked by its own affront, the animal bolted to the opposite end of the palaver house and ensconced itself in the corner to the right of the men. Kortuma rose with indignation and sat down, looked right and left in search of a man to catch the goat. But the overwhelming downpour did not permit anyone to be outside.

"It's hard to forgive this kind of affront," he said under his breath, clenching his teeth. "If some young men were around, they could kill it for the feast."

With swinging arms and a harsh expletive, the Master drove the goat out. Returning to his seat, he said:

"Animals are lawless. They are our soup, so they can die at any time. That's why they don't care about laws."

Looking at the rain once again, Kortuma recalled with pride that water was a symbol of honour. "The Ancestors are honouring him," he said. "Of course, the rain could also mean that he is crying, but he was not the kind of man to entertain tears." He crossed his legs, leaned back in his chair, and gazed towards the Chief's house. But the rain blurred his view.

"What rain!" cried the Master, looking out. "I hope the Elders are in control of things."

"There's a new, undaubed house with a roof near them. I'm sure they have taken him there."

· After a time, the rain stopped abruptly, as the Master had predicted. The sun came out again. Shortly after the sun came, Kortuma and the Master saw the Elders accompanying the corpse to the palaver house. Four strapping middle-aged men of equal height shouldered each corner of Chief Gbolokai's bed. When they entered the palaver house, Kortuma and the Master stood up in reverence, gazing solemnly at the corpse. The men placed the bed in the centre of the palaver house. The Chief, who used to be a huge man of towering height, looked like a tiny piece of log. Two Elders, fly swatters in hand, sat on low stools at the foot and head of the bed and drove flies off the corpse.

The villagers gathered in the square. A few wailing voices

sounded, but were soon drowned in songs and drum beats. The funeral dance which should last at least four days had begun. Leaving the Elders and the Master by the corpse to commence the vigil, Kortuma went to his house.

He ran into the players on the way. They danced around him, several young girls wiping his face and neck with headties which they whisked off their heads. Gently raising his arms, he stopped the dance, thanked the players for their kindness and promised them two demi-johns of rum which he had wisely put away when the Chief's sickness worsened. He ordered two men to follow him to his house to get them.

The dancing continued all day and all night. Because of the enthusiasm of the players, Kortuma postponed the burial till the next morning. He had wished to bury his father at sundown the very day on which he died because the sickness had ravaged him. But he judged that one more day would not make much difference.

The ceremony was simple. Early the next morning, mist still hanging in the sky, the Chief was taken to the river bank where a grave had been dug for him. Kortuma, the Master, the village Elders, and a large crowd of players accompanied him on his last journey. Except the players, everyone walked with solemn, calculated steps to the grave in the cold morning breeze. The river roared, birds cried in the surrounding bushes.

Upon reaching the grave, the men placed their precious burden on top of the red earth dug from the grave. Two grave diggers, dressed in tattered pants and soiled with red dirt, immediately jumped into the grave and were handed the body of the Chief amidst blasts of musket. They laid him gracefully in the grave.

Around the grave and back in the village, players sang and danced. Drums thundered.

2

After the Chief was buried, everything turned gloomy for Kortuma: a heavy weight settled all over his body; severe pain and grief descended upon him, and he felt lost and lonely as nearly everyone abandoned him and went his own way to cope with the tragedy. A large sheet of black-and-white-striped country cloth slung over his shoulder, he dragged himself about the village, perplexed. Tears flowed profusely out of his large bloodshot eyes; he blew his nose repeatedly and wiped the tears with his palms. He thought his last grip on life was gone. The harrowing fact that it was *his* father who had actually *died* and been *buried,* and would never be seen again, except in a dream or vision, left him thoroughly broken.

Members of his family and the village Elders gathered around him and fruitlessly reasoned with him to conduct himself like a man.

"The old Chief did his lifework with honour and courage," said Gbada, a reputable sage who had lost an eye in a battle with the Gola long ago. A painful look on his creased, leathery face and dressed in tattered clothes, Gbada continued in a companionable voice, "Now it is your turn to be brave, for you must complete his unfinished task. If you fall, everyone will fall." As Gbada spoke, he touched Kortuma by the shoulder and gazed solemnly in his face.

Though many voices spoke to Kortuma as he walked to the river in the gathering dusk, Gbada's voice stood out clearly above the others and touched him deeply. Here was a man with one foot in the grave appealing to him to accept death as a fact of life! But the wound was so fresh and painful that no words of reason could assuage it. Kortuma's mind helplessly dwelled on his father. While the Chief was not buried, Kortuma could not imagine that he was actually dead and would soon be out of his reach and sight. How could he die? Someone who was a part of him! Someone without whom the sun, the stars, and the moon would refuse to shine! But with his burial, the Chief was now lost beyond rescue. Everything in and around the village — the people, the houses, the very ground on

15

which he walked and the river that roared in the forbidden jungle — all reminded him of the Chief. He scarcely ate. Even when his wives prepared his favourite dish which was rice and cassava leaves boiled with dry meat and palm oil, Kortuma would only eat a piece of meat and several spoonfuls of rice and soup. Then he would drink a great deal of palm wine which old Sumo, a reputable Elder, brought him each evening. Afterwards he would go to bed alone, and sleep without waking until the next morning.

Kortuma conducted himself in this fashion for the entire four days that had to elapse before 'killing the chicken' and 'pounding the sand' for Chief Gbolokai. After numerous unsuccessful attempts to rouse him out of depression, his wives resigned themselves to his state. In order to avoid worsening his condition, they refrained from crying and talking excessively loudly when he was around.

Early in the morning on the fourth day after the burial of the Chief, the Master, dressed in medical clothes and looking solemn, called on Kortuma who was still in bed. Kortuma's three wives who slept together on a large bamboo bed in the central room, and his daughter who slept on a mat by the fireplace in the same room, were busy building a fire to heat his bath. The Master greeted them briefly and went into the bedroom.

On hearing the room door screech open, Kortuma rose and sat in the bed. Thinking that it was one of his wives who had entered the room, he said:

"Is my bath ready?"

"It's I," said the Master. Opening the window, the Master sat in a chair near the head of the bed. He rose again and closed the window as no light poured into the room.

Yawning and twitching uneasily in the bed, Kortuma said, "Where have you been? I haven't laid my eyes on you for days!"

"You have not been your real self," the Master whispered. After a long pause, he added in a loud voice, "That's why you haven't seen me. But I've found out the cause of your trouble." Clasping his hands and leaning forward, his arms resting on his thighs, he said, again in a whisper, "Well, we got confused! You should have confessed any serious connection you had with the Chief just before he was buried. Not even his headwife made a confession! In fact, the proper burial ceremonies were not performed. I don't know why the Chief's death made everybody so confused and so disorganised. Perhaps nobody expected him to ever die . . . well, that's over now. I've found out that the Chief's head and your head are going in the same direction." The Master stopped talking for Kortuma to feel the weight of the revelation. He closed the room door and, returning to his seat, continued, "The ties between you and him must be broken. Otherwise, he will carry you."

Kortuma grew sober. The incredible revelation unnerved him. He could not deny it; neither could he argue it away, because a Master had admitted it. Arms folded on his lap, he gazed silently at the room door, a jumble of ideas racing about his mind. He was fully aware of his close affinity with his father during the Chief's lifetime. For the many years he had lived with the Chief, he had absorbed all his thoughts, idiosyncracies, and his hunting hobby. As it had to be, they shared the same taboos: snakes, leopards, goats, snails. Like his father, if he happened to eat any of these creatures, or even touch them, boils and rashes would grow all over his body. He resembled the Chief in appearance and behaviour; everyone admitted that he was his father's direct replica. These facts caused him to shudder with fear. Fear for his life and fear for the future of the land which had been entrusted to his care. A bitter taste welled up in his mouth.

"I don't understand it," he declared after a long silence, and spat out. "How could he wish to carry me after instructing me to save the land? If anything, he should be my guiding spirit in the world beyond." He sighed and said, "Whatever you can do to break the ties, do it." Then he stood up and put on a pair of black short pants and a baggy, white shirt.

Meanwhile, Lorpu, bent double out of respect for the gentlemen, and gripping her knees with her hands, poked her head into the room and said, "Are you ready to bathe?" She spoke in a quiet voice, momentarily scratching her black and white headtie as she waited for Kortuma's reply.

"No, no," Kortuma said curtly and closed the room door. "Do your duty," he instructed the Master.

Taking a small black object out of his pocket, the Master gave it to Kortuma. "Put it in your pocket," he said. "And remember to take it with you wherever you go."

When Kortuma put the medicine into his side pocket, a wave of relief and reassurance came upon him. The cause of his intense depression seemed to have been discovered and completely uprooted.

"Does it have any laws?" he enquired.

"No," said the Master, "only the general law for all important medicines: wash your hands thoroughly with soap and water after handling a lime before you touch it."

Kortuma suddenly became aware of the urgent task before him, a task that required immediate and undivided attention: to 'kill the chicken' and 'pound the sand' for his deceased father. He grew anxious on realising that this task must be performed before sunrise. Something in him warned him against having any more dealing with the dead Chief. But how would he live with himself if he failed to perform this sacred rite? It was a rite ordained by the Ancestors and nobody can safely ignore it. As the pepper birds, the true harbingers of dawn, made no sound in the bushes behind the house, he gathered that dawn had not yet arrived, though roosters crowed everywhere in the village. His suspicion was quite correct, for when he impulsively pulled the piece of stick out of the rattan loop that served as a lock for the square bamboo window, and pushed the window aside, he only scanned the black night. He thought he heard drums and voices in the distance.

Heaving a sigh, he said, "Ah, so the play has commenced. Ah, you were right; I've been living in a different world. Since when have they started playing?" He said all this to the Master in the same breath while fumbling his side pocket for the charm. There was a tense expression on his face, but it quickly disappeared when he touched the soft contrivance. He sighed deeply and drew his large, black, wooden box from under the bed.

Arms akimbo, the Master stood near the room door, watching.

"Players, masked dancers, Chiefs, Zoes and people from every corner of the Chiefdom are here to honour Chief Gbolokai," said the Master. "They called here several times during the night, but you had either gone to some unknown place or were sleeping."

"If you had not come to my rescue, there would have been another corpse to bury."

"Nonsense," said the Master. "I will stand by you the same way I stood by your father. He saved my life. And while I am with you, you can rest assured that all will be well."

"Well, I trust no other Zoe more than you. As I told you before, a medicine man is not greater than God. And what God has ordained must happen. He alone can change the night into day, and it would be foolish to lose your sleep because the day is taking long to come. I have full confidence in you. You, too, have saved my life, and I am eternally indebted to you."

Meanwhile, Kortuma groped in the box for a well made gown with the usual black and white horizontal stripes. Upon discovering it, he put it on. The gown had a cone-shaped pocket with beautiful, golden embroidery that depicted a plucked fowl. Recalling with relish and pride the occasion on which he had acquired it, he gracefully adjusted it on his body, inhaled its stale odour, and repeatedly glanced at the embroidery. The gown was specially made for Chief Gbolokai and was presented to him several years before by the people of Lorla Clan when the Chief paid them an official visit.

The matter which had demanded the Chief's presence in Lorla concerned a man of Saamai who had carelessly exposed some secrets of the Poro to his girl friend during a moment of ecstasy when he was under the influence of palm wine. After the local authorities had thoroughly investigated the offence against the tribe, a verdict of guilty was passed, but Chief Gbolokai had to confirm it before the offender was executed. During a short welcome ceremony in the palaver house in Digei, the Capital of the Clan, Clan Chief Porkpaa had presented the gown to Chief Gbolokai, who, in turn, presented it to Kortuma.

"He is now your Chief," Gboloaki had declared in jest to the roaring laughter of his excited audience. "These old bones of mine will soon be laid to rest."

Kortuma had accepted the gown with a smile, completely taken aback by his father's jest. Now the prophecy was fulfilled, though he felt that he was the same man and Gbolokai was still the real Chief. The royal regalia, however, gave him a commanding presence and some reassurance. He took the next symbol of power which his father had also passed onto him: a black cowtail which hung on a piece of sapling that was nailed to the wall at the head of the bed. His father had passed it to him when the Chief could no longer preside over court cases due to illness. Kortuma remembered the old Chief's dexterity in wielding the cowtail when dismissing a case, or passing a judgment, or emphasising a point. When Clan Chief Porkpaa related to him the findings of the investigators at the Assembly of Elders, Zoes, and men of the Poro Society, Chief Gbolokai had stood up with force, waved the cowtail in the air authoritatively, and declared that the judgment was upheld — the offender must die. There was no comment. The Assembly simply murmured and began dispersing slowly while the executioners tied up the offender.

The Master beside him, Kortuma hurried out to the yard with determined steps. As it was dark and misty, they only saw vaguely the thatched mud houses; the meandering goats, sheep, and cows; the giant beleh, palm, and kola trees on the outskirts which made a circular, shadowy mass around the village. The two men walked swiftly towards the outskirts, their splayed feet padding over the

19

loose white sand that covered Kortuma's yard and stretched all the way to the outskirts. They suddenly came to a halt when an explosion of drums and voices assaulted them near the outskirts under a huge kola tree with thick foliage shaking gently in the cold morning breeze. Accompanied by the sporadic sound of a horn, the song was apparently for a Gbetu, an acrobatic masked dancer with raffia skirts and a large conical head upon which stood a long, wrinkled neck with a miniature head of its own. The rapid drum beats and the crisp rhythm of the chorus responses reverberated in every nerve and fibre of the two men. The joyous sounds grew louder and more animated and drifted towards Kortuma's house, evidently to wake him up and pay him homage.

"Suppose we receive them first?" suggested the Master.

But this matter on hand must be attended to before sunrise by all means, and so Kortuma turned down the suggestion and ordered the Master with a gesture of his right arm to follow him. They resumed their journey with wide strides and were soon at the grave site in the shadow of kola trees. It was surrounded by a group of men who had already covered it with white sand collected from the river bank and stuck flat pieces of rock around it. As a greeting to the approaching sunrise, wrens and pepper birds chirped and squeaked in the surrounding bushes. Kortuma stood erect at the head of the grave, the flowing robe covering his arms down to the wrists.

"Gbolokai was my father," he began in a clear, impassioned voice. "Now that he stands before the River, we have come to speed him on his way to the place of truth. He outlived nearly all his relatives, so there is no nephew of his to give the words of blessing. But this cannot prevent the sacred rite from taking place . . ."

"Certainly not," cut in a voice.

"I am his nephew," declared Gbada who had had close ties of various sorts with the fallen leader. A white rooster under his left arm, he stood by Kortuma.

Gbada's intervention touched Kortuma. This spontaneous act of the old, decrepit Elder conclusively proved that his father would live in the memories of many people for years to come. Gbada was about to relate the many generous deeds which the deceased Chief had done for him, but Kortuma interrupted him with a gentle wave of the cowtail.

"Men," he said, "the sun will soon be here. What is your opinion on the matter?"

Meanwhile, Korlibaa the Hunter, musket in hand, walked to the soft grasses west of the grave and commenced a struggle with the gun. In a moment there was a loud blast that echoed down the river, the resultant smoke twirling over the heads of the men and spreading in thin waves over the bushes until it disappeared in mid-air.

"Let Korlibaa give the words of blessing," a voice cried out.

"Is this our word?" Kortuma said, but there was no reply.

All eyes were trained on Gbada who stepped forward, frantically pressed the wings of the chicken together and placed them under his left foot while the poor creature fought in agony and cawed with alarm. Then he grasped it by the head, put the legs under his right foot, and began plucking its neck. In a matter of seconds he took out a knife with a crude, black, wooden handle and a sharp, curved blade from his side pocket and cut the neck of the chicken to the bone. The blood gushed out and before much of it could splash in the grass, he took the chicken by the head and wings and gently waved it all over the grave, sprinkling the white sand with the blood. The chicken initially struggled fiercely in his hand, but was suddenly overpowered by lassitude. It gave one last fitful jerk and was dead. Gbada laid it on one of the jutting pieces of flat rock at the head of the grave. Standing up and looking with a fixed gaze into the sky, he raised both arms in the air and made the following remarks to the deceased:

"Gbolokai, farewell. May you cross the River in peace and be well received by the Ancestors in Dornya-taa. You took good care of us: you performed rituals, made sacrifices, and even risked your life in numerous battles for the land; you loved and respected all sons and daughters of Fuama, and you were kind to all of us. May the Ancestors give you your full and just reward. As you pass from labour to reward, watch over us with eyes of grace and benediction. Let the darkness stay behind us, and before us let there be light. Protect us from pestilence and all disasters. When we plant rice, vegetables, and life-trees, let them grow and bear fruits in abundance. Let no tool or weapon make the slightest wound on a son or daughter of the land. Do not appear to us in the day or in the night, and when we dream of you, let the dream bring forth good luck. Shower us with blessings, increase the children of Fuama and give them good health. Take our greetings and best wishes to the Ancestors, and guide us in our feeble attempts to serve them. Let prosperity and peace reign in the land. May we defeat our enemies in every battle. Prolong our lives and give us strength to work hard for survival and to defend ourselves against wild beasts which live either on the land or in the water. Life is short and its sorrows are

21

many, but there is joy. So give us joy that we may be able to bear life. If we err in making our sacrifices or paying our tributes to you or to the Ancestors, let our errors be forgiven; for the reckless, erratic, and stubborn child is still dear to its parents. Though you lived with us, worked with us, and played with us, do not interfere directly or indirectly with our day-to-day life so that we may not experience mishaps or fear. Let Kortuma be as great as you were so that every creature will tremble at his word and presence; and let his hands be strong enough to save the land. Gbolokai, it's hard to say goodbye, but let this be our farewell. Whatever I have said, whether right or wrong, whether true or false, may it be acceptable to you and the Ancestors."

"Let it be so," everyone declared.

Gbada, who was not known for making utterances at grave sites, succeeded in moving his audience out of gloom and despair. Each pair of eyes lit up, and the men engaged in lively conversations as they picked up their ragged shirts and singlets from the surrounding bushes where they were placed while the ritual was in progress.

"This is one thing you can be sure of," said Kpenkpa, a slim Elder with a cluster of red teeth. "We will all go one by one like this."

"If only God had given man a cure for death!" declared Dogbakoli, a young man of medium height who sacrificed a white ram each year upon the advice of an unscrupulous Zoe in order to save himself from death. He usually sought the ram at all costs throughout the entire Chiefdom, and he was prepared to pay any price demanded of him. As he was known for this habit, owners of white rams took advantage of it and charged excessively for their rams. Of course this drained his meagre resources and caused confusion between him and his wife who openly told him that he would die anyway in spite of the sacrifices.

"I don't know why we always worry about death," a voice said from among the group of men. "Man is nothing. So it doesn't matter whether we live or die, but that we do the will of our Ancestors so that in the end our spirits may join them on the other side of the River."

The conversation continued in this vein until the men reached the outskirts, each person reflecting on the meaning of death and defining its role in life. Some said it was a natural deterrent to pride. Possessions, good looks, power and influence often inflate man with pride and cause him to despise his fellow man. But death always intervenes as a corrective for this false egotism. Some considered death as a natural occurrence which was to be expected. As each day had a morning and an evening, life too had its morning and its evening, and these corresponded to birth and death. But death was not conclusive, for it released man's vitality so as to enrich the earth which in turn provided sustenance for scores of God's creatures; consequently, life was the beginning of death, and death the beginning of life. Others maintained that death was merely a transition from one form of existence to another. The spirit of man gets tired of living in the flesh, which is imperfect and limited in many ways; therefore, the spirit eventually takes flight from the flesh to the world beyond in order to assume a perfect mode of existence. Finally, some believed that life was a gift from God and God had the right to take it away whenever he pleased.

Gbada who had been listening to these remarks without interest or comment (perhaps because it would not matter, now that he was close to death), cut into the conversation with a trifling down-to-earth remark: "Gbolokai and I will have a grand feast today." Beaming with a broad smile, the skin around his eyes wrinkling, he weighed the dead chicken in his hand. Several men laughed in guttural voices at his unpretentious remark, for it was clear to them that he would eat nearly all of the chicken, offering only a token piece of it to the spirit of the deceased. Only a very old and brave man, as he was, could venture to eat a sacrificial chicken which must be shared with the spirit of the dead. For one who ate with the dead ran the risk of sudden death if he harboured hate or jealousy in his heart against anyone, or if he engaged in witchcraft. Old as he was, he was supposed to be beyond such things, for what more would he want from life! And so his understatement was simply a curiosity and could only arouse laughter.

The sun had come out in full, bringing the jungle to life: the cries of Blue Wings, palm birds, and Fong now mingled with those of wrens and pepper birds. The animals in the village were now grazing on the outskirts and uttering sporadic, moaning cries, while chickens chased crickets and bugs everywhere. Children ran about, shouting with innocent glee, and women hurried to the river, greeting each other with repressed laughter, zinc buckets swinging and creaking in the crooks of their left arms. They loosened their lapa and retied them more firmly.

As the men took leave of him and went to their houses, Kortuma hurried to his own house where he found Lorpu standing on the threshold. Dressed only in a headtie and a lapa, she held the doorframe with one hand, with the other she slapped her back and breast, looking in and out of the house in a preoccupied fashion.

Climbing the dirt stairs with heavy steps, Kortuma asked her, "Anything?" She wore a sullen and fearful expression on her face. Without replying, Lorpu only made a curt remark to her daughter and to the other women: "We'll soon be back," beckoning Kortuma.

They went to Gbolokai's house where Kortuma found, to his amazement, all the Chief's widows, except the headwife, sitting dejectedly on low stools in the central room. He and Lorpu walked with caution past them and went into the Chief's bedroom. Kortuma's heart missed a beat. Lorpu opened the window and a wave of sunlight poured into the room.

"She's been like this since this morning," she said as she bent over the figure lying prostrate in the bed. She removed the bedclothes from the figure. Kortuma recognised Gwator. She breathed slowly, her eyes closed. Without saying a word, he went for the Master who, upon closely examining her, said, "This is to be expected." He wiped the sweat from his face with his forearm and continued: "As you know, she was at his side throughout his illness; and so she might have had an unpleasant dream about him."

The Master ran to the outskirts for herbs, and was back in no time with an assortment of old and young leaves which he put in a bucket of cold water and rubbed briskly with his hands. The herb water foamed like soap water. Murmuring incantations, the Master rubbed some of it on his own face, then sprinkled some on Gwator's face. She showed no sign of wakening. It was when the Master rubbed her breast vigorously with the herb water that her face cringed; heaving a deep sigh, she shook her head sideways and managed to open her eyes. Unsatisfied with her progress, the Master forced her lips open, scooped a handful of herb water, and poured it into her mouth. She spluttered out the water, but some of it managed to find its way into her throat and she swallowed it with difficulty. She tried to speak, but her lips only shook briefly, forming no words. All of a sudden, Gwator sat up and looked about in bewilderment as if she had unexpectedly found herself in a strange land.

"Lie down," the Master told her. Holding her left shoulder with his left hand, he pushed her gently with his right hand and eased her onto the bed. "Keep quiet," he said. "You'll soon be all right. Nothing will happen to you." Then he told Lorpu, who stood fearfully by the bed, to stay with her while he and Kortuma stepped out.

Kortuma felt that since the Chief must be subject to many unexpected and strange experiences of this kind, he should not allow any one incident to overwhelm him. He had learnt this from Chief Gbolokai who could pass a death sentence with the casual waving of the cowtail as if it were nothing important. Of course, Kortuma had the unwavering, callous spirit of the warrior, but he knew that war was an entirely different matter which made individuals do incredible deeds of cruelty without the slightest qualm of conscience. It was strange to see a man who could spear another man to death at war, but was completely incapable of mustering the courage to kill a fly with his own hand. Thus, with the assurance that his father would not have done otherwise, Kortuma wilfully cast the incident with Gwator out of his mind and absolutely refused to allow it to make unreasonable demands on him. In fact, such an incident was to be expected as the Master had said. For some time after a death had occurred in a family, members of the bereaved family (especially the women) repeatedly reported that they had seen the deceased on the farm, at a dance, on a road, or in their dreams.

Kortuma fingered the charm in his pocket.

"Well, we'll see in the evening," he told the Master as they parted in the centre of the square. Before he had taken half a dozen steps, Kortuma called to him, "Look, I want you to wash the women."

"No problem," the Master said. "Whichever you prefer: I could wash them as you said, or simply plant horns at the doors."

"Wash them, for I am sure the sickness will spread to the others. They need the cure and not merely the prevention."

It was not long after Kortuma went to his house and sat in a creaking rattan chair to relax that the players called on him. Evidently they had decided to rest and gather strength until the new Chief could be at their disposal.

It was a large crowd of people, varying in age from the very old to the very young. Led by a Gbetu as Kortuma had thought, the crowd danced gracefully. Women shook their hips, men shook their bodies, and the Gbetu now rolled on the ground, now stood erect and made itself tall and short — all to the explosive rhythm of the samkpa and gbongbon and the occasional, moaning sound of a cowhorn. Before the porch, the crowd made a semi-circle and beat away while the Gbetu continued to dance with increasing verve. At length it crashed to the ground to rest. Now and then a man or a woman came forward to demonstrate genema.

Without warning, a group of women, dressed in colourful fanti, singing and dancing to the rhythm of keeh, hurried past the drum players, rushed to the porch and surrounded Kortuma. The song leader was a beautiful girl with red lips and a very black complexion. She was called 'Bird of Fuama'. Her beautiful lyric moved Kortuma almost to tears:

> He's now in the house of earth,
> Earth must take its own,
> If one could be rescued from death,
> I would rescue Gbolokai.
> Kortuma, listen to these words of mine:
> One's relative is never hidden to him in a crowd,
> A stranger is not greater than his host,
> Man has always died and man has always remained,
> One doesn't last; it's one's grave that lasts,
> A man may die, but his name doesn't die,
> However pitiful you may be, death won't escape you.
> The dry palm branch told the young one, "Don't splash me with
> dew drops, for where I am, there you'll also be."
> Let the young girls open their lapa, for goats are never satisfied
> with the scanty leaves that stick out of the cassava fence.

Visibly moved Kortuma stood up and waved the cowtail, at which sign the playing ceased. Just before he brought his hand down, a young girl with springy, bare breasts, her face lit with a smile, hugged him; she tossed her headtie off her head and wiped his face and neck gracefully. His arm fell over her shoulder and reached to the small of her back, but he gently pushed her aside and addressed the crowd. He thanked them for the honour, warning that anyone who caused trouble during the play would be punished. Then he offered to slaughter two cows for them in honour of his father and in appreciation for their kind gesture. He also promised them four demi-johns of rum.

Toward evening an ivory stool draped with country cloth and white linen was placed in the palaver house. Chiefs, Zoes, and Elders of the five Clans and each major town in the entire Chiefdom led Kortuma to the palaver house. A hurricane lantern that hung on a rattan rope tied to a crooked beam in the roof lit the palaver house. Kortuma sat on the stool, holding the cowtail firmly in his right hand which rested on his right thigh, the Chiefs, Zoes and Elders sitting on either side of him. Suddenly, a group of maidens rushed into the palaver house and formed two lines before him. Their faces were painted in many designs with white chalk and pona. Tied on their knees were bunches of rattles made of dry nutshells. The rattles rang at regular intervals as they tapped the dirt floor with their feet; holding rolled white headties in their hands, they bent low, swung their arms sideways, and danced gently to the rhythm of a song. The song, though different in tone, carried nearly the same words as that of the Fuama Bird.

As the girls danced with animation, six fanga players rushed into the palaver house all of a sudden. They were dressed in short, coarse country cloth shirts, with tasselled red skull caps drawn tight on their heads. They tapped the fanga in their armpits in a fiery manner, singing the praises of Chief Kortuma, wishing him good luck, long life, the death of his enemies. Musket blasts reverberated through the village.

Soon the ceremony was over. All that mattered was that Kortuma mount the ivory stool which many Chiefs before him had mounted. This shrine was kept in a hidden place and was guarded by a special Zoe, for if an unauthorised person should sit on it, even by mistake, he would automatically become the next Chief. But the guard was an exception. He could sit on it at will and would never be considered as a Chief, for he was the 'sacrificial chicken' of the Ancestors and the 'nephew' of the tribe.

At midnight Chief Kortuma left the palaver house quietly and went to bed. The players continued dancing, drinking, and singing. He listened to their throbbing drums and their riotous voices. To them the day meant feasting, but for him it meant loneliness and recollection. He groped under the bed with his left hand until he touched the bowl of white rice powder which Lorpu usually kept there for him.

Polang! The name of his third wife flashed in his mind. He remembered telling Lorpu that he would initiate Polang into womanhood the night he mounted the stool. Young, fresh, and innocent, she should bring him good luck.

"And when will that be?" Lorpu had said sharply. "If you keep her in suspense too long, she'll not feel at home here." But he had resolved to wait for this night. That was six months ago.

Shoving the bedclothes off his six-foot body, the Chief sat up, and wrapped the bedclothes around his waist, his hands shook with desire. The house was extremely dark, not even the glow of embers showed in the fireplace. Kortuma felt his way with his feet to the central room where Polang slept in a bed behind the fireplace with Lorpu and Korlu. His daughter, Yembele, lay by the fireside.

He shook Polang briskly and told her in a whisper that he wanted her in his room. She stretched, yawned, and said: "Who's that?" This was the first time someone had woken her so late at night.

"Let's go in," the Chief repeated. She recognised his voice and tried to say something, but the words would not come. Kortuma grasped her with his hands. She screamed and fought to free herself. He held her tight, whispering in her ears and pulling her from the bed. But she continued fighting, and doubtless woke up the other women and his daughter. Nonsense. Giving up on her, he returned to his room, put on his short black trousers and medical shirt, and took the bowl of rice powder.

Alarmed, Polang squeezed herself in a corner of the central room, sobbing.

The Chief stepped out into the harsh cold night. He saw only a knot of players dancing and singing in the distance. He walked to the sacrificial spot on the river and scattered the powder there, murmuring supplications to the gods:

"Accept my sacrifice of peace," he murmured. "Approve my inauguration. It's not by my own choice that I have become a Chief; neither do I presume to be qualified for this great position. Guide and help me save the land."

Chief Kortuma returned to his house and went to bed, feeling assured that all would be well. He fell asleep at once and had a dream.

He dreamed of meeting his father on the outskirts of the village. Chief Gbolokai was clad in the Shirt of Honour in which he had been buried.

"Father!" Chief Kortuma exclaimed, embracing his father.

Withdrawing from his embrace, Chief Gbolokai looked at him with pity. "I sent for you," he told him, his eyes glistening. "I'll never forget you because you were good and kind to me in the world of mortals. When I said, 'Save the land,' on my dying day, you probably thought the Gola question was uppermost in my mind. You were quite correct, but I'm sure you can take care of the Gola. My main concern is the survival of the House of Gbolokai. You need a boy child if this House will not pass away. Korlu, your second wife, will give you that child. Go to Kekula of Kuntaa early in the morning. He will tell you what to do." Chief Gbolokai suddenly vanished.

Kortuma stood still for a long time, trying to make sense of the incident. He couldn't believe that Chief Gbolokai, in all seriousness, could say that Korlu would bear a child. She was supposedly barren. He had consulted every known herbalist and Zoe in Fuama Chiefdom for help — to no avail. Korlu had lived with him for some eight years and was still childless. Other women often ridiculed her for it.

Chief Kortuma returned to the village, planning to see Kekula first thing in the morning as he was told. Unexpectedly, he saw two men, knives in hand, running towards him, their arms raised to strike. He ran for his life, but suddenly stumbled and fell in a heap and wriggled helplessly on the gound like a dying hen, screaming breathlessly.

Chief Kortuma, disgruntled and alarmed at the last scene in the dream, felt relieved when he jerked awake, and found himself lying in his bed, perfectly safe. He sat up and groped all over the bed to make sure he wasn't deceived. He rubbed his eyes with his hands, squinted in the dark room without seeing. Noticing the knock at the door at last, he asked:

"Who's that?"

"Korlu."

"Come in."

"The door is locked."

"Oh, wait."

3

Putting on a pair of short blue denim trousers and a khaki shirt, Chief Kortuma unbolted the room door. The saffron light from the fireplace danced in his face. On entering the room, Korlu opened the window for the morning sunshine, then she leaned with her left hand against the table that stood below the window and looked enquiringly at the Chief.

His head bowed, Kortuma scratched his stubby beard absently and said, "I had a dream . . . close the door." He listened for a moment, but heard no sound in the central room. He thought the privacy was complete because the other women and his daughter must be out. To make sure, however, he asked Korlu, "Who's in there?" nodding towards the central room.

"No one," Korlu replied in a quiet voice. "Polang and Lorpu have gone to the river to bathe and bring some fresh water. Yembele has gone to throw trash away; and I stayed to heat your bath water."

"Oh, you don't have to go through all that," Kortuma remarked. "I simply wanted to make sure we had some privacy. Sit down." As Korlu sat before him in the chair near the table, she felt a wave of heat permeate her body, the blood rushed to her head, and her heart beat violently. She could guess the news her husband had for her. And she wondered why that insoluble problem should come out at a time like this.

"Well," Kortuma began, "maybe you think this is another waste of time. But it isn't. My father himself assured me that you *will* bear a male child. He said I should go to Kekula in Kuntaa right now to see about it." Korlu hung her head; her face grew cloudy and tears formed on her eyelids. "I don't want you to cry about it!" the Chief warned, flourishing the index finger of his right hand at her. "To be barren is no crime, and I don't think you are. Some witch might be bothering you — so there's no reason for you to burst into tears whenever someone tries to do something about it."

"Go and see Kekula as your father told you," she said with a sob.

Kortuma cast a severe look of disapproval at her, whereupon she quickly wiped her eyes dry with the back of her right hand, gave a short groan, and tried to look normal.

Satisfied with the change in her look, the Chief said, "I'm going to Kuntaa right now. You women take care of yourselves." He then took his sheathed sword that leaned against the wall at the head of the bed and left.

In a hurry to meet Kekula before he left for his farm or went hunting, Chief Kortuma walked vigorously all morning on the forest trail, climbing steep knolls and sloshing through swamps. About halfway to Kuntaa a wren flew with a twitter over his head, a sign that Kekula was preparing to leave the village. Kortuma pulled a handful of leaves from both sides of the road, looked anxiously for a black anthill until he found one and placed the leaves on top of it.

"Let . . . bad, bad luck stay . . . behind me," he stuttered. "Let good . . . good luck, and daylight . . . be in front of me."

Before he realised it, he was already on the edge of Kuntaa. He could tell by the round and square mud houses with black thatched roofs poking into the sky in the distance. Much to his dismay, he saw no one in the village; he only saw animals and chickens meandering about. This was to be expected for it was farming time. However, he was hopeful, though slightly apprehensive, for he knew that a Zoe, unlike ordinary men, must tend to his medicines in the morning before leaving the village. He went at a trot to Kekula's house which stood under a huge cotton-wood tree at the opposite end of the village. It was a small, insignificant, round house, but he approached it with reverence as if it were a shrine.

"Kekula, how do you do?" he said in a loud, clear voice as he climbed the blunt dirt stairs, smiling. A whiff of the characteristic, acrid odour of the medicine man's house blew in his face and filled his nostrils. He sneezed. "May I get good luck in this house," he said ceremoniously.

"Who's that?" Kekula, who squatted near the doorway concentrating on a group of charms, asked irritably. "Don't you see me busy with medicines?" Turning around to view the intruder, his face instantly assumed an apologetic look. "Oh, Chief Kortuma!" he exclaimed, a bright smile on his face. "Come in! You are lucky to see me. I'm about to complete washing the charms and go to the bush. Sit down." He motioned to a rattan chair without a backrest that sat against the wall before him. Flinging the fetish he had in his hand to the dirt floor, he stood up. "You should have sent a messenger instead, or sent for me!" He still wore the apologetic smile on his face. Without hesitation, he slapped his calloused, dusty hand into the Chief's hand, and they snapped fingers heartily.

A man of medium height, corpulent, with unsteady, large eyeballs, Kekula was well known and respected as a powerful Zoe, though Kortuma had never taken a problem to him before. A fixed, penetrating gaze on a charm or on the face of a client would probe the secret behind a problem. Depending on the nature of the problem, the eyes would roll in terror, or relax in peace or be resigned in despair. These expressive eyes could have made him frightening and repulsive, but he had charming, bushy eyebrows that almost concealed them. He had a round, fleshy face without protruding cheekbones. His charms were appealing, but unlike most beautiful people, Kekula wasn't aware of them. In order to attract notice and admiration, he carried an air of medical authority wherever he went.

At that moment his heart surged with pride because a new Chief had called on him just after his inauguration. Pointing at the rattan chair, he again told the Chief:

"Have a seat."

The Chief sat down, took off the sword that hung on his left shoulder and laid it near his feet. Kekula sat on a low stool opposite him.

"I came to you," the Chief said in a flat voice, careful not to betray his worries. "If you still lived with us in Haindi, things would have been easier. However, I'm happy to meet you. Maybe . . . the great Zoe village called you." He laughed briefly. Kekula had lived in Haindi before, but, like other Zoes in many parts of Fuama Chiefdom, he had been attracted to Kuntaa, the centre of medical activities in Golaland. "When Zoes live together, they test each other to see who is fittest," the Chief remarked, taken aback by his own joke. Kekula might take it badly.

But Kekula only grinned, knitted his brows and said, "What Zoe can beat me?" Then chuckling and knotting his fingers, he stared fixedly at the Chief: ". . . do you want me to do something for you?" he asked, clasping his hand between his thighs.

Chief Kortuma gave a nervous laugh. "Why do you think I came to you this early all the way from Haindi?" he said. Tucking his own calloused hand into his pocket, he took out three white coins and gave them to him. "My wife, Korlu, has lived with me for some eight years and she hasn't had a child. We need your help."

Kekula stood up and pushed the door forward enough for privacy, which was hardly necessary as nobody else was in the village.

Realising the discrepancy, he ascribed his action to the fact that, for better results, the medicine must be done behind closed doors. However, he left the door slightly ajar to let in some light and air.

"That's nothing," he assured the Chief as he squatted again and tinkered with the charms. "If I told you how many women have received babies from my charms, you won't believe it. But I simply ascribe all my successes to the Ancestors, for if they are not behind you, all your efforts and medicines will achieve nothing." He swung his arms over the charms, his fingers stretched out. Then he clasped his hands, stretched his fingers again and commenced tinkering with the charms. "Let's pray to the Ancestors for them to stand behind our feet . . . you said that your wife is called . . ."

"Korlu," the Chief snapped.

From a little black bag lying near the charms, Kekula took out two kola nuts, split them in four halves, juggled them in his scooped hands four times and cast them to the floor, snapping his right hand fingers. Three halves of the kola nuts bent down; one sat up. Unsuccessful. "Well, as you know," he cleared his throat, a trifle embarrassed, "it's normal to try the charms four times for a male client." He picked up the kola nut halves with one hand, with the other he broke a straw off a broom of rice straw. "This is our new Chief," he addressed the charms, tapping them with the straw as he spoke. "He is in a scrape and knows not how to get out. Do not fail him, I implore you. If an evil spirit or an evil man or woman, or a witch is responsible for Korlu's trouble, let the culprit go down with the river far away." He threw the straw southwards, the downward flow of the river. With both hands he once again juggled the kola nut halves four times and cast them to the floor, snapping his fingers. "Chief," he said with delight, "it's over!" A rare success. The second try and he made it! Two pieces of the kola nut halves had sat up and the other two had bent down. "I'll now cut the sand," he said, loosening a rope from the mouth of little cloth bag which he picked up from among the charms.

Quite impressed by his success, the Chief said, "Thank you so far," giving him a few more coins.

Kekula took the coins and cast them casually to the floor. All his interest and attention were focused on the rite. He poked his hand into the cloth bag and scooped out two handfuls of sand which he spread on the floor. He levelled the sand with his hand and made some strange fingerprints in it: dots interspersed with curves and horizontal lines. He held his legs with his hands and read the prints: "Hmm . . . someone is eating Korlu's stomach. I see the person," he admitted, tilting his head sideways, "But he's caught. Does Korlu have enemies in Haindi?" He looked critically at the Chief.

"Sure!" the Chief said. Who doesn't have an enemy? he thought.

"Is she allergic to anything?" Again nearly every tribesman or woman had an allergy. Chief Kortuma, however, decided to answer Kekula's unassuming questions without further protest in his mind. His father could not possibly recommend a trickster to him.

"Yes, quite a few things," he replied. "Leopard, goat, snake, catfish . . . if she eats catfish her stomach aches terribly."

"Women's usual trouble — I mean the catfish," Kekula remarked. "Has she had a child before?" he asked.

"I am her first husband. Well, no. She hasn't had a child in her life."

Kekula erased the prints and made new ones. With beaming eyes, he read them, nodding his head repeatedly as if he were listening to instructions.

"The problem is complicated," he said after a time. "It involves you as well. First of all, be on your guard. People envy you. They don't want your wife to bear a male child to succeed you. Your father who died recently told you in a dream that Korlu would bear a male child in order for the House of Gbolokai to survive . . ."

"Catch my hand!" the Chief shouted as he snapped fingers with Kekula. Exactly how the Zoe managed to know about the dream was a mystery to him. This caused him to place full confidence and trust in Kekula.

"Thus they have tied her stomach through witchcraft so that she may not bear this child," Kekula continued without excitement as if he expected the Chief's reaction. The Chief watched him with amazement, his lips agape. His eyes still pinned on the prints, Kekula continued: "Three things you must do. First, have an old woman bless four pieces of white kola nuts for you, and give then to four elderly friends of yours. Next, let the same old woman bless a white chicken for you, and keep it round your house. Lastly, kill a white sheep and make a feast for everybody. After eating, let small children wash the pans and spill the dirty water at the beginning of every road leading from Haindi. By giving kola nuts to your friends, you will create a wall of love between you and your enemies who may pose as friends. And no amount of hate or witchcraft can break down that wall to harm you. The sacrificial chicken is important for more protection. If anyone tries to kill you with a bad medicine, it is the chicken that will die. Whenever the chicken dies or gets lost, replace it at once. Finally, the food you will cook for the feast will be kperor in the stomachs of all those who will eat it. I'm sure many people, knowing the purpose of the feast, will refuse to take part in it. But they, too, will be vulnerable; for anyone who has entered or will enter Haindi by the various roads leading to Haindi, and who has evil in his heart against you — that individual will be struck by the dirty water which the children will spill. Believe me, Chief Kortuma! That person will surely die! And before dying, he will come to you on his knees, begging for mercy."

Kekula stopped talking all of a sudden, went to his dingy bedroom and returned in no time with a little black gourd filled with black powder. Pulling off the tiny wooden stopper, he poured some powder into his left palm, licked it, creasing his face and twisting his thick lips. He closed his eyes tight and took a deep swallow. Then he poured some powder into the Chief's left palm.

"Lick it," he said. "It'll protect you from poison. You're now a great man, so you need this kind of protection. If anyone should poison your food or drink, the poison will become cold and harmless like water. Furthermore, if you happen to touch a cup or a pan containing poisoned drink or food, that cup or that pan will crack." The Chief obediently licked the powder. It was bitter. He had thought it would burn his mouth, considering Kekula's grim expression when he licked it.

The investigation over, Chief Kortuma thanked Kekula, gave him four more coins and left for Haindi. Stunned by the incredible revelation, he hurried back to Haindi, seriously reflecting on all that Kekula had told him. He reached home late in the evening. The moon was shining, and crowds of children sang and danced in the square. He went to his house and saw Korlu sitting by the fireplace, a pot of rice was boiling on the fire. Korlu raised her head and spied him in the doorway. His steps were heavy. Korlu could not wait to hear what he had to say. She repressed a choke, tears ran down her cheeks. With the tip of her lapa, she wiped the tears away. But Kortuma did not notice this, for he hurried past her and went into his bedroom to undress.

"Where are Yembele and her mother?" he called from the room.

"They are bathing behind the house," Korlu replied in a heavy voice.

"So you've been crying today?" Kortuma asked.

Korlu said nothing.

"Where's Polang?"

"Po . . . Po . . ." Korlu faltered.

"Run away again?" the Chief said. Coming to the door, he placed his right foot on the doorframe and held the door with his left hand.

"In the morning Polang said she was going to the river for water," Korlu explained. "We did not hear her complain of anything. Rather, she was quiet, going about her chores as usual, but she never returned from the river." Korlu spoke all at once in a loud, clear voice.

"Well," the Chief said, "it's nothing new for her to run away. I won't worry about her now. Come in."

Korlu first lit a bamboo splinter in the fireplace. Scooping her hand around the flame in an effort to save it, she went into the bedroom and lit the hurricane lantern on the table; then she threw the splinter into the central room after blowing out the flame. Finally, she sat in the chair by the table, cupped her chin in her hand, her elbow resting on her thigh. The Chief placed his sword back at the head of the bed, took off his shirt, and sat on the bed. He bent forward, supporting his head with one hand, and slapping his back with the other.

Like a good wife, Korlu understood. "The food is almost ready," she said. "There's some hot water in the pot . . ."

"Everything is over," the Chief interrupted, ignoring her remarks. Though he was hungry and needed a bath, he considered the problem on hand more important.

No longer depressed, Korlu said in a lively way, "I knew that Kekula would take care of everything. He's an important Zoe."

"All one needs is to know the source of the trouble," the Chief said. "We'll catch the witch. Kekula told me that they have tied your stomach so that you won't bear a male child to succeed me."

Korlu started and stamped the floor with one foot. "I used to warn you, but you never listened to me," she said. Before he became a Chief, she used to advise Kortuma about whom to trust, but he used to dismiss her fears and suspicions as 'woman talk'. Now he was convinced that he had enemies.

"If a man should attack me with a sword . . . but, but who is crazy enough to try it?" Kortuma declared sternly, slapping his back and scratching his shoulders. "It's a wife of mine they turn to. The witch will be killed and the child will be born. Tomorrow we'll perform the sacrifice which Kekula prescribed." He reported Kekula's findings to her in detail.

Korlu heaved a sigh and said, "Lorpu or Polang might give you a boy child. How do you know if I get a child it'll be a boy?"

"It isn't an ordinary man who made the prediction. Unless you think you are wiser than the poor one and the medicine man. Why, you too can have a boy child."

"Who am I to say that I am wiser than an Ancestor or a Zoe?" Korlu said, rising to see after the Chief's food and bath.

Presently Lorpu and Yembele entered the central room. Yembele had the empty bath bucket in her hand and was behind her mother. Lorpu sat on a stool near the fire, poking splinters and pieces of sapling into it. Yembele set the bucket in a corner and sat on another stool opposite her mother. The water steamed on their skins. The Chief had heard them come in.

"I've always warned you people about bathing at night," he said in the bedroom. "You'll end up bathing with spirits and you know what that means." They were silent, for they knew what it meant. Anyone who bathed in the open at night ran the risk of bathing with spirits, and this could cause bad, incurable skin diseases.

"See about the food," Korlu told them. "I'm going to the Crier's." She stepped out.

In a moment she was back and the voice of the Crier brayed outside:

"Nobody should leave town tomorrow! The Chief will make a life sacrifice! Nobody should leave town . . ."

Lorpu had dished out the food and put the Chief's portion aside. Korlu took it to him. He hardly ate. Taking a quick bath, he went to bed.

The following morning, the villagers gathered before his house. Dressed in a wide, flowing robe with alternating black and white stripes, Chief Kortuma walked slowly and firmly and stood on a patch of elevated ground before them. A faint smile on his tightly drawn lips, his eyes swerved blandly over the crowd. The smile suddenly lapsed into a stern expression. He raised his arms with authority and told them about the sacrifice, told them how some witches had bewitched his wife. He wanted to know why.

Unexpectedly, Sumo the Elder shambled out of the crowd and stood by him, nonplussed, staring at the crowd with anger. His eyes were caved in, the loose flesh shaking on his high cheekbones, and his head was covered with white hairs. An important kperor Minister, Sumo was overwhelmed with rage. He looked around for a long time and finally managed to speak in a crisp voice:

"We still support our Chief! Any Chief, no matter how small he is, no matter how young or old, deserves his people's fullest support and respect. It is the tradition of this land. To plot against a Chief is a great crime. The culprit should be caught and killed," he ended dramatically and staggered back into the crowd.

Everyone was struck with consternation. The news had hit the villagers like lightning. Murmuring and arguing among themselves, they returned to their houses.

The village was still and lifeless all day as the sacrifice was performed. The Chief had Younkor, an old woman who had supervised five sessions of the Sande, bless four pieces of white kola nut for him. These he gave to four friendly elderly men. Then she blessed the white chicken, wished him long life, prosperity, peace, and the death of all his enemies. The Chief slaughtered a fatted white ram which was cooked; a large quantity of rice was cooked as well. A number of adults and a large group of children ate the food. The children, who took the occasion as an opportunity to overeat, washed out the pans and, running joyfully about with their bloated stomachs, spilled the dirty water at the beginning of every road leading from Haindi.

4

"... tell them to come without delay, for it's an urgent meeting. If a Chief is lying in bed, wake him up and tell him to start on the road to Haindi; if he is sitting or standing or even hunting, go after him in the bush and tell him to hurry to Haindi; otherwise, he will pay a heavy fine. I want you to fly like birds and be back before sundown tomorrow . . ."

It was early in the morning, and Chief Kortuma who had his bedclothes wrapped around him like a toga was dispatching a group of strapping young men to all parts of the Chiefdom to summon all Clan Chiefs to Haindi for an Extraordinary Council which would tackle the main task of his chieftaincy: to defeat the Gola and restore peace and security to the land. Indeed, he was encouraged in this effort, for his recent dream of the deceased Chief assured him of the Ancestors' full support. And he believed that once he had this support, every problem he faced, however difficult it might be, would be easily resolved. He remembered with pride and relief Chief Gbolokai's grim determination to defend the land. He had fought with him in numerous battles with the Gola, throwing spears with both his right and left hands, bawling at his warriors. Twice they had beaten the Gola, but these victories were short-lived. The Gola once again resumed their ambushing spree when Chief Gbolokai took ill. They ambushed more than a dozen travellers from Fuama Chiefdom, and robbed them of their goods. Chief Gbolokai had tried to negotiate peace with them, but they had paid him no attention up to his death. Though the Chief had played down the Gola threat in the dream, Kortuma believed that it was his greatest concern, for without peace prevailing in the land, nothing would be achieved. His last words, "Save the land," constantly rang in Kortuma's ears. And the last words of a dying man must be taken seriously. With the problems of Korlu's barrenness and the quest for a successor almost resolved, Kortuma felt that it was time to pay full attention to the Gola threat.

After dispatching the messengers, he dressed hurriedly, took a bowl of rice powder and hastened to the sacrificial spot on the bank where he sprinkled the powder, murmuring prayers to the gods and to the Ancestors.

For the next few days, Chief Kortuma behaved in a strange and peculiar fashion to the amazement of his entire household: he slept alone, ate sparingly, and spent the days on the river bank, pacing up and down. When he began losing weight, Lorpu became concerned. She thought that he was either worried about Polang's sudden disappearance or perhaps the sickness that attacked him after his father's death was returning, for he was sullen and withdrawn as he had been at the time. One evening, she braved a question.

"Kortuma, what has happened?" she asked.

Surprisingly, he bawled, "We have the Gola on our backs again, Lorpu. The road to the coast is closed. We must open it, or else the graduation festival for the Sande will be a bad failure. There will be peace and happiness, but we have to fight for it. We must deal with the Gola! Teach them a lesson they'll never forget!"

In preparation for the Council, the Chief had the Kpaan cleared, four new bamboo benches built there, and a lamb leashed to a post by his house.

The men he assigned to clear the Kpaan did their work promptly and efficiently. Of course, the festivities and ceremonies that usually accompanied the clearing of a Kpaan were not performed because the land was officially in the hands of women, since their society was in progress. However, when the men cleared the Kpaan and hung a gate of bamboo thatch, interspersed with torfa, across the path leading into it, it was evident that the men were in action once again, for the gate showed that the mystery and power of manhood were evoked. Women, children, and non-initiates of the Poro fearfully averted their eyes from it as they passed by.

In a week the Chiefs of the five Clans and every major town in Fuama Chiefdom gathered in Haindi. Several of them were reportedly sick and could not come, but were represented by the important Zoes of their areas. Chief Kortuma welcomed them and expressed happiness at their prompt and favourable response to his call. He had the lamb slaughtered for them on the morning the Council convened.

As they went to the Kpaan that morning, Chief Kortuma and the Master walked side by side several paces behind the group of Chiefs and Zoes, chatting. Dressed in their medical clothes, the two men looked sprightly and resplendent. The Master had a horn of

40

medicine hanging on his left shoulder; he kept adjusting it with pride. Chief Kortuma had the cowtail in his right hand. It was now plaited with red and black leather all the way down to its tuft of hair, a leather strap was fastened at the end through which he poked his hand and held the tail. They walked with dignity into the Kpaan and sat in two rattan chairs before the Chiefs and the Zoes.

Without preliminary remarks, Kortuma launched upon the matter of the day. The Elders who had expected the usual introduction of rambling remarks, not particularly connected with the matter for which they were called, grew curious and quiet.

"I called you Elders for a special reason," said Chief Kortuma, rising, briefly adjusting his medical shirt, and pacing up and down before his audience. "I want you people to help me decide what we should do about the road. As you know, the Gola closed it when the poor one took ill, for they knew that a man on his deathbed could not go to war. I'm very certain that this action of theirs was also meant as a direct challenge to me. The success or failure of my reign depends on how I meet this challenge. I am determined to meet it! Meet it like a man! Furthermore, the Sande is in progress. If we don't open the road for us to take our produce to the coast to trade, the graduation festival will be a bad failure. Our children will never forgive us if we leave them at the waterside. No one who calls himself a man can afford this. The House of Gbolokai has always stood for honour and courage, and I will not be the first Chief of this House to break that tradition . . ."

Members of the Council grew increasingly uneasy as the Chief continued to speak. It was Chief Guladia of Yarbaryong Clan who interrupted him. Standing up impulsively, he gestured with his right arm and exclaimed:

"May the Ancestors stand by us!"

Before the Council could reply, Chief Kortuma waved the cowtail forcefully, a stern expression on his face, and declared:

"Do you want to be slaves?"

"No! Not by a long sight!" came a rousing reply.

"Do you want to be free?"

"Yes indeed!"

"Are we men or women?"

"We are men!"

"Well," he grew slightly relaxed, "that's what I called you for. Think about this problem with a sober mind for us to make a wise decision. Think about your wives and children. Think about the land. And finally, think about your own safety."

41

As Chief Kortuma returned to his seat, the Elders scratched their heads and the napes of their necks; they wrung their hands impatiently. The speech had been provocative, and they were prepared to flare their rage at the Gola, but with the Chief's call for sobriety, they commenced a general discussion in order to let their excitement cool off before giving their opinions.

"When last did we lose a man on the road to the coast?" someone asked.

"Let's see," someone else tried to remember. "Yes. It was two months before Gbolokai's death when Boakai braved the dangerous road and was killed."

"Oh yes! I don't know why some people wilfully go after death."

"Well, to be a man is no joke," Chief Kortuma said. "I talked with him shortly before he went on that fatal journey. He told me, 'He who is poor has to suffer. I can't afford to wait for the last moment before looking for clothes and perfume and beads — and if I fail my children because of fear, will they be proud to call me their father?' I fully understood his dilemma. However, I advised him not to make the trip alone, but he said that nobody else was ready to travel to the coast; and as the rain-time was fast approaching, the sooner he made the trip the better."

After Chief Kortuma related his conversation with Boakai, there was a moment of silence as if he had paid a tribute to the memory of the dead. Boakai's death began to make sense to everyone. Hitherto it had been considered as the result of a reckless action on his part. But now everyone understood the sacrifice he had had to make.

It was Chief Guladia who again came forward and turned everybody's attention to the problem at hand. This time he walked with calculated steps from the second bench in the row and stood before Kortuma and the Master. Short, burly and dressed in a white country cloth shirt and a pair of short black pants, Guladia stared around with a solemn face, cleared his throat, and, speaking with controlled passion, addressed the Council.

"The Gola know that we are strong and brave," he said, striking the air with his right arm. "There is no tribe under the sun that can attack Fuama Chiefdom and expect to win. For many years, the Gola have posed the only serious threat to us, because whenever we go to war with them, we do not fight for total victory, but only push them to the point where they would give us the white chicken. This is why they menace us so often. But let us resolve now to fight for conquest — and have them pay us tributes. Otherwise, they will continue to harass us forever. This is my opinion."

When Chief Guladia took his seat, Chief Korlibaa Yekeh of Zuwulo Clan, a good-natured man of medium height, stepped forward to make his own observations. Also a Zoe, he wore a long, sleeveless blue denim shirt that extended all the way to his knees; bulging under his left arm was a horn of medicine which he carried with him at all times. He kept it concealed under his shirt so that he would be approachable like the Chief he was. Speaking in a guttural voice, he fully agreed with Chief Guladia, and declared that there was no substitute for total conquest. The Gola, he said, should not be permitted to continue strangulating the people of Fuama Chiefdom. He admitted that Chief Kortuma was right in saying that they had launched renewed hostilities on Fuama Chiefdom because they saw that Chief Gbolokai was sick, and was fighting for his life. "The old Chief had no choice but to try to make peace with them," he said. "And what did Chief Dadie of Golaland do to the two emissaries Chief Gbolokai sent to him to start the peace negotiation? To the first emissary, the poor one gave four white coins and told him to take them to Chief Dadie as a symbol of friendship between the people of Fuama Chiefdom and the people of Golaland. Dadie took the money, had the emissary whipped mercilessly and driven violently out of his village, telling him that there was no man in Fuama Chiefdom whom he respected. Again Chief Gbolokai sent another emissary. This time he took a white rooster as a sign of peace and good will. Dadie not only had the second emissary beaten; his men tied his hands behind his back, tied two torches of bamboo splinters on his head in broad daylight, and chased him out of the village, pointing at the road to Haindi, saying, 'This is the road to your village. With these torches you won't miss your way. And never come here again.' This was absolute impudence. Gentlemen, we have offered love and received insult. You can't dig love and respect out of a person with a hoe. What more can we do? So far as I am concerned, there is no way out but total war." Chief Yekeh sat down.

Everybody knew the story of Kwesee, the second emissary, and its intimate relation by Chief Yekeh could have caused a general display of anger had Chief Kortuma not called for sobriety during the discussion. Though Kwesee's story seemed ludicrous, it was serious. A short, temperamental man and a known boxer, Kwesee had beaten his breast in anger and volunteered to take another message to Chief Dadie when the first emissary reported the cruel treatment he had received in Golaland. Chief Gbolokai had preferred to let the matter rest for a time, give it some thought, before taking any action. But Kwesee would not hear of this. He personally caught the first white rooster he found in the village, took it to the Chief and said, "This is a sign of goodwill and friendship. Let me take it to Dadie and see what will happen." The Chief nodded his approval and was about to make a remark, but Kwesee flew out of his sight like a bird, and was on the way to Golaland.

The next day he returned to Haindi in tattered clothes, ran to the palaver house where Chief Gbolokai was judging a case, and fell at the Chief's feet, grovelling in agony on the dusty floor.

"Chief . . . Chief . . . Oh Chief!" he panted. His entire body was soon covered with yellow dust.

The Elders plied him with questions.

"Did a snake bite you?"

"Did you see a strange creature?"

"Were you ambushed?"

"Were you beaten?"

"Are you hurt?"

Some Elders attempted to pick him bodily from the floor.

"No," the Chief protested. "Leave him! Kwesee, get up and tell us what happened to you!"

Kwesee sat up and spoke self-consciously in a frantic and incoherent voice.

"When I gave the chicken to Chief Dadie, he grasped it from me and told his men to beat me up and chase me out of his village! Quo! He did not even listen to what I had to say! The men pushed me around as if I were a fool! Quo! One of them pinched my ears, another hit me on my back and I fell flat in front of the villagers! Quo! They handled me like a thief! When I fell down, they rushed upon me and beat me up and stood me erect, tied bamboo torches on my head, tied my hands behind my back and pushed me out of their village! Quo! Chief, what the people did . . ."

Everyone recalled with anger Kwesee's humiliating experience. The fact that the incident had occurred long ago made it more painful and provocative. At the time Kwesee reported it with wild antics in the palaver house, opinions were divided, though it was the general consensus that the Chief of the Gola had acted badly and deserved severe punishment. Some Elders were of the opinion that Kwesee was merely putting on an act of provocation in order to cause war between the two lands, because, as a boxer, he could have defended himself and escaped. The incident he reported was therefore exaggerated. Others maintained that he was really ill-treated and that an appropriate reaction from Chief Gbolokai was necessary. However, everyone was against rash action; rather, it was agreed that the matter be given careful consideration. But now the leaders of the land felt that the incident was the final test of their patience and endurance. The pain of Kwesee's humiliation became overwhelming as if it were taking place right there and then. Sending another emissary to Golaland was out of the question. They began regretting the fact that Chief Gbolokai had been unable to take action against the Gola for this rude and reckless behaviour of their Chief. Sickness and death had prevented it.

The discussion continued all morning, each Elder throwing in a parable here, an anecdote there, to justify war with Golaland as the only practical solution to the incessant Gola threat and menace.

Again it was Gbada who brought an end to the long discussion. How he managed to sneak into the Council was not known. Dressed in a tattered, dirty singlet and an old visored cap, he had sat silently through the discussion as if he disagreed with everything that was said, but wanted to avoid a violent clash by withholding his own opinions. Standing before the Council, he boxed the air impulsively with his fists, and gave three cheers:

"Sina-ooooooooooooooooo-sina!" he cried.

"Ho!" the Council responded.

"Sina-ooooooooooooooooo-sina!"

"Ho!"

"Sina-ooooooooooooooooo-sina!"

"Ho!"

"May the Ancestors stand by us!"

"Let it be so!"

"May the Ancestors protect us!"

"Let it be so!"

"Everything we mortals say or do, whether right or wrong, whether true or false — may it be the will of the Ancestors!"

"Let it be so!"

"We have been violated. The Gola should not go unpunished! They can't continue violating us and getting away with it. We don't like war. It's not because of cowardice, but because we believe that, as decent people, we should rather devote more of our time to farming, cleaning roads and villages, hunting, performing initiation ceremonies, and preserving the sacred traditions handed down to us by our Ancestors. To be destructive is no mark of strength or courage. Those who live responsibly and try to be good are few — and they are the only hope of any land. I am proud to say that we are among the number of such people. But now our good hearts must give way to violence, because we can't achieve anything of value while there is no peace." Gbada stopped talking for a moment and watched the Council. Everyone listened to him with undivided attention. "As for me, I am almost gone," he continued. "Do you see my white hair? War and peace mean nothing to me now, but we must fight for our land. Don't let us spend all day dragging things out. We don't know what the Gola are planning right now! If you see a man running, he's either chasing something or is being chased by something.

"Before sitting down, let me give my blessings — I'm apparently the oldest in the group." Brief laughter.

"May the future be full of sunshine."

"Let it be so," all responded.

"May we win victory in every battle we fight."

"Let it be so."

"May the courage which we inherited from our forefathers never leave us."

"Let it be so."

"Any man or woman who wishes us evil, any witch or evil person who tries to poison us or destroy our crops and homes — may God foresake him that he may fall in our hands."

"Let it be so."

As if he had performed an unusual acrobatic feat, Gbada walked with pride to his seat while the Council cheered him.

Chief Kortuma did not cheer. Rather, he laid the cowtail on his lap, clutched his head with both hands, his elbows resting on his thighs, and reflected. When the cheering stopped, he said:

"What will we do now?" Gbada's impressive and courageous speech had evidently made further discussions unnecessary.

"Fight!" came the rousing reply.

"Who will be our Kulubah?" he asked. Without a strong and reliable general, all the talking would be in vain.

The Master stood up and tugged at the horn of medicine hanging on his left shoulder. Chief Kortuma straightened up in his seat and watched him.

"From Upriver all the way down to Seghai, I see no Zoe who is equal to me," he said with emphasis, gesturing with his right arm. He paused slightly, gazing at the Council with a stern face. "And so it'ld be absurd for me to be here while you people look for a Kulubah. I volunteer my services to our Chief and our land. If I lead this war, it'll be the end of the menace of the Gola people."

"Thank you," said Chief Kortuma, smiling. He rose up and shook the Master's hand. "Nobody else is better prepared for this task than you . . . is this the consensus of all?"

"Yes!" the Council answered with one voice.

"Well, gentlemen," said the Chief, "this is the time for action and not words. Gbada has cut a long story short. Let's prepare for action! I trust the courage and power of the Master. We'll win the war."

"Let it be so!" the Council answered again.

"I now command the Master to lead the warriors! May the spirits of our Ancestors be with you."

This was the end of the meeting. The Master chatted with members of the Council, while Chief Kortuma walked away.

It suddenly grew dark, though it was mid-afternoon. A shaft of lightning pierced the sky, and was followed by a blast of thunder. The Chiefs and Zoes whispered among themselves, spying the Master. They ascribed the sudden turn of weather to his medical powers, though in the dry season, sporadic thunderstorms were not uncommon. What seemed at first to be a light breeze gathered force and shook the kola trees on the outskirts, and blew the village thatched roofs fiercely. It lasted only a moment and the day became clear and bright again.

"You're prepared for the Gola," someone said to the Master. Chief Kortuma overheard the comment, but continued walking away, heading to his house.

In the yard he met Yembele who ran to him with outstretched arms. She looked depressed. Her head with beautiful plaits was thrown backwards, her broad face with snubby nose, small eyes and thin lips, looked enchanting even with its depressed look.

"What happened?" he asked. "Let's go into the house."

She was in her early teens, and the Chief sometimes thought it absurd for her to be so fond of him. He held her by one arm and pulled her from his waist. She bowed her head and fumbled with his gown.

"Don't you know that you're no longer a baby?" he chided her. "You're a grown woman now. Do you know that?"

"I . . . I . . . I . . ." She was obviously frustrated. Chief Kortuma surmised this whenever she embraced him in a depressed mood.

"What happened?" he asked again.

Lorpu came to the door and said, "Children don't usually know when their parents are in a scrape. Leave your father alone! She's been brooding over your absence all day."

They went into the bedroom. Chief Kortuma took off his gown and put on a shirt. Yembele stood against the yellow wall at the foot of the bed.

"What happened?" the Chief asked again. "How will I know what to do for you if you don't talk?" He held his arms forward. Casting a moody stare at her fidgeting hands, she walked into his arms. Stooping, the Chief hugged her.

"I put my horse into the basket, tied a string on its leg, and tied the string to a splinter in the basket," she said in a thick voice. "Later I went to see my horse, but it wasn't there." Streams of tears rolled down her fat cheeks.

"There are many horses on the outskirts. We'll get one," the Chief said in a paternal voice.

"I don't know what happened to my horse. All I found in the basket was one leg tied to the string. I did not see my horse." She continued to sob.

"You won't get another one by crying," the Chief said soothingly. "Let's go to the outskirts and find one."

He was fond of encouraging Yembele's childish ways against the wishes and advice of her mother who said if he did not stop, she would grow up as a big baby. The horse she referred to was a grasshopper which she had caught on the outskirts and strapped to a splinter in a bamboo chicken basket. He had spoiled her with baby rats, squirrels, and birds — her favourite pets — which he used to bring her when he returned from hunting. As he no longer hunted, she could not get any more pets. She had gone after grasshoppers.

The Chief went with her to the outskirts where they saw many grasshoppers flying about in the tall grasses.

Meanwhile, members of the Council were sauntering back to the village. The Master had told them the number of warriors each Clan should send, how they should dress, what weapons they should have, and so on. He ordered that all warriors be in Haindi in ten days.

The Master was the first to see Chief Kortuma chasing grass-hoppers. Bursting out with laughter, he said:

"See your Chief chasing grasshoppers!" Everyone watched the Chief, laughing.

"Children make fools of us," someone chuckled.

The Master walked to the Chief, told him the orders he had given the Chiefs and Zoes, and then walked with them to the village.

Yembele absently plucked grass stems as she stood on the edge of the tall grasses, watching her father. The Chief ran backwards, forwards and sideways, snapping a grasshopper here and there on plants. No sooner would he catch one than it would fly out of his hand, leaving its legs behind. He covered a distance of more than a dozen yards from where Yembele stood, the grasshoppers popping up in his way and flying about. At last he decided to stalk one of them which he saw pressed neatly on the stem of a firestone plant. It was large and had a green coat and long antennae. The Chief stretched his hand towards the insect with care so that the air around it would not stir. Besides, the plant was thorny; he could not safely thrust his hand at it. When his hand was within several inches of the grasshopper, it crouched to fly away, but he picked it off the plant in time. A thorn struck the back of his hand. He pulled it off, a small trickle of blood shot up where it had struck. He felt no pain because he bubbled with joy at pleasing Yembele. Yembele ran to him and grabbed the giant grasshopper. It struggled to get free, but she held it carefully and walked slowly away from the grasses, the Chief following her. With a sudden burst of excitement, she jumped up and down and ran home.

"I have a big horse! I have a big horse!" she cried.

Chief Kortuma met Sumo the Elder sitting on his porch, a gourd of palm wine at his feet. White foam poured out of the mouth of the gourd that was stuck with a rolled bamboo thatch and flowed down the body of the gourd, making a puddle on the earth floor.

"Thank you, Sumo," the Chief said, entering the porch with heavy steps. "I really need some wine." The tightness in his throat eased. Lorpu brought them two white, enamelled cups.

Sitting in a chair by Sumo, the Chief poured a cup of wine and gulped it down. A wave of relaxation spread through his body.

"You tap good, strong wine," he complimented Sumo.

"At my age if a man can't tap good wine it would be surprising," Sumo said in a throaty voice.

Chief Kortuma laughed, the flesh on his face creased and two dimples appeared at each corner of his mouth.

"We've taken the greatest step," he said. "When we win the war, everything will be all right. Then we won't drink to relieve tension, but just for fun."

"A brave step," Sumo remarked. He drank one cup of wine after another, his pot-belly protruding under his brown shirt. "It'll be a legend. To become a Chief and declare war first thing is no joke."

"To declare war is one thing, to win a war another . . . you see, Sumo, my main concern is to have peace in the land in order for us to do our work. Without peace you can't do anything." The Chief knitted his brows and took another drink.

"Sure . . . but I've been thinking — what will you do with the women Chief Gbolokai left behind?" Thinking that the Chief might be angry with him for being inquisitive, Sumo grew tense.

Chief Kortuma became quiet and sober for the moment. He had not thought of the women as yet. He drew his legs together, then crossed them and leaned back in his seat.

"Well," he said, "I don't think one man can fight on two fronts at the same time. It's better to turn them over to their people."

"That's a wise way to go about it," Sumo said, becoming relaxed. "To be a success you must put woman palaver at the back of your heart and not in the middle."

The Chief grinned at the ancient admonition.

"Believe me!" Sumo maintained, bobbing his head emphatically. "You know the story of Chief Nanporlor very well — how he once betrayed this land because of women."

"I haven't thought of it that way. I can keep any number of women, but the job I have — this war — will not permit me. I don't even spend that much time with the few I have. You know what it means."

"I know. Women are good, though. They can build a man up."

Yembele jumped out of the house, the 'horse' in her hand, and ran to the square.

"You had better take care of that one," the Chief warned her. "There's no more time to hunt for another one."

"As I was saying," Sumo continued, "one must know how to play this woman game in order to survive. Otherwise, nothing you want to do will ever be done. Your body and your mind get weak." He talked rapidly and stopped abruptly as if he had caught himself exposing a secret.

"You know," the Chief said with a determination to put an end to the issue, "when some men see a woman the next thing they think about is the bed. But if you take them as people, they won't pose a great problem." He leaned back in his seat, satisfied at giving his idea about women so precisely.

The gourd was now empty. Sumo, who had nothing more to drink or say, rose to go.

"I don't think we can settle the women question tonight," he admitted, laughing. "You've been busy today. I'd better let you rest."

"Thank you for the wine," the Chief said. He looked sleepy.

"I am your wine tapper. I wish I could be of more service to you."

"Don't say such a silly thing," the Chief glowered. "You are already serving me well. I appreciate anything you can do for me. Goodnight. Sleep well."

Sumo looked outside. It was dark. "Goodnight," he said, taking the empty gourd and stepping down from the porch with care.

5

After Sumo left, Chief Kortuma sat awhile on the porch, reflecting

After Sumo left, Chief Kortuma sat awhile on the porch, reflecting on the discussion he had had with the Elders and the conclusion they had reached. Now and then his daughter or one of his wives broke his train of thought as she shuttled to and from the house. He thought of the fear and uncertainties the war would bring, but he knew that his people were capable of any sacrifice. Furthermore, since a Master would conduct the war, using natural and supernatural forces, he was reasonably certain of quick victory, which should be achieved at no great cost because the Gola would not be able to withstand the surprise attack for long. The entire prospect of the war looked encouraging. This completed his relaxation which the wine had partly induced.

When the sun sank beyond the horizon and the evening shadows fell on the village, the Chief decided to go to bed. Sodden with wine, he stood up with a stagger, adjusted his gown absent-mindedly and scanned the dusk. Then he went straight to bed, forgetting to bolt the bedroom door.

Lorpu who grew uneasy because he had gone to bed without eating or bathing, lit the lantern in the bedroom, and looked at him in a preoccupied fashion. She wanted to wake him, but upon second thoughts, decided not to bother him for he was already asleep; and even if he should wake up, he would be of no use to himself. This was the first time in many months that he had drunk so much wine.

In the middle of the night, the Chief felt jabs in his ribs. He jumped up with a start and sat up in the bed, blabbered, and rubbed his heavy eyes with his hands. Opening his eyes, he saw a figure wrapped up in a lapa lying on the edge of the bed. He thought it was one of his wives, but he could not tell which one, for he did not remember asking any of them to sleep with him that night. Perhaps it is Polang, he thought. Perhaps she has returned at last.

Removing the lapa from her naked body, the figure turned out to be Fita, one of Chief Gbolokai's widows. Taken completely by surprise, the Chief sighed, took off his gown and placed it at the head of the bed for a pillow. Except for a slight feeling of nausea, the scent of wine on his breath, and an upset stomach, he was normal.

"Fita," Chief Kortuma called the girl. He got down from the bed without touching her, put the lantern out, took off his pants and went back to bed.

After some time, Fita managed to say, "You told Korlu I should come."

"I don't remember telling her that," the Chief said. He lay in the front of the bed, Fita behind him.

"So you've been deceiving me?" Fita said, sighing deeply and making a slight movement. She now lay flat on her back, looking up at the invisible, matted ceiling.

"You should have waited until I made up my mind about all of you."

"What have you decided?"

"Well, I must blame myself for making a hasty promise."

"Tell me what you have decided."

"Nothing yet."

"I am sure you have decided to send us away because you are afraid of your wives."

The Chief chuckled mildly. "Is that what you think?" he said.

"But what else would be the reason?"

"Let me tell you one thing: I fear no one. I do what I believe is right."

"I know . . . I know . . . that you have fought many battles — and killed many wild beasts, alone. You have also performed many other brave deeds. But do you know one thing? The most powerful and courageous man can be a slave in the hands of his wife."

"That's true. I love my wives and I sometimes let them have their way, but I make the final decision in everything. So if you hear me say no or yes, believe that it is *I* saying so . . . and remember, whatever happens, I love you."

Fita was silent for a long time. Then she said, "That's nothing new to hear from a man. You must show it if you love me." She fondled his hand for a moment.

Chief Kortuma's heart beat violently. He grew stiff and breathless, but something in him argued against any rash move. He thought of those moments, many years ago, when Fita's engrossing charms would arrest him most powerfully and he would tell her, "When the old man dies, I will inherit you." Then he would look at her large tuft of hair; her big, round hips; her springy breasts; and her hooded eyes.

"I remember all you used to tell me," Fita said in a mean voice. "Probably you have changed your mind now because you think if I get into your house I will cause trouble. But you know me very well. While I lived with your father, did you ever hear that another woman and I had the slightest misunderstanding?"

"Well, no," he said. "But don't you think it would be better for you to get your own husband?"

"But you're already my husband! Are you not pleased with me?" she asked in a loud voice. Then she added, "If you love a man, it doesn't matter how many other women you share him with."

"As I said before, whatever happens, I want you to remember that I love you," he said. "I love all the women of Fuama Chiefdom."

"I am not all the women of Fuama Chiefdom!" Fita protested sharply and sat up, turning her back to him.

"But, but — Fita, don't misunderstand me! You're pretty and hard-working. I have no doubt that you can make a good wife for me."

Chief Kortuma put on his pants and groped for the hurricane lantern on the table. He took it to the central room and lit it. When he returned to the bedroom, he saw streaks of tears on Fita's cheeks. She stretched one leg before her on the bed, the other one dangled by the bedside. She stroked the leg that was on the bed with one hand and with the other she wiped her eyes. He watched her for a time. He had not thought it would come to this; it dawned on him that it was foolish and dangerous to make a promise one was not sure of keeping. In an effort to make some amends, he placed the lantern on the table, sat beside her, and hugged her shivering body.

"Well, I won't bother you any more," she sobbed. "That's the way of men. They don't love the woman who truly loves them."

"I know that you love me, Fita," Kortuma admitted. "But give me a chance to make up my mind."

Fita thought for a long time and said emphatically, "If you don't love me, tell me! How long will you take to know if you love someone?" There was no reply. All of a sudden she said, "Goodnight. I'll see you in the morning," rising and tying her lapa on her waist in a frenzy, and walking quickly out of the room.

Closing the door, Chief Kortuma sat on the bed, cupped his chin in his hand, stared about the room which was cluttered with plunder, and thought of the problem of having many wives. He recalled his father's numerous battles with his ten wives who had lovers in every corner of the village, and even in far-away places. Whenever he asked them to confess names of lovers, they would confess hordes of them. Had he not played the 'great Chief' that he was, he would have gone crazy. After his encounter with Fita, it became clear to him that he could not take this woman question lightly. To evade it with a shrug of the shoulders amounted to falling in a deep river and absolutely refusing to swim. He remembered some occasions on which woman palaver had seriously embarrassed him. Once a girl had told him that she would call on him before midnight. He was about to attend an urgent society meeting, but he had sent in the excuse that he was sick and could not be present. He had lain in bed all night, anxiously expecting the girl. The rustling of mice in the thatched roof, the sound of a cat running into dishes in the central room — all indicated the arrival of the girl. But she never came. The next day he had had to pay a heavy fine, for the Zoe of the society could not accept his sudden illness.

He lay in bed, in the dingy room, listening to the rain pelting onto the crisp, thatched roof. He did not know how long it had been raining. Usually he enjoyed the music of the rain. But now it stung him like bees and he tossed in bed. He would think awhile of the imminent war, and then the question of Chief Gbolokai's widows would spring up like a cobra and stare at him in the face. Wouldn't he be avoiding responsibility by sending them away? Everybody expected him to inherit them. He remembered Sumo's reassuring remark that women can build a man up. But it seemed to him that the three wives he already had posed enough problems. Polang had proved intractable. Korlu needed a baby. Lorpu sometimes got lost in the night only to turn up early in the morning with the flimsy excuse that she had gone to the outskirts to relieve herself. She might be carrying on an affair with a man somewhere.

Chief Kortuma lay calm and placid in bed and thought of Chief Nanporlor's ludicrous story to which Sumo had referred. It was funny how some men allowed passion to control them. "Ah, Nanporlor," he thought, "you dug your own grave and buried yourself in it."

The story of Nanporlor was a popular ballad in Fuama Chiefdom. Women sang it when they pounded rice, scratched farms, washed clothes, or danced in the moonlight.

Nanpolor was a great Chief,
Nanpolor was a strong man,
'Twas just woman palaver,
That made him fall.

It stood to reason he had to fall. It was said that he was a tall, dark, intemperate man with beady eyes and thick lips. His harem comprised ten houses and thirty young, beautiful wives. To make sure the right thing was happening, he built his own house at the entrance to the harem. It was a large house with a hallway running through it. Only by means of the hallway could one enter the harem, and he was always in the hallway. At night he made sure the thick, heavy wooden door was latched firmly and his fierce black dog placed in the yard.

He was surprised to learn from his watchmen one day — and he had many of them — that his wives escaped over the walls of the harem by means of ladders while he slept and went to their lovers. He couldn't believe it because he used to check their houses more than a dozen times each night. However, he had an ordeal minister examine them, and he surprisingly discovered that a couple of them had lovers. Chief Nanporlor became speechless, restless, and extremely irritable. He refused to eat, and he wandered from place to place, not knowing what to do. After several tormenting days of indecision, he had the lovers whipped severely, and he made them work for him one whole year; he killed the dog since it had proved to be a mere puppy. It was also said — Kortuma shuddered at this — that he took the lunatic attitude of staying outside at night to be his own watchman. One night some Gola strong men kidnapped him and demanded a high ransom. The Council of Chiefs and Elders simply ignored the incident and elected a new Chief.

As usual when he faced a crisis or when he had to make an important decision, Chief Kortuma fetched the bowl of powder under the bed in order to give a peace offering to the gods early in the morning. He did not find it. However, he decided to take a stroll to the river in order to think through the problem. He felt that the problem was not as serious as he imagined it to be. It was a matter that merely called for firmness and a clear-cut decision.

When he reached the river, the sun was up. It glared imperiously on the choppy waves which sent spirals of spray into the sky. After pacing up and down for a while, he returned to his house. The first person he saw in the yard was Fita, a bucket of water balanced on her head, going into the house. Kortuma fixed his eyes on her lovely figure as she swung her arms and twisted her body to maintain balance. She climbed onto the porch, raised her arms, and bent backwards — her breasts, with streaks of water, stood up — and took the bucket off her head by the handle. Every movement she made pierced his heart like an arrow shot. When she spied him over her shoulder, she grinned.

"I came to make hot water for your bath," she said. She made up the fire, placed the hot water pot on it and filled the pot with water. "Your wives and daughter are at the riverside," she added. Kortuma walked past her and went into the bedroom.

That morning he dispatched a messenger to Digei to summon Polang and her parents to Haindi in order to settle the woman question in one grand discussion. He then summoned his father's widows to the palaver house and told them politely that he was grateful for the good services they had rendered the poor one. He could not thank them enough. In a few days, he would decide their future; and they should always remember, whatever the case may be, that he loved them to the bottom of his heart.

The Chief waited for Polang and her parents for two days. They did not come. After two more days of waiting, he decided to go ahead with the household affair.

It was a cold evening. There was no moon in the sky, so the village was quiet. The Chief had a hurricane lantern hung in the palaver house. The lantern light summoned the village Elders, who chatted and laughed, trying to figure out what the Chief wanted to consult them about.

Chief Kortuma went to the palaver house and sat before them in a high rattan chair. Crossing his legs, he buried his hands in his gown and pushed the gown over his legs until it reached his ankles, the tip falling to the floor. His splayed left foot poked out of the gown, dangled several times, and became steady. There was a placid expression on his round face with its large eyeballs, a nose too large for the face and flat at the base. Leaning on the backrest of the chair, he took his arms from under the gown and clasped his hands on his lap. He bent forward and then leaned backwards again. Growing restive, the Elders shuffled their feet and looked at each other in suspense.

"I called you people," the Chief began at last in a rather flat voice, yet it carried weight. "I want you people to help me decide the future of Chief Gbolokai's widows. My own idea is to let them find other husbands. The poor one gave me a job to do. I owe it to him and to the land to do my very best. And besides, my hands are already full. I won't be able to do my job well if I have to run a houseful of women." He spoke matter-of-factly.

Inscrutable! The Elders stared at one another in disbelief. They could not imagine a Chief, healthy, full-grown, and strong, refusing beautiful young girls as his wives.

"I have never seen this kind of thing happen before," said Seward, a short, slim Elder. He walked to the centre of the palaver house and stood near the lantern, his shadow falling at the entrance. A born orator, his voice was strong, loud and clear. "I want to tell the Chief," he continued, "don't get into a leopard skin and act like a cat. The principal mark of a Chief is a haremful of women. Suppose a stranger came here and asked, 'Where are the Chief's quarters?' Will we tell him, 'That house?'" He pointed aimlessly in the darkness. "Chief," he turned to the Chief, leaning forward and hitting his chest with the tips of his fingers, "we can build you as many houses as you want. Don't send the women away. Women are the builders of men."

Other Elders came forward and said the same thing with varying degrees of emphasis. Chief Kortuma would attempt to interrupt them, but would restrain himself to let them speak their minds. The speaker who impressed him most was Old Man Momolu who spoke with grace and sincerity like a father — urging, advising, pleading. He was a slim, bald-headed man. Kortuma could not help thinking of his own father as he watched him, though he was a direct contrast to the departed Chief who used to be a huge man until sickness struck him down. The last word spoken, Momolu sat down and Chief Kortuma rose to make some observations of his own.

"I understand why you Elders feel as you do," he began. "I too feel the same way because I have the greatest respect for our sacred traditions. But at a time like this, one must use one's best judgment. As a war Chief, I would be doing a disservice to the land if I permit woman palaver to prevent me from giving full and undivided attention to the protection and security of my people. By taking on these women, I would be creating another front in my house. Furthermore, when I die, I don't want to be remembered for how many wives or children I had, but for how well I fought for the land." Having made himself clear on the matter, Chief Kortuma sat down.

Moved by this patriotic appeal, the Elders no longer argued their case; they simply smiled at each other with pride.

"Then your name should be on them until they're remarried," one of them said casually. "You know how it is. If they don't have your protection, men will take advantage of them."

"They'll be my wives until they're remarried — even then . . . every woman in Fuama Chiefdom belongs to me."

That closed the meeting. The Elders now engaged in a general discussion of the war, farming, and household affairs. Chief Kortuma enjoyed the jokes, fables, and wise sayings which they used to illustrate and emphasise their points.

While they were talking a man and a woman entered the palaver house. Chief Kortuma recognised them at once. They were Polang's parents: Kpenkeeh, a tall, bright-skinned man with a frowning face; and Femeh, a shy woman who was dressed in a colourful lapa that was tied over a dress of the same colours, a black headtie firmly fixed on her head. They looked weary after the day-long walk. Kpenkeeh took off his hat and held it in one hand, raised above the midriff, and looked around, searching for a seat until an Elder gave him his stool. But he did not sit down; instead, he commanded his wife with a nod to take the stool. Bending double in honour of the Chief and the Elders, she took quick, short steps to the stool and sat down. Kpenkeeh looked over his shoulder at the entrance to the palaver house for a long time until he saw Polang climb in disdainfully and stand by him. Another Elder gave her his stool. She sat down and turned her back to the Chief, looking at the big toe of her right foot which dug into the earth floor.

"It's good for me to see Elders with you," Kpenkeeh said. The Chief glanced at him and looked away absently as if what he said bored him. It had been said on so many previous occasions.

The father of Polang spat out a pinch of snuff and continued in an apologetic voice. "We have come to apologise for all the troubles our child has been giving you, Chief," he bowed to the Chief who gave him a lopsided glance again. "We gave you this woman as your wife with all our heart. We own her, and we mean for her to be your wife! If she misbehaves, punish her! What man or woman in this land can you not punish? You own all of us, and it is unfortunate that a child like this is giving you so much trouble . . ." His voice broke.

"It's my word, too," Femeh said in a low voice, her only remark on the occasion.

Chief Kortuma agreed that Kpenkeeh and Femeh were true friends, and sincerely wanted him to keep their daughter as his wife. Polang was indeed beautiful and he loved her, but her resentment of him could not be interpreted as an ordinary feminine caprice. Perhaps she wanted a different man.

"Don't put that idea in her head," Kpenkeeh protested vehemently.

"Let me finish talking," the Chief said. "Well, many of the things I've been saying and doing of late appear to differ from our traditional ways. But my aim is the good of the land. What can you get from chaos? You see, I'll never impose love or marriage on any woman . . ."

"Chief," Kpenkeeh interrupted again, "I can't give you the pants and the legs to wear them." There was general laughter. "You are a man like the rest of us. Once a man gets a wife, it remains with him to be strong enough to handle her. I have given you the full right . . ."

"Let me finish talking," Chief Kortuma said again. "Maybe I sound ridiculous, but I believe that a man should have a chance to make his point. I love women. Don't misunderstand me. I could have inherited all the women my father left, for I'm strong enough to keep them. But I have decided to let them find other husbands . . . this matter of forcing someone on somebody else is not my idea of marriage. Anyway, let's hear from the girl herself. I want her to say here and now all the wrongs I have done to her which have caused her to run away from my house so often. I'm fully prepared to apologise to her for my wrongdoings."

"That's it, Polang," Kpenkeeh said to his daughter. "What has the Chief done to you that is so bad that you have to run away from his house all the time?"

Polang only grunted and remained silent. Kpenkeeh stared around in misery like a defeated man.

"I think Kpenkeeh had a point," said Bhenda, a witty Elder. He stood up and spoke seriously. "The girl merely needs advice. All girls act like that. As this is the first time a man is keeping her . . . all she needs to understand is that there's nothing wrong with it." He turned to Polang and said, "My child, don't refuse the Chief. He is a good man. He is able to take care of you better than any man in all the land. Many women wish to have the opportunity which you are throwing away. Probably some irresponsible young man is misleading her," he added.

Polang especially resented Bhenda who often threatened her with fables that had bad endings. She could not recall how many times his reproachful voice had assaulted her. When he first addressed her, she turned her back even more from the Chief and her parents, twitching in her seat. She was in love with Dogba, a handsome, hard-working boy in Digei, but her parents, in a hurry to ingratiate themselves with the royal family, had given her to Kortuma. Whenever she ran home, she would think of stealing into Dogba's zorba, but would think twice about it, for it would endanger his life.

"I am waiting for your answer," Kpenkeeh told her. She still maintained complete silence. "I am sorry that slavery isn't practised any more," he remarked. "She wants all our sufferings to go in vain."

"Don't frighten her," Bhenda said. "Women are like children. One must persuade them, coax them until they see their mistake. You see, my child, probably you're thinking of some good-looking young man, but beauty isn't everything. Long, long ago there was a young, beautiful girl who vowed never to marry a man with any scar or defect. She turned down dozens of suitors whenever she discovered the slightest scar on them. This went on for many years until a dragon heard about it. He borrowed the best of all possible features in the world and went to this girl's village. She fell in love with him at once and they got married. Do you know what happened next?" Bhenda asked Polang, smirking. "My child, in this world the worst often appears to be the best. This dragon of a man took the girl to the middle of an evil forest, transformed himself into a dragon — he had to give back the features which he borrowed, you know — he turned himself into a dragon and devoured the girl. So you see, we're only seeking your own good."

Bhenda returned to his seat, highly gratified that he had clearly shown wisdom.

"Chief Kortuma and you Elders, hear my voice," Kpenkeeh said. "I think we should cut this matter short as the Chief himself suggested. Let us ask Polang to state definitely whether or not she wants to stay with the Chief. No more advice, no more threats. Let her plainly tell us what she wants to do and we'll go by her decision."

He turned to his daughter, watched her sadly as if he was about to offer her as a sacrifice to some god unknown.

"Polang," he called her in a clear, loud voice.

"Hnn," Polang said.

"Do you want to live with Chief Kortuma as his wife?

"Yes," she said quietly.

"Think twice before answering, because if you make a fool of us again, I'll never approve any other marriage of yours, for I'll take it for granted that you don't want to marry. You are not compelled to stay here. Are you willing to live with Chief Kortuma as his wife?"

"Yes," she said again.

6

Having abandoned his routine of rising early in the morning, bathing, and paying Chief Kortuma a visit or going with his family to the farm, the Master now sauntered silently about the village each day. He could not eat half of any dish his wife prepared for him. This aroused the curiosity of the villagers who now and then cast puzzled stares at him. At first, Yata thought his unusual behaviour was a sign of an approaching illness, but as he continued to behave like this for several days and complained of no fever or pain, she ascribed it to his acute involvement in medical affairs. She had learned through the years that a Zoe lived in two worlds: the world of everyday life, and the world of the supernatural. It was normal for him to lock himself up in the bedroom all day, dealing with medicines. But on the contrary, the Master was simply reflecting on the turbulent life which he had led and how it had inexorably culminated in the present situation. He often felt sorry for his wife who had to endure his peculiar way of life and all its attendant anxieties, pains, inconveniences, and dread. Doubtless, she was deeply concerned about his present mood; she might have had hints of the impending war, but did not know what part he would play in it — or if he would play any part in it at all. He would attempt to break the unwelcome news to her, but his lips grew heavy as if they had turned to lead.

How strange life is, the Master thought during these days of intense reflection. After leading a tumultuous life, wandering all over Lomaland, encountering numerous and unexpected disasters, he had come to the conclusion that a man's life is a unit, regardless of the turns of fortune. If a man is destined to be poor, he likely remains poor all his life even if he happens to accumulate fortunes for himself. He remembered the story of Bima, a War Lord of Wozi, who conquered nearly all of Lomaland. Bima accumulated immense wealth, but he buried all his money in the ground somewhere in the deep forest, and nobody ever discovered it after his death. Bima never slaughtered any of his large herd of cattle for food, he never wore an expensive gown as becoming a Chief. He thought of the poor man who happens to acquire wealth and who might ruin himself with over-indulgence. He tries to kill the poverty that is in him with too much of everything, ending up in misery. And finally, the man who is marked for poverty who may find himself deprived of all the nice things of life in spite of all his efforts to overcome poverty. He works hard for many long years to defeat poverty, but all in vain. No sooner would he acquire some prized possession, such as money or cattle, than he would waste it on trifles that bring him no respectable social status or lasting satisfaction. Similarly, the Master's own life had followed a regular pattern that was characterised by violence and danger. And it had continued to be so in spite of his assiduous and uncompromising search for peace, security, and joy. Whatever reprieve he had had from misfortune had been deceptive. It appeared to him, to all practical purposes, that his life must be offered as a sacrifice for others, regardless of whatever he did to escape this fate. And he could have had no better opportunity to make this supreme sacrifice.

As a boy he had fled from Fisebu in Liberia to Masanda in Guinea when war broke out between Gizima and Wubomai. The war came because of boundary disputes. Hellingi, the powerful War Lord of Wubomai, had decided to extend his Chiefdom all the way to Zorzor, the Headquarters of Gizima. But Chief Guzeh of Gizima could not accept such an arrangement. The two Chiefdoms, therefore, went to war. In the dead of night, his parents had fled with him and his little sisters and brothers. It was a hideous journey which took several weeks as they had to hide themselves in the dense forest among the outcropped roots of giant beleh and cotton-wood trees during the day and could resume their journey only at sundown. For many years they lived in Masanda where their journey took them. They returned to their homeland when the Liberian Government managed to pacify the north and erect barracks in Zorzor.

Upon returning home, they decided to live in Baloma where they made farms and hunted in the surrounding forests. A full-grown boy now, the Master was initiated into the Poro Society in Baloma. It was during this time that he began to practise medicine. And he met with modest successes. It had been predicted at his birth that he would be a Zoe because he was born with great difficulty. His mother had spent three consecutive days 'behind the house' before he was born, and he was born only after the intervention of a Gbon

Zoe. Probably because of jealousy of his success with medicines or because of vengeance, the Elders of the land asked his father for 'the chicken' to be sacrificed to the shrine of the Chiefdom which was located in the heart of the forest. Their eyes were on the Master. This practice of killing a brilliant male child for the mysterious shrine was carried out once every seven years, and it was his father's turn to offer the best of his offspring for the sacrifice. But the Master's prescient mind came to his rescue. He noticed a change in his father's attitude; the old man became sullen and he frequently cast a look of despair and dejection at him. Eventually the Master got the message. One night he disappeared from the village and went to Borkeza where he lived with a distant relative. There he was hidden for some time until reports of the end of the Elders' anger had reached him. His father had offered them another 'chicken', the brother that was next to him.

The Master married a beautiful girl in Borkeza, but she died in child-birth after several years. The child did not live. Undaunted, he continued his medical practice there until a crazy old man claimed one day that it had been revealed to him that he should be sacrificed for the protection of the village from some unspecified, imminent disaster. His next flight took him to Kpelleland, to Chief Gbolokai. Gbolokai had received him with both hands and even offered him a wife who bore him a beautiful daughter. In a bid to repay in part the Chief's generosity, he became his private Zoe. He had put up a grim struggle to save the Chief's life, but one could not be saved from death. Now he was preparing to make the greatest sacrifice anyone could make for his fellow-man. If only Chief Gbolokai were alive to witness it.

On the eve of the tenth day when the warriors were expected in Haindi, the Master 'washed' his medicines. It was then that Yata suspected that he would play an important part in the war that was to come. But she held her peace. The Master gathered all his medicines in a large rattan fanner and placed them at the door. Squatting before the fanner, he took a red rooster from his wife who stood apprehensively behind him, cut its neck, and sprinkled the medicines with the gushing blood, then gave the dead chicken to her to cook. Yata watched him keenly, her eyes wide open, as he held his hands over the medicines and muttered supplications. Much to her surprise, the ceremony was already over, and the Master carried the medicines hurriedly back into the bedroom and returned to the central room where Yata was busy plucking the chicken. He broke the news to her. For a moment, she sat still like a statue, and stared at him with a long face, her thick lips parted in disbelief. Beads of sweat suddenly grew on her forehead below the rim of the black headtie which was tied firmly on her head. As if she had assessed the situation and accepted the inevitable, she grew slightly relaxed and resumed her work without comment. The Master stood over her with a baffled expression on his face.

"When is it?" Yata asked him in a subdued voice.

"Tomorrow," he said quickly and walked to the door.

"There's nothing a woman like me can do about it . . . but, but be on your guard," Yata called after him.

Unexpectedly, a loud uproar of voices and foot thuds detonated in the Kpaan. The Master became suddenly convinced that the warriors had arrived. Leaping out of the house, he almost collided with Kulah, his daughter, who ran with alarm from the square where she had been playing in the moonlight until this strange clamour drove every child from there. She buried herself in her father's bosom for a moment and then rushed into the house, banging the door shut.

Running to the Kpaan, the Master met the warriors who immediately gathered around him as they continued to dance jubilantly in a vicious and frantic manner. There was no chance to say a word, so he only greeted them with a faint smile. After a time they ran around the village that was all but deserted, eventually gathering in the square and performing a mock battle as a way of spending the night since they were no longer permitted to enter houses. Their mournful song, *The spear and the sword,* shattered the silent, cold night. Swords clashed and clattered, spears flew in the sky. Shortly before dawn, they scampered back into the Kpaan at the blare of a ram horn.

While the Master and the warriors were so engaged, Chief Kortuma, prayers on his lips, slaughtered a spotless, white ram and sprinkled the bank with its blood, threw the dead ram into the deep river and hurried back to the village. When he reached his house and touched the door, a rooster crowed. Without realising it, he had spent the entire night, for the first time, at the shrine.

Opening the door, he heard Yembele's quavering voice call him, "Data!" She rose from her mat by the fireside and grasped his legs in a frenzy. The Chief's three wives who slept in the bed behind the fireplace, stirred and groaned, trying to wake up.

"Keep quiet, my child," Lorpu told Yembele in a low and fearful voice. Yembele obediently left her father and sat on the edge of the bed, trembling.

The Chief dressed quickly, took his cowtail, and joined the warriors who had gathered before his house. On seeing him, they grew quiet and calm — gazed at him eagerly, adjusting their raffia skirts with their left hands while holding spears with their right hands, swords slung on their shoulders. Chief Kortuma walked with confidence and dignity, waving the cowtail, and stood before them on an elevated patch of ground, a broad smile on his face.

"Warriors of Fuama Chiefdom," he declared in a loud, clear voice, "once more war is on us." The warriors' faces lit up as they watched him; apparently considering themselves as the best of the land, they waved their rippling arms in the air with each word he spoke. The Master, a musket hooked to his back, walked up to the Chief and stood beside him. "We're not the cause of this war, though we'll be the first to strike," the Chief continued. "Well, the story is well known to all of you. I need not repeat it. But let me say one thing: prove to the Gola once and for all that we are men! Life is sweet, but death is better than the shame of humiliation. Man lives for honour, and once honour is at stake, it's better to die. Let this be the last war we'll fight with the Gola, for I want complete victory. May the Ancestors be with you and give wisdom to the Master to lead you to victory."

"Let it be so," the warriors declared in one voice.

The Chief waved his cowtail in the direction of the Kpaan, and the warriors walked in that direction.

The day was cold and misty. The harmattan held sway over the land, even though the morning sun rose rapidly. Pepper birds and wrens twittered and chirped in the kola trees, greeting the sunshine. Animals walked sluggishly in the square, sniffing at crumbs of cassava, eddoes, sugar cane, and banana peelings which careless villagers had scattered around. Littering up the village with dung, many of the animals actually grasped the crumbs of foodstuff with their powerful jaws and chewed briskly, shaking their tails to drive off the tsetse flies that roamed about them. Women and children, who usually came out at this time of day, laughing, calling each other, exchanging greetings, and going to the river to fetch fresh water, were still indoors.

Chief Kortuma and the Master stood together awhile, chatting and looking about the lifeless village. On an impulse, they gripped each other's hands very tight and snapped fingers. Then each man went to his house at a fast pace.

When the Master entered his own house, his daughter who was plump and highly sensitive became aware of his presence in her sleep. Yata had tried to cuddle her to sleep, and had succeeded only after a long struggle. Kulah had cried for her father when she told her that he would soon go to war. Though such a matter ought to remain a secret to a child, Yata could not avoid revealing it to her, for she had harassed her continuously with the painful question, "Where's Data? Where's Data?" Like the average mother, she could not stand the plight of a child asking for its father. It was a relief for him to enter the house. On seeing her father, Kulah impulsively jumped out of her bed which was by the fireside and grabbed him by the legs. The Master stooped down and tried to gather her in his arms — to no avail. Standing straight, he quickly pushed the musket to his back with a shrug of his left shoulder as it began to slip down his left arm.

He glanced at his wife who sat motionless on a stool; the elbow of her left arm that was decorated with an ivory bracelet was placed on her raised knee, her chin and lips cupped in her hand, the fingers wide apart.

In an effort to dispel the gloom that descended on him upon watching Yata's melancholy look and to show that he was in control of the situation, the Master glowered at his wife:

"Get the child!"

But Kulah started crying, and her piercing, frantic voice mingled with her father's command: "You won't go to the war, Data! Will you?" she kept saying.

"Nothing will happen to me, my child," the Master said absently, watching Yata with a baffled stare. A tremor shot through his head and he began to feel a severe headache, though he managed to look composed.

"But Mama said that people get killed in war!" Kulah maintained, writhing in pain and stamping the dirt floor with her small feet in frustration as she continued to hold her father by the legs. "I don't want you to die, Data!" she said again. "Please stay, Data!" She was now sobbing, and the tears welled up profusely in her eyes and flowed down her fat cheeks.

"Nothing will happen to me . . . nothing . . ." the Master stuttered.

"Let the other men go, Data!" Kulah pleaded in a hoarse voice.

Pulling the girl forcefully from his legs, the Master carried her in his arms, looking reproachfully at Yata with red eyes. Yata roamed irresolutely about the room.

"You didn't take care of the child!" the Master quarrelled. "Instead, you've been giving her ideas."

"The child has been crying for you," Yata said sharply. "What could I do?"

Kulah in his arms, the Master went into the bedroom, managed to take down the musket and place it in a corner of the room at the foot of the bed. Returning to the central room, he told his wife:

"Come for the child. I must get ready quickly."

"So you men are about to go?" Yata asked in a shrill voice as she tried to get the child, but Kulah clung to her father desperately, holding him firmly by the neck.

"Almost," the Master said. "We're about to consecrate the weapons . . . Kulah, go to Mama."

Yata pulled her from the Master with force as she fought and cried and called her father. But the Master, paying no further attention to her, quickly went into the bedroom and closed the door.

He pulled the fanner of medicines from under the bed, squatted by it, and examined each piece of medicine. First he took Gaiyomoi, which was in a black deer horn. It supposedly had the power to uproot witches wherever they might be and punish them severely or kill them. The Master recalled some of the many occasions on which crones had come to him, crawling on their bellies, and confessed that 'the horn' had caught them. He laid this medicine back in the fanner. Then he took Naatuwoi, which if placed in the path of an enemy could cause the enemy's feet to swell with pus. He decided against this as well. After going through all his medicines undecidedly for a time, he finally chose a small, black gourd filled with the brown 'lightning' powder, which the initiate could manipulate in any desirable way to cut an enemy down. He resolved to take it with him. Removing the wooden stopper from the gourd, he put some powder under the nail of the index finger of his left hand, then he placed the gourd in his side pocket.

Yata who never intruded upon him when he dealt with medicines, presently rushed into the bedroom, looking bewildered.

"Will you see a sand-cutter?" she reminded him, holding the door tentatively, her small eyes rolling in their sockets in her oval face, waiting for an answer.

The Master replied almost immediately, as if he were already engaged in a conversation with her:

"If you are a Zoe and know that you are a Zoe, there is nothing to fear." He spoke with extreme conviction.

Yata's lips twitched uneasily for a time. Remembering in a flash that the food was ready, she managed to say:

"Make haste and eat."

"From now on, we're not supposed to eat anything that is cooked at home," the Master replied as he continued fingering his medicines.

"At least you should eat something, Gayflor!" she said bluntly, suppressing a sob, and sitting near her daughter on the bed by the fireside, her hands clasped on her lap, looking with dismay at the pot of rice that was now on the embers.

Without saying a word, the Master continued to rifle through the charms, much more to be busy than to make another selection, for he had decided on the most powerful charm he knew. At length he stood up and said:

"Remember to take good care of the child. Do not grieve, for grief is meant for the dead. You are a gbolokpolo. You know very well when men are in action their wives must behave as if all is well. Find something to do while I am away, and when you need help, see Chief Kortuma."

Yata gave one fitful wail, but, not knowing how she would justify such a display of grief if crowds gathered at her door, she kept quiet and sat helplessly on a low stool by the fireplace, watching the cold, grey ashes. Assaulted by loneliness, she pulled her daughter gently by the arm from the bed, and placed her between her knees. Unable to understand the drama unfolding before her, Kulah simply laid her head on her mother's breast, and held her own legs with her small, delicate hands. Yata began to think of the fate of the Master who had never fought a battle before. How will things work out for him? she thought. He was too proud to consult a sand-cutter. Perhaps he would not even take any medicine along for protection. It was his stubbornness, and not his going to the war, that piqued her. She had the greatest reverence for medicines and believed that sheer force was insufficient to counter real danger, whether natural or supernatural. Her concern for her husband was suddenly replaced by fear for her own safety. She could not tell how long it would be before she would be able to go to her farm for food. She could not determine how safe the village would be, for an enemy warrior could sneak through the surrounding tangled undergrowth any time and set it ablaze. Dry thatched roofs, highly inflammable, would not protect anyone if set on fire.

Kulah was almost asleep. Yata shook her briskly. "Wake up!" she said. "Day has broken! Wake up and let's go to the river for water!" Kulah rubbed her eyes weakly and stood up. Trying to cheer her up, Yata said, "Don't worry about your father. Nothing will happen to him." Then they left with empty buckets for the river.

Meanwhile, the Master went to the Kpaan and commanded the warriors to assemble before the blacksmith's shop, a little shed flanked by tall kola trees and thick bushes on the western outskirts of the village. Now fully prepared for action, the warriors were dressed in baggy, sleeveless country cloth shirts, raffia skirts, amulets studded with cowries — sheathed swords slung on their left shoulders, spears with pieces of wood stuck at the sharp points in their right hands. The Master inspected them briefly as they now walked silently to the blacksmith's shop. In the village, women and children were still indoors.

When the warriors had assembled at the blacksmith's shop, the Master walked with determined steps to the entrance of the shop, where he stood and declared in a slightly hoarse voice:

"I, Gayflor, declare war on Golaland!" He strained to make the greatest possible emphasis.

Though he expected this development, the blacksmith appeared to be taken aback. A slim, grizzled man with rolling eyeballs and constantly flapping eyelids, he held the tough, brown leather on the bellows with one hand, with the other he held the handle of a hammer that lay near a large piece of rock before him. His lips were agape, his quick eyes gazed uncertainly at the crowd. Now and then he added more charcoal to the fire between two low mud walls into which the two pipes from the two bellows were stuck. The Master's words sent a chill through him.

After the Master repeated his declaration of war three times, the warriors cheered him, "Eeeeeeeeeeei!!", danced jubilantly, and sang loudly. He joined them 'to blow the wind of war' over the village. They beat the dusty earth with their feet at regular intervals, sending whirls of dust into the air, and moved around the village, killing several chickens and goats. They were soon buried in dust. As they returned to the blacksmith's shop, they slackened their fury until they came to a standstill. The gentle wind blew the dust away, and the silence that usually follows a wild celebration or a lightning storm fell upon the village which lay bare in the bright sunshine.

The Master emerged from the crowd of warriors, walked proudly, and stood before the blacksmith, who now pounded a piece of red hot iron with his hammer on the rock. All of a sudden, a little boy, about twelve years old, jumped into the shop and began manipulating the bellows eagerly, to the satisfaction of the blacksmith, repeatedly spying the warriors over his shoulder. As the iron got cold, hard and dark-grey, the blacksmith would place it back into the fire with the tongs; it would get red hot again, and he would hammer it some more. It began taking a definite shape, something like a cutlass.

"Good work," the Master told him as he watched him.

The blacksmith put the cutlass back into the glowing fire, laid the tongs and the hammer near the rock, and told the Master to have a seat. The Master sat on a low stool opposite him. Perspiring slightly, the blacksmith repeatedly wiped his forehead with his right palm.

"You know me, Master," the blacksmith said, scratching his arched right knee self-consciously. "I can do better than this, but the iron is brittle. I don't know how good that cutlass will be." He looked at the iron in the fire.

"You make good spears," the Master flattered him.

"Any child can make spears," the blacksmith said, gazing at the Master.

"Not good ones, though."

The blacksmith looked at the cutlass again. It was burning out.

"That's enough," he told the boy who was pumping the bellows with all his might.

The blacksmith took a piece of vine with a frizzled end, dipped it into a rusty cup full of water, piled the charcoals together with it, and dipped it back into the cup. He watched the warriors curiously and then watched the Master.

"So you're ready for the war," he sighed, looking into space briefly; he took the cutlass out of the heap of burning charcoals and laid it near the rock.

"We're ready, Flomo. We're as ready as we can ever be. We're ready for the ritual."

The warriors gave a loud cheer.

"Where's the white thing?" Flomo said.

As a Zoe, the Master thought it debasing to seek nelp from another Zoe. Here was a man using the same gimmicks he himself used on others. He knew that, whatever Flomo did or said, it was their courage and strength that would sustain them in war. However, in deference to tradition, the blacksmith must consecrate and bless the weapons before they were used in war. The Master tucked his right hand into his pocket, took out ten coins and gave them to Flomo.

"That's the white thing," he said.

"Thank you," Flomo said, putting the coins into the side pocket of his tattered, black, short pants. Then he took down his bag of medicines which hung behind him on a rafter stick.

He swept a circular spot on the dirt floor with a small rice straw

70

broom, and took the fetishes out of the bag one by one, laid them carefully in two straight rows, stretching his right arm to the east, his left arm to the west, his right arm to the south and his left arm to the north. He stood up and scanned the warriors, his bloodshot eyes rolling in their sockets, his lips parted in a smile, his brown teeth, a few of them missing, showing. Sitting down again, he addressed the medicines in esoteric words, cheering them, challenging them, imploring them. After a time he became quiet, watching the medicines with a fixed gaze. He looked up, turned to the boy and told him to go to his wife for a red rooster and some red kola nuts.

A slight cloud hung over the quiet village. The nervous twittering of wrens and pepper birds was no longer heard in the kola trees and the surrounding bushes; only the fresh smell of leaves and grasses prevailed.

The boy soon returned, running, with the chicken and the kola nuts. Flomo grabbed the chicken, plucked its neck, cut it with a sharp blade, held it tightly by the head and the feet while it wriggled, sprinkling the medicines with its gushing blood. At the same time he made more esoteric remarks to the medicines. When the chicken died in his hands and the blood ceased to flow, he laid it down and took two of the kola nuts from the boy and split them in four halves and laid them by the medicines.

"Bring your spears and swords," he told the warriors who looked solemn as if paying homage to the sacred rite. They immediately unsheathed their swords, placed them with the spears, ends-together, over the medicines. Those that could not make their way into the shop sent their weapons in.

Rising, Flomo put a kola nut into his mouth, chewed it briskly, blew the mixture onto the weapons, giving a loud cry. He danced all over the weapons with his calloused feet until sweat streamed down his cheeks, the creases on his forehead, and his bare back. When he became exhausted, he sat down, panting.

"It's over," he told the Master, wiping his face with a piece of cloth. "God will stand behind us. I have done this twice and have been successful twice. God does not forsake you if your heart is good to others. My heart is not bad to anyone, so all I do is always success-ful." Standing up, he gestured with authority. "I will stand behind you! Depend on me! So long as you fight with the work of a blacksmith and it is the will of a blacksmith that you win, you will win. May the spears and the swords serve you well."

"Let it be so," the Master and his warriors replied.

"If you hit anyone with any of them, may he die instantly."

"Let it be so."

"If by accident any of you get cut by a spear or a sword, may the wound be very slight and of no consequence."

"Let it be so."

"Take your men to war. God will bless you," Flomo ended on a firm note.

"Thank you," said the Master. "We will do the best we can. Goodbye."

They left for the river bank, dancing majestically, singing, *Goodbye to the old maid.* The river bawled and cried at the ripples in an unusually monotonous tone. Below Luen it looked calm and placid, but unapproachable. Except for the sound of waves dashing against the bank, birds squealing, squirrels jumping from bush to bush, it was quiet. They entered the dark, lonely forest and walked down the river with full confidence towards Golaland.

7

Chief Kortuma did not know whether he was going to or coming from the river. All he knew was that he was placing one foot before the other, floating in space where everything looked clean, bright and beautiful. The sun was sinking rapidly beyond the horizon and when he reached the outskirts, he stood still and watched its last brilliant flare of red and yellow colours. Of late he had developed a penchant for watching trees, green grass, birds . . . now the enchanting sunset. In the purview of the flare of the dying sun were hawks, Fong, palm birds, and Blue Wings hovering like leaves in a whirlwind above the azure forest. Soon the sun was buried in darkness. He looked briefly at the early stars that began to appear in the sky, and resumed walking, feeling relaxed and cheerful.

Crickets and rodents rustled in the grass on both sides of the path. Chief Kortuma deeply inhaled the fresh scent of the river and the refreshing warm breeze that blew over it. He sat on the back of an old, broken canoe that was out of service and was used mainly as a seat, crossed his legs and took a deep breath. Prayers and offerings no longer helped. In fact, he did not wish to bother the gods any more, but simply to be alone. He looked at the river glistening in the starlight that grew brighter as the darkness deepened. Like the sunset, the choppy, rolling, silvery waves arrested him as if it were his first time of seeing them. As he watched the river, his eyes suddenly caught sight of a blurred, tall, dark figure on the opposite shore. Riveting his eyes with fear and suspicion on the nondescript figure that defied all scrutiny, he said to himself, "It must be a man." He looked at the shore on his side and saw the canoe which looked like a long piece of log floating on the river. Maybe he wants it," he thought aloud.

In a loud, clear voice, he called, "Uuuuuuuuuuu-wi!"

No reply.

He called again, "Uuuuuuuuuuu-wi!"

No reply.

"The canoe is on this side!" he declared. "If you need it, I can bring it for you!" he called again, feeling a trifle sorry for the poor traveller.

No reply.

The figure grew tall and bulky and then vanished from sight like a spurt of dust blown by the wind. A ghost!

Chief Kortuma had come to grips with reality. Near him, on the upper bank, was the cemetery of Haindi, where a ghost, no doubt, sat on top of each grave. Beyond the river was a ghost. His heart pounded his ribs violently, a bitter taste welled up in his mouth, but he quickly calmed down. As he was now vulnerable, fear was useless. In order to make sure the ghost had not cast an evil spell on him, he called out his own name, testing to see if he still possessed his voice. The first disaster one experienced on talking to an evil spirit was to lose one's voice. But his voice was loud and clear; he judged by this that it was a good spirit he had seen and addressed. Could it be his father's spirit? he wondered. Most unlikely. The poor one had no qualms about appearing to him directly. An ample proof of this was his dream of his father shortly after his burial. The more Chief Kortuma thought about the whole affair, the more tense, confused, and disconcerted he became. He therefore resolved to go home. As he walked through the quiet village, he suddenly remembered his mother telling him, when he was a child, that whenever a village became quiet like this, it meant ghosts were flying over it. He had never taken her seriously, but now he did for he had just seen one.

Chief Kortuma tried to forget his encounter with the spirit and think about his warriors. It seemed that he had done everything, short of going to the war himself, that could be done for men at war. He had given numerous peace offerings to the gods and to the Ancestors, he had made blood sacrifices, and he had taken care not to meddle with the warriors' final preparation for the war. He had not even attended the consecration ceremony at the blacksmith's shop, for he could imagine exactly what the warriors would have told him had he been there: "We will not go to war if you don't leave us. It is better for the Gola to take the land than for you to die." If the Chief were killed or taken prisoner, it would mean their discomfiture. They would automatically stop fighting and surrender, whether or not they had an advantage in war. The warriors of Fuama Chiefdom had never lost a war in this way, and he was not prepared to make them take the risk. Had he a full-grown son to succeed him in case he died or disappeared, probably the risk could have been taken . . . why this excessive preoccupation with the war? the Chief suddenly asked himself. Why the impatience? Although he had full confidence in the power and performance of the Master, he longed for the customary periodic reports from the front. For a whole month he had received none; the suspense had an unsettling effect on him: he became dazed, his head heavy, his heart beat violently, and a severe wave of heat — almost of paralysing proportions — spread through his body, his eyes grew dim, his legs grew weak and unsteady. He realised that there was no avoiding the problem by taking refuge in day-dreaming.

Chief Kortuma had hardly entered his house when he turned around abruptly, deciding to spend some time with his headwife and not continue to be alone with his thoughts. It appeared to him that he was reaching the danger point and must consequently discuss his problems with someone who was close to him. And he knew nobody else who was more suitable.

Lorpu lived in one of Chief Gbolokai's houses which was located at the beginning of the road that led to the part of the river where women bathed and got water for household use. In order to avoid congestion, Kortuma had given her that house, where she lived with her daughter; he promised to give Korlu and Polang the house in which the widows lived. Then he would live by himself and call in his wives by turns to sleep with him.

As he entered Lorpu's yard, Chief Kortuma had another misgiving: perhaps it would be better to see a sand-cutter instead. But he decided that that would be the next step after talking with Lorpu. All he needed at the moment was someone to talk with. When he entered the porch, a group of goats that had been lying there scampered about and then clattered down the dirt stairs. A whiff of their nauseating odour blew in his face. He wondered if Lorpu was already asleep. As for Yembele, he knew that she usually went to sleep as soon as she touched the sleeping mat or bed. He had never knocked on their door this late before. Thus they might mistake him for a ghost or a Gola warrior and refuse to let him in. However, he inched his way to the door, knocked softly, straining his ears for any sound of movement or response. There was none. He knocked again, "It's I, Kortuma — Lorpu, open the door!" Painful silence. Could it be that his wife heard him, but deliberately refused to open the door? the thought flashed in his mind. The Chief knocked on the door very hard this time, saying in a loud voice, "Lorpu! Lorpu! Lorpu, open the door! It's Kortuma . . ."

Unexpectedly, the door flew open and slammed against the wall. There wasn't a flicker of light in the central room. The Chief was stunned.

Groping in the grim darkness, stubbing his toes against firewood, he made his way to the fireplace and searched in the ashes with his hands, blowing frantically on the hearth, until he discovered a live charcoal. He put pieces of bark and bamboo splinters on the charcoal, still blowing, until a blaze of fire shot up, lighting the central room. Chief Kortuma scanned the room, gathered more splinters together and made a torch. Torch in hand, he went into the bedroom that had a long sheet of black cloth for a door, and saw his daughter lying in the bed, alone. Snuggled in a blanket with blue and white stripes, she lay flat on her back, her left hand poking out of the bedclothes and lying casually on her breast, her face turned to the yellowish, rough, mud wall. The Chief sighed in dismay and guessed that his headwife had probably gone behind the house to the bath fence in order to pass water. With the torch he lit an oil lamp that was on a wooden table which stood near the head of the bed. Then he sat on the edge of the bed, waiting for Lorpu.

Yembele stretched, kicked him lightly in the loins with her left foot, turned over and lay on her right side. Then she pushed the bedclothes down to her waist, leaving the upper part of her body bare. Chief Kortuma briefly gazed at her shapely figure and became overwhelmed with paternal feelings. The thought that Lorpu might be gone to a lover, leaving his daughter exposed to danger, unnerved him. The Chief went to the central room and threw the torch into the fireplace. After standing in the central room undecidedly for a moment, he went out to the porch and looked around in the darkness, seeing nothing, or at least seeing only that disdainful and nondescript figure with his mind's eye. "Why should it continue haunting me?" he thought.

"Lorpu has no right to stay this long away from my child," he said under his breath. "It doesn't matter where she has gone or why."

Running down the dirt stairs, he called her in a loud voice, "Lorpu! Lorpuuuuu! Lorpu!" He stubbed his toe on a clump of dirt below the last stair, staggered and almost fell, but managed to regain balance.

Having been in the darkness so long, he could now see clearly. Chief Kortuma decided to check the bath fence; he called Lorpu as he went there, his voice echoing strangely through the village. But Lorpu was not in the bath fence. It became clear to him that she had gone to a lover. He remembered warning his wives about the problem of engaging in love affairs. "You'll be making me small in other men's eyes by lying with other men," he would tell them.

He paced up and down in the yard, waiting for Lorpu. After some time, he heard Yembele call:

"Mama! Mama!"

The Chief rushed into the bedroom and saw her on all fours, feeling urgently in the bed, her eyes closed. She was about to spring out of the bed.

"This is Data," the Chief said, touching her by the shoulder. "Don't cry. Sleep." She sat in the bed, rubbed her eyes with her hand, yawning. "It's I, Yembele," the Chief said with reassurance. "Don't be afraid." He spoke in his usual flat voice which he thoughtYembele would recognise. But it was only when she opened her eyes and looked at him up and down that she recognised him and grew relaxed.

"Where's Mama?" she asked, still yawning and rubbing her eyes.

"I just came," the Chief said. "I don't know where she has gone."

"Will she come back?"

"I don't know . . . lie down and go to sleep."

Yembele lay down and wrapped herself in the bedclothes, the Chief helping her. She tried to sleep. In a moment, the front door flew open and slammed against the wall. Lorpu rushed into the house as if she were pursued by a brigand, calling Yembele breathlessly. Yembele answered in a weak voice, sitting up in the bed. Lorpu halted at the room door, winced, and stared coldly at the Chief.

"Where have you been?" the Chief asked harshly. Her thick lips twitched uneasily, but the words did not come. "Tell me where you've come from!" His eyes poking out sharply, the Chief stood up.

Yembele began to kick and scream in the bed. Lorpu tried to go to her, but the Chief blocked her way with his massive body. He posed to strike her, but thought better of it because she could scream and everyone would think that a Gola warrior had attacked her. What a shame if the villagers came to find their Chief fighting his wife!" But Chief Kortuma could not help himself. For the first time, as far as he knew, he slapped Lorpu in the face, pushed her violently into pots and pans, and dashed her against the wall.

"You animal! You slut! You dog!" he said in the same breath, panting.

Lorpu neither fought nor cried. Chief Kortuma shook her briskly by both shoulders, asking her to reveal her lover's name. But she neither defended herself nor said a word. Leaving her in anger, the

Chief went to the door, highly irritated. "I will know that man tomorrow," he said over his shoulder and stepped out.

He walked among cows, goats, and sheep that lay leisurely on their bellies in the village square, chewing the cud. He could not recall how many times he had walked in the night, alone. It seemed to him that he spent as much time outdoors as indoors and that life behaved in unexpected ways. Would he be able to redeem his promise to his father? Even the simple problem of managing his household was proving insoluble. With all the sacrifices, with all the worries and effort, things remained as complicated as ever.

On entering his house, he saw the lantern burning. He did not remember lighting it when he left. Well, it did not matter — thanks to whoever had been so thoughtful for him. He turned the wick down and prepared to go to bed and rest. He had failed to find consolation outside his own resources.

"Where have you been?" He, in turn, got the question which he had asked Lorpu. The voice seemed to come from the bed. Turning up the wick and looking apprehensively at the bed, Chief Kortuma surprisingly saw Polang lying on her back in the bed, her round, supple breasts standing up. Silhouetted against the saffron light, the breasts made two conical shadows on the wall behind the bed. A smile on her face, Polang said:

"I've been waiting for you ever since!"

The Chief grew relaxed, for when he first heard the voice, it was the image of that detestable creature that flashed in his mind. He sat on the bed and Polang began to scratch his back.

"You want to bathe?" she asked.

"I'm all right," he said with a sigh.

Polang sat up and then laid her head on his lap. He absently fondled her soft, warm breasts.

"I thought you didn't love me," he said with passion loosening up, and smiling broadly. For the moment he felt that all his troubles were over.

"I love you," Polang said in a cute voice, turning up for him to have full access to her breasts. He fumbled at her waist. Polang pulled the bedclothes over her naked body.

He now understood her fear and judged that it was normal. He had been too insensitive and impatient.

"Put out the light, let's go to bed," she said. "You need rest."

He undressed, blew out the light, and got into bed.

The morning came quickly. He wanted to rest some more, but a man could not afford to lie in bed while crowing roosters and hissing voices all over the village indicated that day had broken. Polang was already up. She and Korlu who slept in the central room began making warm water for his bath. With an effort he roused himself, got dressed, went out to the porch and sat in his creaking rattan chair.

The morning was different from the usual mornings of Haindi when men bustled out of their houses, the wooden handles of cutlasses poking out of their armpits, hurrying to their farms or traps or wine trees. He only saw an old man in tattered clothes going towards the southern outskirts, the handle of a cutlass pressed against his ribs, its blade poking behind him.

"People, when they grow old usually don't care about death," he thought. "Warriors don't kill old people anyway." He remembered Chief Gbolokai. It seemed as though whenever he saw an old man he had to think of his father.

Presently, Polang came out of the house, a bucket of warm water in her hand.

"Are you ready to bathe?" she asked. There was warmth in her voice like the warmth he had felt in her body. He feigned a dignified look, the look he was fond of showing underlings. She now acted like a wife. Chief Kortuma felt guilty for he had not made love to her as passionately as he should have done that first night. Maybe she thought he was still angry with her. He had only had her and lain beside her without passion, as if nothing had happened. She was so inexperienced, he could not discuss personal problems with her.

"Yes," he said casually, "I'm ready to bathe. Take the water to the fence and get me my rattan brush."

An empty bucket in her hand, Korlu left for the river.

Polang walked down the dirt stairs with care, the bucket of warm water swinging slightly in her hand. With her left hand she rolled up the edge of her lapa tightly, making a bun, so that it would not fall into the water. Chief Kortuma admired her tender, youthful skin, her round breasts, her hair plaited in beautiful rows. Soon she returned to the house and brought him the long piece of rattan with a frizzled end.

He took it absently and said, "Call Sumo to me. Tell him it's something very important." Then he began brushing his teeth vigorously.

Early in the morning, Lorpu went to Kona, a slim, pensive, old woman with white hair always tied neatly with a black headtie. She lived on the eastern outskirts of the village. Having had the misfortune of outliving her children and her husband, she lived alone in a dilapidated house, supporting herself mostly by making baby medicines and with the generous gifts of kind villagers. Mothers often brought her rice, meat, fish, palm oil, clothes, and money in gratitude for her services.

Lorpu knew that Kona would be able to help her because she was a master herbalist. Many girls in her situation had consulted her before and had received help. She would confess everything to her without being modest, for that was the only real requirement for success in trying to find the solution to such a problem.

As it was her habit, Kona had risen early in the morning and was strolling in her yard. When she saw Lorpu rushing to her with a frowning face, she asked:

"How is Yembele?"

"She's well," Lorpu replied shyly.

"What happened then?" Kona maintained, standing still, her arms akimbo, watching Lorpu with her tired eyes.

"Kortuma caught me last night," Lorpu confessed. "I'm sure I'll take kperor this morning. I'm not afraid for myself but that poor man, you see. I promised to cover up for him. I don't want to put him in trouble at a time like this." Tears stood in her eyes.

They stood near each other in the grassy yard, their backs turned to the small, round mud house crowned with a black thatched roof loosely held together with rattan ropes. Kona looked into space as if she didn't care in the least for Lorpu's confession. As she waited for Kona's reply, Lorpu dug the black top soil with the big toe of her right foot, looking at her toe with a fixed gaze.

"If you know any antidote to kperor, please help me," she pleaded. From under her headtie in her plaited hair she dug out a silver coin and gave it to Kona. "This is the white thing," she said, sobbing.

"Don't cry on me," Kona protested, taking the coin. "You young women must be careful how you live with your husbands. It's no problem. It takes only a piece of leaf. But the best remedy is to stay away from other men. I've passed through so many things in my life-time, my child. One man is enough."

"I'm just a wife to him in name."

"What are you talking about?" Kona creased her forehead in disbelief, looking at Lorpu in the face. "Chief Kortuma is still a young man!"

"That's not what I mean. True, he is a young man. But since he took two new wives, he's never been in to me."

"He's a Chief, Lorpu. He has a lot to think about."

"I know, " Lorpu said with impatience.

Kona walked into the tall grasses that were sodden with dew, scanned leaves, studied leaves, here and there snipped a few and cupped them in her hand. Eventually she got what she wanted and went into her house, took a piece of kola nut and returned to Lorpu. She gave her a few leaves and the kola nut to eat. Lorpu bit off a piece of the kola nut and chewed it with the leaves briskly as if she were starving to death. Then she took a deep swallow.

"Eat it all," Kona told her as she gave her the rest of the leaves. "You're not the first girl to eat it. Keep calm and remember to close your eyes tight when you take the kperor. Just before you take it, drink some palm oil. If you have any cooked rice, mix the oil with it and eat it. That's it. Good luck. Be a brave girl."

"Thank you," Lorpu said when she took the last swallow.

"Hnn," Kona murmured. "Go now. He might be looking for you."

At her house, Lorpu saw Polang sitting on the porch. Apparently she had come to call her.

"They say you should go," Polang said, rising and coming down from the porch.

"Where is he? Who's with him?"

"Sumo and a few Elders are with him at his house."

"Tell them I'm coming."

As Polang returned to the Chief, Lorpu ran into her house and rummaged all over in search of palm oil. There was no cooked rice nor a chance to cook rice. She only drank some oil from a green bottle and stepped out. Yembele, a bucket of water balanced on her head, met her in the yard.

"I have been looking for you, Mama," she said with a faint smile.

"I was attending to an important matter somewhere," Lorpu said without looking at her. Wondering what was up, Yembele went into the house, put the bucket down and followed her mother as she walked to the Chief's house.

Chief Kortuma was sitting in a rattan chair in his yard, several Elders perched on a long bamboo bench near him. Sumo sat on a low wooden stool before the Chief and the Elders. At his feet was the kperor bottle, a black teaspoon hung on the small bottle which was plaited like a checkerboard with black strings made of palm thatch fibers. When Lorpu saw the bottle, cold sweat broke out all over her body. Nervously she loosened her headtie, wiped her face with it, and walked to a stool opposite Sumo and sat down. She tied her head again with the headtie. The Chief stood up and waved his hands authoritatively. Standing apprehensively at a distance, Yembele watched the scene.

Presently Korlu, a bucket of water balanced on her head, walked past them and went into the house. Soon she returned to the porch where she sat on a stool and watched the proceedings.

"I called you," the Chief told Lorpu who sat with a bowed head. "I called you for something simple. You may or may not be guilty, but we must make sure." Turning to the Elders, he said, "Sumo and you Elders, hear my voice. This is my wife," he pointed at Lorpu. "I feel that she has a man in her belly who must come out."

"The matter has reached you," Sumo said to Lorpu.

Lorpu looked at the bottle again. Her heart escaped a beat. She was running a risk and if she failed she would surely die. For a moment, she remembered Madia, a friend of hers, taking the kperor a year ago. Madia had confessed her lover's name. Not wishing to take a chance, her mother had taken her aside and asked her if she had any more names. "Do likewise," a voice seemed to urge her. "If he's truly a man, he'll take it."

Yembele rushed upon her mother all of a sudden, hugged her desperately, crying bitterly.

"Go to your father," Lorpu told her. But she wouldn't leave her. Her crying disturbed the ceremony until the Chief grabbed her by the left arm and pulled her away; he dragged her to his seat and placed her between his legs.

"If you don't keep quiet, I'll beat you," he said, raising his hand to strike.

"Leave her alone," Sumo intervened.

"No, Sumo. She's big enough to have sense. If she wants to be a baby all over again, I'll teach her a lesson." Yembele kept quiet, choking and wiping her face with the back of her right hand.

Lorpu looked at the black liquid in the bottle again, wondering what it tasted like. If only she had a friend whom she trusted with her at this moment, everything would be bearable. She felt lonely and forsaken.

Sumo stared at her. "If there's something in your belly, don't be afraid or ashamed to bring it out. Disgrace is better than death," he said all at once. "We could call some elderly women if you want privacy."

Lorpu was looking down as Sumo talked, thinking of her past innocence when such a moment was unthinkable.

"I'll drink it," she said bravely.

"Chief, do you want me to give kperor to your wife?" Sumo asked, raising his eyebrows, his eyes poking out.

"Let it be so," the Chief replied.

Yembele cried and kicked the hard, red earth with her feet, squirming and struggling to get free from the Chief's firm grip. Chief Kortuma slapped her repeatedly until an Elder took her from him.

"Do your duty, Sumo," he said, his face frowning in anger.

Sumo took the teaspoon from the bottle, poured some of the kperor into it, drank it, and poured some more into it. Lorpu tied her lapa tight over her belly. Then Sumo poked the spoon of black liquid into her mouth, her head thrown backwards, her eyes closed tight. She swallowed it quickly. It was tasteless. She threw her head forwards. Sumo laid the empty spoon on her head. It fell to the ground with a tinkling sound.

Yembele continued crying, fighting to get loose from the Elder's grip to go to her mother. Lorpu took her by the hand.

"Don't cry," she said. "Nothing will happen to me. Let's go to the house and cook. I'll give you a fish head."

The next day Chief Kortuma decided to put an end to the woman question once and for all. In the evening he called Chief Gbolokai's widows to the palaver house in the presence of Elders and bade them farewell, giving them the full right to remarry. The women cried and beat their breasts, for they could not imagine a future without Chief Kortuma. How would they fare outside the royal household after living there so long? In order to help assuage their fears and ensure that men would not take advantage of them, the Chief told them that they would continue to be his wives, wherever they might be, until they had acquired husbands. Then he gave Polang and Korlu the house in which the widows had lived. He thought that settled his household affairs.

8

After receiving no word from the war for almost a year, Chief Kortuma came to the point where he abhorred even the mention of war. Feeling that the gods had deserted him, he stopped making sacrifices to them or giving them peace offerings. On several occasions, he simply stood over his father's grave and wept. What could he tell the poor one? Could it be that he had lost the war and thereby betrayed his father's trust? He refused to believe it. At times, he would decide to go to the war, but his wives, the village Elders and his own judgment would argue against it, for this would entail organising another army which the Chiefdom could hardly afford. Furthermore, he would be endangering the survival of the House of Gbolokai. But the Chief never took these considerations seriously because he was prepared to make any kind of sacrifice for his people, even if it meant the end of the Gbolokai dynasty. And he was prepared to make it alone. It was his people's suffering that restrained him from going to the war.

The people of Haindi — doubtless, like people throughout the entire Chiefdom — were starving to death as they could not visit their farms to get more foodstuffs when their food supplies ran out. And probably it did not matter now whether or not they visited their farms, for the crops must certainly be ruined after so many months of no care. The villagers had consumed nearly all the chickens and vegetables they raised in and around the village. Chief Kortuma had offered them almost all of his cows, goats and sheep to slaughter for food, reserving only a few for purposes of sacrifice. But even this had not redeemed the situation. It seemed to him that staying home and facing harrowing starvation with his people was the same as going to war. In an effort to combat the disaster, the Chief had his wives and daughter accompany him to his farm several times to get some food which he shared with other families. As was expected, mice, bugs, and mould had destroyed a large quantity of the rice. However, they managed to salvage a good portion of it which they supplemented with cassava, eddo, and potato. During these visits to the farm, they never encountered any enemy warriors, though the women often expressed fear of such an encounter. Of course, the Chief was always armed with a sword and a spear, ready to defend them in case of any attack. They always walked directly before him, his eyes flitting from one side of the road to the other. His brave act gave courage to many villagers to visit their farms and see after their traps and wine trees.

Chief Kortuma sometimes thought that this was an appropriate time to initiate Yembele into the Sande. A full-grown girl now, she might soon lose her innocence. It would be a great shame if this happened before her initiation. He had watched her flirt with boys on many occasions, and she was growing increasingly conscious of her body; now she wore a towel on her waist in addition to her bonmor. From all indications, she was becoming a woman. While the war had not yet come to the land, it would be best to take advantage of the opportunity to initiate her. Lorpu had admitted that he was right, but she did not want her daughter and only child to be away from her for two full years. Besides, things would have been easier for Yembele had she had at least a sister to accompany her into the Sande. The Chief considered this rejoinder as being tenuous, but he deferred a further discussion of the matter.

Chief Kortuma did not know that another problem, extremely urgent, would come to serve as another important reason for his not going to the war. This happened when it was Korlu's turn to sleep with him for a week. One morning she rose sluggishly from bed without performing her usual duty of waking him. But he happened to be awake. Unable to understand her strange attitude, he lay still and quiet, wondering what was up. After getting up, Korlu went to the central room and commenced building a fire.

The Chief rose resolutely, the bedclothes wrapped around him, and stood at the room door.

"Are you sick or angry with me?" he asked Korlu as she blew vigorously on the fire.

No reply.

The Chief tortured himself with fears, anxieties and doubts until she said with hesitation, "Oo-ei."

"Which one?" he enquired.

"I'm not feeling well," she said weakly as she hitched firewood together.

"And why didn't you tell me? Am I not your husband?"

Korlu said nothing. Rather, she filled the large iron pot with water and placed it on the fire, piling bamboo splinters and dry palm nut husks under the pot. Judging that she was too shy to make things clear for him, the Chief decided to ask Lorpu to get the full story.

When he asked Lorpu, she told him, "She doesn't see the moon."

"Don't tell me Kekula is that powerful!" he exclaimed, beside himself with joy and surprise.

"Well, don't be too hopeful," Lorpu warned mildly. "You can't be sure what's growing in her belly."

"Jealousy," he thought. But another thought made him sober: only a barren woman could be jealous of her sonang's pregnancy. Thus he began to think seriously about the possibility of Korlu being sick. Some symptoms of pregnancy were really symptoms of sickness. But the Chief did not entertain the thought for long because he believed in Kekula and the words of his deceased father; and besides, whatever conclusion he might reach at this stage would be based entirely on conjecture.

"Well, I'll see Kona this evening so that she may give her a horn," he remarked after the sober reflection. "That's the most we can do right now."

"I'm not predicting anything," Lorpu assured him when she observed that her warning had caused him some concern, "but simply giving you friendly advice. If you pass the word around, you never know what witch or witches, lurking somewhere, might get it. And witches can inflict any sort of harm on people, as you are fully aware."

In the evening, Chief Kortuma consulted Kona; upon hearing the good news, Kona congratulated him and said that she was happy Korlu had become one of her clients. She took a hollowed antelope horn from one of her black medical, raffia bags which she kept behind her bamboo bed and went with the Chief to Korlu. As she entered the house, Kona blessed Korlu who sat by the fire, tense and restless.

"Don't tell me you're that concerned about your first pregnancy," Kona told her, laughing. After saying a few more words of blessing, Kona tied the horn to Korlu's hair with a piece of white thread and told her neither to let it fall to the ground nor allow water to touch it. She should take care of it like her eyes until she delivered.

"May it protect the baby from witches so that it is born strong and healthy," she gave the last blessing.

"Let it be so," both Korlu and the Chief replied.

The horn became Korlu's greatest concern. Whenever she was

about to bathe, she would take it off her hair and lay it far away on a piece of cloth. Sometimes she suddenly felt that it was lost and would feel nervously in her hair until she touched it. Then she would sigh with relief.

Chief Kortuma thought Korlu needed good food. It was now his happy lot 'to feed the pregnancy'. One evening he decided to go hunting the next day. Korlu and Lorpu would not hear of it.

"I'm not hunting just for Korlu," he argued. "I want meat in my soup, too."

"We could kill a chicken, or one of your young goats," Lorpu said. "It's dangerous for you to venture into the deep forest, alone."

"Don't worry about me," Korlu said, trying to look lively. "I can eat anything. It's not only good food that makes one healthy and strong, but also peace of mind. I am contented."

The Chief was sitting in his rattan chair on the porch, leaning against the backrest, while arguing with the women who sat in the central room. He wasn't a man of means. All he had or wanted to have must be earned with his own effort. How would he make progress if he continued killing off his few remaining chickens and animals while the forest teemed with deer? A hunting expedition would also give him something else to think about besides his problems.

"I can protect myself," he said, already thinking of where to go hunting. "If anyone comes behind me with a message, let him wait for me. I'll be back in the evening."

Giving up, the women busied themselves with household chores.

The next morning, Chief Kortuma dressed in a tight blue denim shirt and short black pants, took his hunting bag, knife, and musket, examined them briefly and went to the porch. Korlu and Lorpu watched him resignedly as he hung the bag on his right shoulder and laid the gun on his left shoulder, knife in hand, and stepped down from the porch without looking back.

He went to the river bank. Walking down the bank, he saw his fishing canoe tied to a vine. For a long time he had not done any fishing, now he wished to do some. Chief Kortuma put his hunting implements into the canoe, loosened it from the vine, sat at the stern, paddled softly until the head of the canoe turned to the swift current.

A gentle, fresh breeze fanned him as he paddled past Luen which was barely covered with water. He glanced at it and then looked directly ahead. The canoe gathered speed as it went down the swift current. It wobbled precariously until he reached the calm part of the river below the island which was on his right. He thought of building his headquarters on this island some day for it was well protected by the river from surprise attacks.

At this point, the river looked deep, dark and foreboding. The canoe glided peacefully as he paddled swiftly for the opposite shore where palm birds and bats hovered above the treetops. Chief Kortuma looked down the broad river and saw the Island of Bats half a mile below. He did not like bat meat at all, though he loved to see the bats flying in large numbers over the Island. Dobange forest loomed imperiously over the bank; monkeys cried in the forest, jumping from bush to bush. On the bank stood a huge cotton-wood tree which sent balls of cotton wisp flying all over, littering up the shore and this placid portion of the river. When the canoe hit the shore, he quickly collected his hunting implements, got out and tied it to a big, jutting root. The strong, raw, nostalgic scent of the forest blew in his face. He retched. Clambering up the bank, he looked around, remembering not to clear his throat even if he had to. The ground was completely covered with leaves and twigs which were fortunately dampened by the morning dew, making it possible for him to walk without making too much noise. However, he walked with care up the steep hill under the shadow of the forest and stood on the top. Surveying the vast expanse of forest below with his eyes, he saw Haindi from his vantage point.

After walking awhile, he reached a fresh, clear stream on the other side of the hill. He wished it were near Haindi so that he could get his drinking water from it, rather than from the muddy Deyn River. As he watched the stream, he grew thirsty, his stomach rumbled. He should have eaten something in the morning, but it was odd to begin the day with a meal. Laying his knife down, the bag dangling on his side, the gun on his shoulder, he stepped into the stream. With a scooped right hand he repeatedly dipped the sweet, cold water and threw it rapidly into his mouth. Suddenly he heard grunts. He jumped out of the water and grabbed his knife and looked around. "Perhaps it is a wild boar," he thought. The grunts turned into a terrific growl. An elephant!

Chief Kortuma stood still and tried to compose himself in order to avoid making a false move. His eyes pinned on the elephant as it rubbed its neck up and down a huge tree, the Chief opened his bag very deftly, took out the gunpowder, filled the musket barrel, pulled out the ramrod, pounded the powder down, and placed it back into its socket. Then he took out three pieces of iron, cut from the legs of an old iron pot, and dropped them into the barrel. Finally, he placed 'the fire', a piece of tiny copper cap, at the end of a bit of jutting iron rod on the left side of the gun. All this happened in a matter of seconds. The beast stopped growling. Chief Kortuma bent on his knees, cocked the gun, and stalked it. He had never shot an elephant before. Stories of elephant hunts sprang up in his mind at random. Some said the hunter should be directly under the elephant before shooting. Others advised that he should use a spear at the mouth of the gun rather than bullets. Now within six yards of the elephant, Chief Kortuma aimed at the heart and pressed the trigger. The ensuing blast and cloud of smoke blinded him for a moment. He did not know how he managed to be sitting in the crotch of a sara tree the next moment.

The elephant danced all over, growling fiercely, trampling the bushes and seemed to move in every direction at the same time. Tugging at his hunting bag, Kortuma feared for his gun and knife which he had flung away in the frenzy. The thought of going back without arms alarmed him. Suddenly the elephant ran up the stream. Blood was splashed all over where it had been fighting and marked its trail.

Chief Kortuma sat in the tree for a long time and then came down. He rummaged about for his gun and knife, and found them pressed in the soft, alluvial soil. The elephant's weight had simply pushed them into the soil without breaking them. Digging out his weapons, he went to another part of the forest where he sat nearly all morning cleaning them.

Carefully avoiding the elephant's spoor, he walked through the briery wilderness all afternoon, breaking a plant here and making a notch on a tree there in order to be able to find his way back. Monkeys howled, jumped from tree to tree, fell into bushes, gathered into groups on boughs, but he fought the temptation to shoot any of them. It would be a waste. The sun climbed rapidly overhead, making the monkeys quite noisy. They dropped half-chewed nuts to the ground and screamed. When he got tired of walking, he hid himself among the outcropped roots of a huge tree and looked around keenly. He was weak and hungry, but he refused to eat wild fruits. Marks of grass and sticks were all over his arms and legs. His chest ached. Opening his shirt, he saw bruises on his chest, an aftermath of climbing the knotty tree.

At length he thought of a large swamp along Mawo, a tributary of Deyn. He walked towards it with all his might in an effort to reach it before dark. Hogs usually rambled in that swamp, carrying on nocturnal ruts, chewing the palm nuts that fell from ripe bunches.

He reached the swamp late in the afternoon; there he saw fresh spoor and followed it for a good distance, stood awhile, looking around and listening. Suddenly a red, lithe deer sprang out of the bushes before him and stood in the open, whisking its tail and swinging its head sideways. Chief Kortuma squatted behind a hedge and loaded the gun, held it across his lap with his left hand, and with the right hand pressed his nose and hummed like a deer. The deer walked daintily towards him, blinking its large eyes. When it was close enough, the Chief held his gun tight, the butt resting on his shoulder, cocked it, took a good aim, and tugged at the trigger. The big deer had not gone more than a few yards when it fell down. Knife in hand, he ran to it, but it was already dead. The shots had cut through its breast and severed the joints of the front legs. As it was too heavy to carry alone, he simply cut off its short, black and red tail, put it into his pocket, and hurried back home.

The Chief fought his way towards the roaring sound of the river, the only hint of direction he now had for it was completely dark. He no longer felt hungry but numb. On reaching the river bank, he sat on an outcropped root to gather strength before calling someone to carry him across, for he was too tired out to paddle a canoe in the strong current.

When he had rested long enough, he called, "Uuuuuuuuu-wi!"

"Uuuuuuuuuuuuu!" came a reply. Or was it his own voice coming back to him? He called again and there was a reply. Now confident that it was someone else responding to his call, he sat quietly and waited in the cold night air. After some time he called again and there was a reply, closer to him, and distinct. He could hear the *wuuuuup wuuuuup* of the paddle in the water.

"Is it Chief Kortuma?" It was Sumo's voice.

"Yes," he answered weakly.

The moon was now shining. Chief Kortuma's eyes caught sight of Sumo's silhouette at the stern, bending forwards and sitting upright as he paddled the canoe. At length the canoe came to shore. Going down the bank, the Chief caught it by the head.

"Korlu told me you went hunting today," Sumo said, laying the paddle across the canoe before him. "You didn't even tell a man about it. I thought of waiting at the riverside for you. How long have you been here?"

"I have just arrived," the Chief said.

"How was the hunt?"

"Rough. I got something, though." The Chief squatted in the middle of the canoe. Sumo began paddling again.

"You must be hungry. What did you get?"

"A red deer."

"Full-grown?"

"Yes."

"You were lucky. Leaves and twigs are so brittle these days one can hardly walk without them hearing you."

"I wanted a hog, though."

"Red deer meat is better. It's more delicious. Hog is just a bunch of fat . . . sit straight. This canoe is light and scary."

"Did anyone bring a message for me?"

"No."

Chief Kortuma held the edges of the canoe tight as Sumo paddled with all his might. They were now going against the strong current.

"Where did you kill it?" Sumo said.

"Near Mawo. A good trapping place. Deer ramble all over there. Go with me tomorrow for the one I killed. You'll see what I mean."

"Certainly. I'll like to."

"I hope leopards won't bother it . . . after all that trouble."

"I don't think they will. When they hear a gun shot in an area, they stay away from there for many days. Leopards bother only animals that are trapped."

"We must leave right away. It's already day."

"Don't you want to rest?"

"I don't rest. I could eat something, though I don't feel hungry. I'm too weak and tired out, I have to eat something."

"That's hunting, and you've been out of practice for a long time. So you have to feel like that."

They glided past Luen and hit the landing stage. After they got out of the canoe, Sumo tied it to a vine and they walked to the village.

"Don't be long. I'll soon be ready," Chief Kortuma said.

"All right," Sumo said, hurrying to his house.

Knocking on his door only once, Chief Kortuma heard footsteps in the house and the door opened slowly.

"So you didn't sleep," he told Korlu who opened the door; he walked past her and went into the bedroom.

"Sumo and I have been sitting on the porch nearly all night, waiting for you," Korlu said, going to the fireplace. The fire had died out, and the big, iron pot of hot water was probably cold. Dipping her fingers into the pot, she found out that the water was still hot. She fed the fire with wood and bamboo splinters and blew on it. A blaze shot up. "Do you want to take a bath now?" she asked.

"Yes," the Chief said, coming out of the room, wrapped in a blanket. "Has anyone brought me a message?"

"Nobody has been here to see you today," Korlu replied formally.

She poured some hot water into the bath bucket and took it to the bath fence. The Chief followed her. It was now dawn. Polang who had slept with Lorpu came to the Chief's house with an empty bucket and asked Korlu if she was ready to go to the river for water.

"When did he come?" she asked.

"Not long ago," Korlu said.

"You mean to say that he spent all the night in the bush?"

"He just came," Korlu repeated, taking her bucket, and the two of them went for water.

On their return, Lorpu had already brought a bowl of cooked rice for the Chief. She did the cooking late in the night. Chief Kortuma who had no appetite, only forced a few spoonfuls down his throat and prepared to return to the bush.

"He might have been unlucky," Lorpu said, sitting by the fireplace. "It's hard to see anything in the bush these dry-time days. Animals have become clever. All a man can do is set traps."

The Chief came out of the room, equipped to go back into the bush, and dropped the deer tail before her. She started and then smiled. Korlu who sat opposite her, looked shyly aside.

"Is it big?" Lorpu said, her eyes beaming.

"Fairly big," the Chief said. Cutlass in hand, Sumo appeared at the door. "Sumo and I will soon go for it."

Taking a short-cut to Mawo, they reached the swamp by noon and found the red deer. As Sumo had predicted, no leopard had bothered it. They butchered the animal, plaited palm thatch kenja and loaded them with the meat. Sumo was delighted with the animal spoor which he saw all over the swamp and hoped to set traps there sometimes in the future. They reached Haindi in the evening.

Yembele was the first person to see them on the edge of the village. She ran excitedly to meet them, and raised her arms smilingly for her father's load.

"Take time," the Chief warned as he gave her the kenja. "The blood is dripping."

The kenja of meat on her head, Yembele hastened to the house. Lorpu, Korlu, and Polang who were sitting around the fireplace, waiting for the meat, took the kenja off Yembele's head and thanked her.

"You were not careful," Lorpu chided her. "Take the bucket and go to the river for water. Bathe and wash your headtie before coming back."

The Chief and Sumo entered the house. Sumo laid his kenja down.

"It's really big!" Lorpu said as she hauled the second kenja towards her feet. It was bigger and heavier than the one which Yembele brought. "Thank you, Sumo," she said. She and Polang loosened the two kenja and put the meat in a large white pan.

"It's just a young deer," Sumo said.

"It's big!" Lorpu retorted.

When every piece of meat was placed in the pan, the Chief sorted out the viscera, the legs and genitals and put them in a small iron pot. Thinking that he meant her to cook a separate soup for him, Yembele who had come just then to the doorway, a bucket of water on her head, said:

"I want to make my own fire and cook Data's meat."

"No, my daughter," the Chief said. "That's gaigai. Sumo, take it to your house and cook it for us . . . . it's for men only, Yembele, initiated men." To Lorpu: "Send a piece of meat to each family. Tell them it wasn't a big deer. Don't bother cooking rice for me. I only want pepper soup. I'll go with Sumo to see after the gaigai."

He followed Sumo outside, walking with relish in the moonlight, and swinging his arms. Since he had become a Chief, this was the first day he could call pleasant.

Yembele was puzzled by her mother's unexplained behaviour throughout the day. Lorpu was at times restless, gentle, aggressive, sullen, voluble, cheerful, and unusually generous. Presently she entered the house in a breezy manner and said:

"I'll cook a chicken for you, Yembele. You did well to wait for me. That's my girl. I don't want you to go out playing tonight because we have a lot of work to do. Go behind the house and get the white hen from the basket — the one that is not laying eggs. Bring it. I'll plait your hair tonight. Do you know that tomorrow will be New Year's Day? It'll be a great day. I want you to look nice tomorrow. Your new clothes are in your father's house. I am sure your father will kill one of his sheep tomorrow . . . go for the hen." She pattered about the central room while Yembele who sat, astonished, on a low stool by the fireplace, rose up slowly and walked to the door, staring at her mother over her shoulder. "No, come back," Lorpu told her. "Leave the hen. Leave it for tomorrow. Let me plait your hair first. Let's leave the hen for tomorrow. Good girl, sweet girl, come now and let me plait your hair. Get the comb. It's on the table in the bedroom. Did you light the lantern? Yes, I see light glowing in the room. My girl is thoughtful. She remembers such things. You're becoming a woman. You'll be a good wife. Get the comb and take off your headtie while I get the mat."

Lorpu took a bamboo mat from behind the wooden door and spread it near the fireplace. She put a lot more wood into the fire and a large, ruddy blaze shot up, brightening the central room. As Yembele returned from the room with the comb, she heard children singing and clapping their hands outside.

"The moon is shining, Mama!" she said, rushing to the door and poking her head outside. She saw the children, like dark shadows, running about the square. "I want to play, Mama!" she said.

"Children are not usually aware when there's trouble in the air," Lorpu said bluntly. Taken aback by her tactless remark, she grew quiet and remorseful. Yembele became concerned about this sudden change in her mood. "Oh, well," Lorpu said, "what I mean is that the children out there are thinking only about the new year." She smiled faintly. "Come and lie down. It's not every night a child goes out playing!"

Yembele stamped the dirt floor in anger, screwed up her face, and scratched her left thigh vigorously. She walked with reluctance to Lorpu who sat on the mat, her legs stretched, holding up her hand for the comb.

"Give me the comb," Lorpu said. "Come lie down!"

"But I want to play!"

"Let's make haste and get your hair plaited. Why are you anxious about playing tonight as though there'll be no more tomorrow? Lie down!"

Yembele gave her the comb and reluctantly placed her head on the soft, fleshy lap. Lorpu loosened her hair gently with the comb.

"Why not wait till tomorrow morning?" Yembele pleaded.

"Now look," Lorpu said sternly, "if you don't let me plait your hair you won't wear the new headtie I've been keeping for you. I won't give you my new beads. Remember tomorrow will be New Year's Day, and you want to look nice. We'll be cooking in the morning; so I won't have time to plait your hair."

"Hurry then!"

"It won't take long . . . lie still."

"Make haste." Yembele's voice was low and imploring.

"If you keep your head still and let me begin, everything will be over in no time."

As her face was turned to the door, Yembele saw the stunted shadows of children running around, and her anxiety increased. She groaned as the comb ran with difficulty through her tangled, kinked hair.

"Do you want to look nice?" Lorpu asked her with irritation.

"But you didn't put oil on my hair!" she cried.

"Go for the hair oil."

Yembele hurried into the bedroom and brought back a bottle of burnt oil with perfume which Lorpu had bought from a Mandingo peddler a year ago. She used it on important occasions only. Now pouring some in her left hand, she sniffed it, and then rubbed it in Yembele's hair vigorously.

"It smells sweet, Mama," Yembele said.

"I'm doing this for your own good, and you want to waste my time," Lorpu said, resuming her work with verve.

But Yembele grasped her hands, and cried, "It's hurting, Mama!"

"Look," Lorpu said harshly, "don't waste my time! I'll leave your hair unplaited if you continue acting like this. And you'll be your friends' laughing-stock tomorrow." She thought for a moment and said in a gentle voice, "Be patient. It has to hurt a little, but everything will soon be over. Girls that look nice bear the pains that go with good looks."

While they were so engaged, Chief Kortuma, dressed in a flowing robe, entered and stood over them in silence. With a start, Lorpu looked at him.

"Look," she told Yembele who had closed her eyes tight in an effort to endure the pain, "your father is here." Yembele opened her eyes and looked at her father who gazed solemnly at her. The Chief took out a pair of silver bracelets and gave them to her, bending down.

"They are for you," he told her, standing straight.

"Thank you! Thank you, Data!" Yembele exclaimed with joy and excitement, trying the bracelets on her wrists. They fitted neatly.

"They are your New Year presents," the Chief said.

"I like them," Yembele said, smiling; she raised up both wrists and stared at the bracelets.

"You see what I was talking about?" Lorpu said. "Your father also wants you to look nice. You might be the only girl wearing silver bracelets tomorrow."

The Chief walked out quietly.

Lorpu combed a lock of hair, her tiny fingers wriggled in it for a moment, and a row of well plaited hair emerged. She told Yembele to feel it to see how well it was plaited, but Yembele was fondling her bracelets, paying her no attention. Lorpu continued fumbling in her hair, roughly now, making haste to finish while she was preoccupied with the bracelets.

"May I go and play with the girls now?" Yembele asked her when the ordeal was over.

They stood up. Lorpu picked up the strands of hair on the mat to bury them on the outskirts in the morning so that they would not be available to a wicked person who could use them to bewitch her daughter. Yembele handed her the bracelets for safe-keeping.

"May I go now?" she asked again.

"You may go," Lorpu said, "but remember not to play with boys. And don't stay long."

Yembele stepped out, tying her headtie on her head, and ran to

96

the children in the square. They had now formed a ring, clapping their hands, singing and dancing gbai.

Yembele liked the gbai dance, but there was no place for her in the ring. She stood and watched the children. Presently a boy, short and strongly built, jumped to the center of the ring: first, he danced around, swinging sideways, made a sharp turn, ran to a girl and stamped the ground before her with force, pointing the index finger of his right hand at her cockily, and retreated to his own post gracefully. The girl he pointed at leaped right away to the centre of the ring. The clapping grew rapid and fiery. Yembele caught the rhythm and started clapping her hands and dancing as she watched the girl. Another girl who was dancing right before her in the ring noticed Yembele with a glance over her shoulder and gave her a place. Yembele entered the ring and looked left and right. She grew embarrassed when she saw Sengbe dancing on her right. She had once met him at the riverside and he had felt her breasts, waist beads, and hair, causing her to be in trouble with her mother. She did not like standing by him. It would encourage him. "Perhaps he thinks I stood by him on purpose," she thought.

At each moment someone was in the ring, dancing and jumping, and stopping before someone else. The boys stopped before the girls they loved; and the girls stopped before each other and infrequently before the boys they loved. At last someone stopped before Sengbe. Entering the ring, he danced so well that the rhythm of the clapping and singing went wild. He stopped before Yembele with such force she drew back about a yard. As he returned to his post, Yembele followed him into the ring, dancing with grace and charm, and winning the loud clapping and singing of her mates. The sweet aroma of her perfume filled the ring. Her breasts, almost fully developed now, shook nervously as she danced. She stopped before a girl.

As soon as she returned to her post, Sengbe walked to the centre of the ring. She thought she had stopped before a girl! But Sengbe did not dance. Rather, he raised his arms and stopped the dance with a shout:

"Let's do demabai because the girls are fond of stopping before each other. They are selfish. Right?"

"Right!" the boys answered in a chorus.

At first the girls wanted to play by themselves, but later changed their minds to play with the boys 'if they behaved', for boys sometimes took unusual liberties in demabai.

Two lines were formed, the boys forming one and the girls

the other. A boy raised a song to which everyone responded warmly:

The town to which I'm going,
Women are so few there,
If I should get one here,
I better hold her fast.

While they sang a boy would leave one end of the line of boys, dancing with abandon, go to the line of girls, survey it with his eyes from one end to the other, and then choose 'a wife' for himself and return with her to his post, holding her by the wrist firmly. At Sengbe's turn, he danced around in his usual graceful manner, moving towards Yembele, who pretended not to notice him. On reaching her, he held her by the arm gently and they left for his post, dancing together. At times he would deliberately lean towards her and her breasts would touch him 'accidentally'. He would relish the fiery elation.

After most of the boys had acquired 'wives', a few of them remained 'bachelors' because there were more boys than girls. These 'bachelors' did not put up a quarrel as was sometimes the case; rather they stood alone, hoping to have a chance next time. The girls went back and formed a line. It was now their turn to raise the song. One of them sang,

The town to which I'm going,
Men are so few there,
If I should get one here,
I better hold him fast.

Everyone responded to the song and the girls began choosing their 'husbands'. At Yembele's turn, she deliberately chose the boy that stood next to Sengbe. That should put him off, she thought. Sengbe's heart burned with jealousy. As if to increase his frustration, she suddenly stopped halfway to her post and said:

"Let's do boa," leaving the boy's arm, highly gratified that she had finally found a means of avoiding Sengbe.

Of course everyone welcomed the change. As the night was far spent, it stood to reason that they should go through their repertoire of dances as quickly as possible before bedtime. Yembele loved the boa dance for its own sake, though, because it was not aggressive and the song to boa was beautiful.

They formed a long line, alternating with boys and girls. Sengbe managed to stand next to Yembele. "Well," Yembele thought with resignation, "I must bear it." She could not afford to be unruly by fussing with the boy and possibly bringing the play to a drastic end. In a shrill, nostalgic voice, a girl raised the boa song:

> *Snake, O snake,*
> *You're too long,*
> *You're too long,*
> *Up and down the hills,*
> *Beneath the waves of waters,*
> *I certainly will follow . . .*

Holding each other lightly by the waists, they bent low, and moved slowly between houses, coiling up, wandering all over the village like a snake. The song leader continued improvising phrases to boa: *O snake, you're so big, You're not really snake, Deer and you are equal . . .* At the end of each phrase came a rousing choral response, a repetition of what the song leader sang.

Lorpu walked up to Chief Kortuma who sat on the porch and said, "The Hawk is ready."

"Already?" the Chief said.

"Yes."

"What does she have to say?"

"She salutes you."

"I wanted to talk with her first."

"Talk what?"

"That's my daughter going, you know."

"There's nothing to worry about. I myself will be there!"

"I know."

"Give me whatever you have without further delay."

"Tell the Hawk I salute her."

"Bring the white things!"

"Here. Three kola nuts and three white coins. That's all I could put my hand on at the moment. The coins are for Yembele. Tell her I wish her well, that's why I decided to initiate her tonight. Tell her not to grieve. I'm here for her."

"See you later," Lorpu said as she stepped out of the porch and quickly receded into the dark night.

The boa dance progressed steadily until the moonlight grew faint. It was now past midnight. But the dance was so engrossing the youngsters did not feel like going to bed. While they were playing, some women gathered around them. Thinking that the women came to witness their performance, they tried to make a good impression. Unexpectedly a woman rushed into the winding line, dipped her index finger into a little gourd filled with black paste and rubbed it on Yembele's left ankle.

Yembele turned, stunned and speechless, wondering why she alone was marked, why her mother had deceived her. She wouldn't see the new year after all. Now she understood her mother's strange behaviour throughout the day. She tried to be brave for she had expected 'the chalk mark', though not tonight. But fear and anxiety had the better part of her. In a loud voice, she cried out:

"Data! Data! Dataaaaa!"

The Hawk pounced on her, said something in her ear as her playmates ran away in terror. Her mother had told her long ago that it was a great thing to happen to a girl. It happened to all girls. It would transform her into a well matured, respectable girl — a new girl. Yembele had looked forward to it with pleasure, though whenever her mother was displeased with her she would say, "Zelei will tear you to pieces," and she would loathe her future encounter with Zelei, constantly afraid of doing wrong, for Zelei was watching her and taking note of all her wrongdoings and would punish her for each one. Now the Hawk had snatched her to take her to Zelei. She bravely wiped the tears from her eyes and tried to look cheerful.

The Hawk's firm grip penetrated to her bones, but she did not fight to free herself. Overwhelmed with curiosity, she wondered what would happen next. Suddenly, kono sounds were heard on the southern outskirts. The sounds increased in volume and drew towards where they stood. Eventually Yembele saw a group of women coming towards them; they were singing and striking kono in diverse rhythmic patterns. Soon they encircled her and the Hawk. An ecstatic smile on her face, her mother danced to her, beating her kono with pride. The wild throbbing of her heart stopped. Everyone moved to the Chief's house, many more women joining the group.

Chief Kortuma came out, walked carefully down the dirt stairs and stood before the women, gazing at them with pride. A woman danced jubilantly, bending and running all over, cupping her breasts in her hands. In a gesture of honour, she bent at the Chief's knees. Chief Kortuma acknowledged her respect by touching her back with the tips of his right hand fingers. Then she stood up. The Chief raised his arms in the air, and the women grew quiet. Before he could say a word, the Hawk came forward, leaving Yembele with her assistant.

"We came to you, Chief," she declared. "The Hawk attacked your quarters and caught a prey. Dry the sweat!" The kono were struck briefly.

"Thank you for the good work which you have begun," the Chief replied. "I'm happy that my beloved daughter will soon become a gbolokpolo. I wish her well in this great adventure. Tell Zelei to bring her back to me, well and sound. All a mortal man can possibly do to please the Big One, I will try to do it." Each sentence was punctuated with applause. Tucking his hand into his pocket, the Chief took out three white kola nuts. Handing them to the Hawk, he said, "This is the white thing. Tell Zelei that I greet her with humility."

The women resumed striking their kono, singing and dancing, going towards the southern outskirts. Slowly they receded into the darkness that had now replaced the moonlight. Chief Kortuma took one last look at the direction in which they went and walked back to his house. For a whole year he wouldn't see his daughter.

The Chief went to bed thinking of Yembele, but when dawn came he remembered it was New Year's Day. He jerked out of bed, dressed quickly, took his musket, and went behind the house. It was misty. The smoke of smouldering fires clouded the black thatched roofs. He had forgotten the gunpowder. He went back for it, loaded the gun and shot it, pointing the muzzle at a clump of dirt. It gave him special satisfaction to be the first person to salute the new year and to hear a loud blast resounding in the surrounding forest and echoing down the river. He reloaded his gun and shot again. When he came in front of his house, he stood for a moment and looked around. Guns were now blasting off all over the village. Men and children leaped to bath fences, women with buckets went to the river for water. "There'll be some life here today," he said under his breath. He hoped the old year which had been shot would go with all its mishaps and misfortunes, and the darkness would remain behind and the future would be bright. He began murmuring the new year prayer as he climbed onto the porch,

May there be another year behind you we'll live to see,
May the blessings of our Ancestors go with us each day and each night,
May no snake bite us in the tangled bushes of the deep jungles, or crocodiles catch or threaten us in the deep waters.

101

May our breath be far from death,
May the sons and daughters of Fuama Chiefdom
increase,
May God stand behind our feet wherever we go;
May he not turn his back to us.
May this year's farms be productive . . .

He continued murmuring the prayer as he entered his bedroom. How careless he had been to forget about Yembele! *May Yembele return to me again, safe and sound,* he prayed in a loud voice.

After the mist had cleared away and the sun was up, Chief Kortuma killed two of his young goats for a modest feast in memory of Yembele, and to usher in the new year.

Polang alone was cooking, for Lorpu had accompanied the women and Yembele to Malamu, where the Sande was established, and the Chief had sent Korlu there in the morning to bring back news of any complications that might arise. It was not long before Korlu returned and said that everything was all right. She then helped Polang cook. They worked hard to finish cooking so as to join the new year plays. All women must rejoice regardless of the rumours of war that pervaded the entire Chiefdom, for their Hawk had snatched another victim — a very important one at that.

By noon bowls of cooked rice and soup were exchanged from house to house as presents. From the Chief's house ten bowls were to be sent to ten important Elders of Haindi. Chief Kortuma, not really hungry, only examined each bowl of food brought to him, tasted the food, and put it aside.

Korlu turned jealous: "You want to fill your stomach in order not to eat our food," she drawled.

"Don't worry," the Chief said. "If I don't taste their food, they'll say their Chief doesn't love them."

"How will they know?"

"They'll ask me to name the types of food they sent and say how they were — don't worry. You may have to cook all day. Today is New Year's Day. Remember?"

"You have to be careful!"

"Not on New Year's Day!" the Chief snapped. "Who'll dream of poisoning someone on New Year's Day?"

"Your enemy can do anything to you any day," Korlu maintained.

Chief Kortuma scratched his head, trying to forget what Korlu said. One could spend all one's life afraid of things that might never happen.

A knock on the door. A gourd of palm wine in his hand, Sumo, who was dressed in a pair of blue denim short pants and short-sleeved shirt made of white drill, said:

"How is the Chief?" He entered the house.

"Oh, is that Sumo?" the Chief said, rising from the rattan chair he sat in near his room door watching his wives cook. Polang had just gone to the river for water. Korlu, who sat on a low stool near the fireplace, blew on the fire strenuously.

"It makes one dizzy," the Chief warned her as he received the gourd of wine from Sumo. Sumo now visited the Chief regularly, bringing him wine.

Holding the gourd with both hands, the Chief tipped its rolled bamboo leaf to his lips and sucked it. The wine was strong and sour.

"Very good wine," he complimented Sumo, smacking his lips.

"I'm not a woman," Sumo apologised. "So I don't know how to cook. But I thought of bringing you some wine. May the new year be good to you."

"Let it be so," the Chief replied.

"May all your enemies die for us to walk over their graves."

"Let it be so."

"May your life be far from death."

"Let it be so . . . Korlu, do you women want some wine?" the Chief said.

"Leave ours in the gourd," Korlu said.

"All right. Sumo, sit down. Isn't there a stool, Korlu?" the Chief said.

"We're busy here," Korlu said.

"Let's go out, Sumo," the Chief said. They took their chairs and went to the porch. People were gathering in knots, all dressed in colourful clothes, conversing and trying to sing. They sat down and watched them.

"People are happy again," Sumo said.

"Not really, Sumo," the Chief said. "We must first win the war; only then will life become normal." He poured a cup of wine and took a long drink. Sumo poured a cupful, too, but only held it in his hand. "Those people you see out there," the Chief continued, "need food and clothes. And the war makes it impossible for them to visit the coast."

"Where will you make your farm this year?" Sumo changed the subject when he saw a depressed look on the Chief's face.

"In Bodua forest. I want to make my farm in the forest area this year. The young bushes, as you know, breed too much weed."

The Chief drained another cup and poured more wine. Sumo is wise and helpful, he thought.

"Let's remember the women," Sumo said, draining his cup.

The Chief shook the gourd with one hand.

"There's enough here for two or three cupfuls," he said. "Korlu, come for your wine."

Presently Polang entered the house with a bucket of water balanced on her head. She placed it near the southern wall where the dishes were kept. Korlu distributed the wine in two cups. She and Polang drank by the fireside. After drinking they dished out the food, put it in bowls, poured soup on each bowl of rice, and Polang took two of them at a time to the different Elders.

Sumo and the Chief had finished drinking and Sumo rose to go.

"Stay, let's eat," the Chief told him. "Korlu was about to send you some food, but since you're here she might have put ours together . . . Korlu, what did you do?"

"Put yours together," Korlu said.

"So stay let's eat," the Chief said.

"All right," Sumo said.

Much to the Master's satisfaction, the warriors displayed unusual courage and discipline: they walked quietly, in single file, on the tortuous forest trail, maintaining a distance of several yards from each other, looking up in the trees and the surrounding tangled bushes for the enemy, investigating the slightest noise to determine its source. Without any orders from the Master, they painted themselves from head to foot with black mud; some went beyond this point (which was adequate in itself) by tying twigs around their heads — all in an effort to make themselves elusive targets. While doing all this, they held their weapons at the ready, formally primed for any confrontation at the shortest notice. Remarkably enough, their performance was superb as if it were a result of long practice.

Because he had to be the symbol of courage during the war, the Master could not afford to disguise himself. In fact, the thought never occurred to him. The mysterious medical clothes he wore and the loaded musket on his shoulder bespoke full protection against natural and supernatural enemies. He walked with pride in the middle of the procession of warriors, from which vantage point his instructions could easily be relayed to the men in front as well as to those behind.

Upon reaching a large glade that was once the site of a prosperous village, the Master ordered the warriors to assemble in order to brief them on his own plans for the war. Beginning with the expected rambling prelude that dwelt on nothing significant, he went on to warn them about the danger they were in.

"A warrior has four eyes — or should I say six," he said mildly. As the dying sun was no longer visible through openings in the enveloping foliage of the jungle, the evening shadow speedily descended on the forest so that the Master could only see vaguely. The forest grew cold and lonely, though the painful cries of birds, crickets, and beasts still gave it a sign of life. Standing tall and erect among the men, the Master held onto his musket firmly with his left hand, while gesturing forcefully with his right hand, emphasising his points: "Well, let's say that warriors have many eyes," he continued. "Thus, as of now, you are expected to look all around you at the same time. Look up in the trees and in the shrubs for the enemy — the rule is, be watchful!" From his medical shirt pocket, he took out a small horn with black paste. Holding the sharp point of the horn with the tips of the fingers of his left hand which held the gun by the barrel, he dipped his right hand forefinger into it and licked it; dipping his finger into the horn again, he rubbed it on his chest under the medical shirt. Then he passed the horn to the warrior who sat directly before him, instructed him to do exactly what he did and pass it to the others. Continuing his warning that began to grow more and more impassioned, the Master told the warriors that the medicine which was being relayed among them would destroy fear in their hearts, though nothing could actually destroy fear but self-discipline and courage. "Remember that war is a serious affair," he said. "It's no child's play. At home, the rituals, the dances, and the loud talks make it look delightful and pleasant. But we are now in the forest, depending on ourselves. Therefore, we must banish fear! To win is not to be afraid. A brave man can knock down any giant — survive any hazard . . . be strong! And never think about defeat regardless of what happens. Forget about defeat! Don't let it come to your mind at all. Whenever you confront a Gola warrior, your first words should be, 'We're in for it. We'll soon see the fittest. When I'm through with you, you'll know the manner of man I am.' Anything to make him afraid. Always remember that it's fear alone that conquers a man. Continue to be brave and wise for you cannot afford to be otherwise."

Before revealing his war plans, the Master ordered a few shots of musket in the surrounding bushes in order to drive off possible Gola spies. But this came too late as events proved later.

The Master had three main plans. The first of these was to conduct a massive search for a lion den once they entered Golaland. The lion den would serve as a bivouac during the entire course of the war. This operation was to be conducted from sundown through the night when farmers and most hunters had returned to their villages. During the operation, the warriors should be far apart; if attacked, they should take cover rather than respond in kind. Also whenever they got to a farm, they should gather foodstuffs and cooking utensils for the den. After this operation, a band of shock troops would be dispatched throughout Golaland with the mission to terrorise several villages and take hostages. In case these initial strategies failed to win the 'white chicken' from the Gola, then the Master would give his 'last command' which was to remain a secret until that crucial stage was reached.

The next morning the Master took the first count of his men and discovered that there were one hundred and fifty-nine. He decided to send an advance force of fifty men to carry out his first plan. As this would begin at sundown, the entire army spent the day digging possums out of anthills, and gathering wild nuts and fruits for food.

Shortly before the advance force departed, a short, sprightly member of the force informed the Master that he had 'cut sand' and found out that they would take Golaland in two weeks. Initially, it would be a grim struggle and there would be some losses, but they would take victory back. To ensure victory, however, they must bury a virgin alive. In a situation like this, every opinion must be respected. Of course, no virgin was available; so the Master simply provided a kola nut which was buried with the appropriate supplications to the Ancestors for them to consider it as a virgin.

Maavi of Mauwa led the advance force. A village of Fuama Chiefdom, Mauwa was located near the border with Golaland. Its inhabitants were, therefore, well acquainted with the Gola forest. Furthermore, Maavi had indicated that he knew the location of several lion dens in the Gola forest. Therefore, the Master judged that he was in the best position to lead the first operation.

Surprisingly, a band of Gola warriors attacked the advance force almost before it had crossed the border. Poisoned arrows and other missiles rained on them mercilessly and they ran in every direction for cover in the tangled forest undergrowth and among the out-cropped roots of giant beleh and cotton-wood trees. Apparently intended to demoralise and frighten away the invading force, the surprise attack lasted only a moment. The fact that it encountered no resistance perhaps convinced the attackers that it was an overwhelming success. Soon they began withdrawing with speed and returning to Golaland.

Just before the attack, Maavi had spied a man with a bow and arrows ensconced in the crotch of a medium-sized sara tree. The man wore a pair of black, tattered short pants. Hanging on his left shoulder was a long, narrow bag stacked with arrows. Completely painted black, an expression of dread on his face — perhaps because he had done such a poor job of hiding in the tree — he aimed an arrow at Maavi. Maavi gave a loud, piercing cry and pandemonium broke out. The arrow flew with tremendous speed, but Maavi dodged it, taking cover in the outcropped roots of a huge cotton-wood tree. The screams and terrifying shouts indicated that he had lost some men. Unable to do anything about that for the moment, he decided to stalk the sara tree in order to catch the Gola warrior. In fact, he made this decision when he first saw him. As the pandemonium began to die down, Maavi crawled on his belly out of the outcropped roots, stealthily making his way to the tree. Though it was completely dark now, he had night vision so that he could see the silhouettes of the objects around him. Halting momentarily and looking up in the tree, he saw the massive shadow of the warrior holding firmly onto the tree trunk with his legs, arms, and body, descending slowly. With each move, the warrior would look down sideways. Except for the rattling and scrunching noise of his departing mates far in the distance, all was quiet. Each time he made a move down the tree, Maavi made several careful moves himself. This continued until Maavi was close to the tree and his movement in the dry leaves and twigs became apparent to the warrior. Whenever he stopped to investigate the sound of Maavi's movement, there was silence. Then he would descend several feet with great caution, and there was the noise again which was closing up on him. As he was now only a couple of yards from the ground, he jumped down with a thud, whisked the bow and arrow bag off his shoulder and crouched to run. But a sudden, overpowering grasp swept him off his feet and dashed him to the ground; he felt a heavy blow on the right side of his head. He saw stars. Then he began sailing down a narrow, weedy stream in a canoe that no one paddled. He inhaled the fresh, cold breeze, feeling nauseated. Fishes splashed sharply to the surface of the stream and dived back to the bottom again. As it made its way through the rocky parts of the stream, the canoe would wobble precariously, coming to the verge of capsizing; but it would become steady again after passing through the rocks. He continued to drift down until the scene changed dramatically. It was early in the morning. Surprisingly, he found himself bound, hands and feet, lying helplessly on the damp ground; shiny, unsteady pairs of eyes gazed at him with amazement, anger, and vengeance all at once.

"Thank you, Maavi, for bringing one of them alive," the Master said, his eyes pinned on the Gola warrior who only had on a pair of tattered short pants. Maavi looked battered: on his broad forehead was a wound shaped like a crescent moon. The blood, having coagulated, covered most of the wound, leaving a small portion of it at the end, over the right eyebrow, open; the red flesh showed in the morning sunshine. Except for minor bruises, torn pants, his skin covered with black topsoil, Maavi had no other visible sign of his grim struggle with the Gola warrior in the dark. When the Master thanked him for his brave deed, his eyes lit up, and he smiled broadly, displaying rows of white teeth.

"Tell us, my friend, where the Gola army is located," the Master asked the bound man in a friendly voice. But the man only raised his head weakly and stared at him without saying a word. A warrior thereupon struck him on his left side with a thorny sapling. He cringed and groaned. The mark which the sapling made on him swelled instantly and blood oozed from it. "Don't strike him again," the Master waved casually to the strapping young warrior who had the sapling. From the sign of resignation and despair which he read in the bound man's eyes, the Master became convinced that he had taken a sacred oath that would never permit him to betray his people. However, he decided to prod him further. Bending down and holding both knees with his hands to support his body, the Master repeated, "Now tell us, my friend — nothing will happen to you — simply tell us if your people are prepared for war." Silence. "Don't make me have the men beat you to death. We don't have time to waste. Talk!" Silence again. The man lay quiet and apprehensive. After numerous unsuccessful attempts to make him speak, the Master ordered that he be killed. Like a flash of lightning, a blade struck him on the neck. The blood gushed out profusely as he wriggled breathlessly. Another blow, and it was over.

This first encounter with the enemy was reassuring to the Master. He became more determined than ever to fight for victory. It was clear that the Gola had been following up events in Fuama Chiefdom and that they were prepared to put up stiff resistance. Doubtless, his failure to send spies to Golaland was the principal reason for this temporary setback. There was every reason to believe that the Gola were guarding their villages. But it takes man to beat man, in the same way as it takes iron to cut iron, the Master thought. Maavi, of course, had demonstrated real courage, setting the best precedent. This made the Master proud. He thought of sending a report back to Chief Kortuma about their progress so far. But how could he, a Master, send his Chief news of anything less than total victory! Taking another count of his men, he found out that he had lost five of them. Evidently he could not sustain losses at this rate for long. Thus he decided to strike deep inside Golaland, for it was too risky to postpone direct confrontation any longer.

Again he divided his army into three divisions. The first and second divisions were to launch simultaneous attacks on both the east and west of Golaland. He was to lead the first division which consisted of fifty-four men, while Maavi was to lead the second division which comprised fifty men. The third division which also consisted of fifty men was to be led by Yasieh Dolo of Gbalala who had once lived in the Gola village of Nyein for many years. Dolo was a huge man who reportedly killed an elephant single-handed some years ago; he became commonly known as The Elephant Killer. His division was to remain behind and patrol the border and would be called upon when needed. Instead of maintaining a bivouac, the Master told his warriors to fend for themselves as best they could in the lush jungle. They could feed on wild fruits, raw cassava, sugar cane, cucumbers, and other foodstuffs they could find on Gola farms. Once the decision was made, everything proceeded with speed. The Master and his troops went west, while Maavi and his troops went east.

For the first month, the Master and his division used famine as a weapon. They would go to a farm towards evening when the farmers had gone home. After helping themselves to their rice, dry meat or fish, and palm oil (which they cooked in abundance), they would burn the rice kitchen, and cut down any banana or plantain trees that bore full bananas or plantains. They would pull out the cassava trees and chop the roots to pieces. In this way, they destroyed a large quantity of food on countless numbers of farms until famine began to take its toll on the Gola. In fact, no Gola could venture to go to his farm once it became known that warriors were roving the land. When these tactics had trapped the Gola in their villages, the Master and his men began burning the villages one by one. First they would terrorise the villagers and after killing a few men, burn the village. It became apparent to them that the Gola, after all, were not prepared for war as they had previously supposed.

After successive, easy victories, the Master and his men encountered their first real challenge in Kuntaa, the historic medical centre of the Gola. Kuntaa was located on the eastern bank of the Deyn River. Several miles up the river from this village was Tinkayan, a tiny island where fishermen usually made their camps when swarms of fish migrated to the rapids around the island during the dry season. The fishermen would catch the fish in large quantities and dry it in their camps. Presently there was no one on the island, for the dry season had just begun and the fish had not yet commenced their annual migration. The Master instructed his men to take refuge there if necessary during the battle of Kuntaa. Knowing that the Gola would do everything possible to defend their sacred village, they planned to launch their attack by night.

Unfortunately, the moon showed up in the night. There it was, large and bright, in the endless blue sky. A whiff of light cloud now and then passed before it with speed. They waited for it to go down before the attack — and when it sank slowly beyond the forest, they moved in three waves down the river to where the women of Kuntaa fetched water, and followed the narrow path, on either side of which the grass had been hoed away. The first wave suddenly broke out in a run towards the village while the others walked with care and vigilance behind them. Soon there was a sharp cry ahead. The first wave of attackers had run into a barricade of warriors! The rear force rushed to the scene.

After a fierce skirmish, the Master and his men withdrew, a tactic that often yielded good results. The Gola pursued them all the way to the river, about a quarter of a mile away. Thinking that they had gained the upper hand and that the enemy had no other recourse but to jump into the river and drown, or take to the forest in flight, the Gola slowed down to see what they would actually do. But in an unexpected turnabout, the Master and his warriors fell upon them: swords clashed, spears flew in the dark sky, some dozen musket shots were heard in the night.

Women and children ran about in disarray in the besieged village, shouting, screaming, calling for help. Babies howled fitfully on their mothers' backs. While some men fetched spears and swords to join the battle, others carried the lame and the aged on their shoulders and backs into the bush beyond the outskirts, away from the battle scene. Nothing much could be done to salvage their meagre belongings.

The Master and his men were now on the offensive. They had pushed the Gola back into the village. The battle was now fought under the eaves of houses and in the square. There were heavy casualties on both sides. When the fighting reached a peak, the Master sneaked into one of the many abandoned houses, lit a bamboo torch, and set the inflammable dry thatched roof on fire. Soon the fire leaped from house to house, making one big torch that lit the sky. Screaming voices were heard in the blaze. Both armies had no choice but to run for their lives.

As he ran back to the outskirts, the Master felt a sharp missile hit him in the back. Everything instantly turned red in his eyes as he fell in a heap and became unconscious. As if he had been under guard, he was immediately whisked off by two of his soldiers who first cut down his cowardly assailant with their swords. He too was stabbed in the back as he ran away from the scene of the assault. The Master on their shoulders, arrows and spears flying over their heads, the two men disappeared in the intense darkness beyond the outskirts. Wading through the broad, shallow rapids, the rushing water almost sweeping them off their feet, the soldiers made their way to Tinkayan where they laid the Kulubah on the ground and began to massage his body frantically.

A little later some dozen other men joined them — all that remained of the first division. On realising that the Master was fatally wounded, four of the new arrivals stood guard at the four corners of the island while the others lent their hands in the effort to save him. But in the darkness, they could do little more than toss the body of the Master from hand to hand, massaging it with all their might. At dawn there was a powerful rainstorm: the thunder rumbled and repeatedly exploded with flashes of lightning. Thoroughly drenched and terrified, the men repeatedly wiped the rain from their faces with their forearms, while preoccupied with the Master. A few of them hurriedly constructed a palisade of palm fronds in which they made a bed of fresh leaves. There they took the languishing body of the Kulubah, undressed him and found the open spear wound. The spear had struck him near the vertebrae in the middle of his back and made a wide, perpendicular wound that was some five inches long. The wound was swollen, a large clot of blood in it. The men bathed it and then the entire body of the Master. One of them surveyed the bushes for herbs, and soon returned with a knotted fist that contained some tender, fresh leaves. He rubbed the leaves in his hands briskly and then squeezed the resulting pulp; green liquid filtered through his large, calloused fingers and dropped directly into the wound. Then he pressed the pulp at the base of the Master's nose. The Master sneezed and twitched his weak limbs. The men grew hopeful.

The rain slackened as the morning sunshine tried to penetrate the eastern cloud. Except for the roaring sound of water at the rapids, all was quiet on the island and beyond the river. Only debris and black mud walls stood where the sacred village of Kuntaa had been. The men looked vainly across the river all day for the rest of the first division, but no one showed up. It became clear that the first division had suffered severe losses. How they had come through it all, safe and unscathed, was a mystery to them.

The Master woke up at dawn and sat on the bamboo bed with its mattress of dry leaves, his feet dangling close to the black dirt floor.

He had spent a restless night as was indicated by leaves scattered all over the floor; except for piles of leaves spanning its edges, the bamboo mat on the bed was bare. Two warriors, loaded muskets on their shoulders, marched around the hut of palm thatch in opposite directions. On approaching each other's silhouettes, they would turn completely around then resume marching, their ears pricked and their eyes squinting in the dark. As the grey, misty sky dispersed and the first rays of sun appeared in the east, the other soldiers who had been on guard at various points on the island, sauntered to the hut for the usual morning assembly.

In a moment, the Master emerged, unexpectedly dressed in his medical shirt. His eyes were red, they emitted a fiery sheen like those of a lion. Leaning slightly backwards on account of the pain in his back, he managed to cast a benevolent stare at his warriors. This strange and perplexing attitude baffled the men who had never seen their Kulubah appear this way for the three weeks they had made the tiny island their home. The Master often gave them orders as he lay in bed; at times he only poked his head out of the bamboo door of the hut or stood casually before them and issued his instructions for the day, forcing a smile.

"Well," he began, "I want to thank you men for the courage you have displayed and the sacrifice you have made during the many months we have been at war with the Gola. We have done all that is within our power to win the war. Whatever may be the result of our efforts, one thing we have done well, for which we deserve congratulations: we have driven the Gola out of their sacred village. Now they are wandering about the forest, frightened, disappointed, and perplexed. The source of their power and strength has been uprooted. Their hope and will to live have been shattered. Henceforth, Golaland will never be the same again.

"As you know full well, for three weeks I have tried to recuperate from a wound that refuses to heal. The spear that hit me had poison. I should have died on the spot, but it takes a real Zoe to beat a Zoe from Upriver. The wound has persisted and even worsened in spite of all the curative poultices I have applied to it. Now the palm of a full-grown man cannot cover it. But I will beat it! My only concern at this moment is the menacing suspense which Chief Kortuma is going through." The Master paused for a moment as a wave of pain, nausea, and debility shot through his body. His gaunt figure grew stiff, the flesh on his cavernous face was drawn tight like the leather on a samkpa drum. His medical shirt, a little too big for him now, shook gently in a burst of wind that blew on the island. He felt that the wind could blow him off his feet for he had become light like a leaf. With his thumb and the middle finger of his right hand he pressed the nail of his right hand forefinger under which he had buried his lightning medicine. He gazed into the sky at the sporadic, faint shafts of light that razed the heavens in a zigzag manner, the aftermath of the thunder storm. Could it be that his power over lighting had deserted him? He wished it were the rain -time when the lightning was frequent and very explosive. He looked at the warriors sadly and then gazed in the distance.

"I had a dream last night," he said. "In this dream, I saw Dadie, the Chief of the Gola, and Bahla, his Kulubah. When I saw the two men . . . well, what I'll tell you is this: we have made life untenable in Golaland. What remains to be done is strike down their Chief and his Kulubah. That I am prepared to do alone!" he said decisively. "Kolleh," he called to a tall, young warrior who had a spear in his right hand. "Go tell Chief Kortuma that the war is won. I will see him in ten days." That was the Master's last command.

Yaa Dadie, the Chief of the Gola, was a short, muscular man with thick, black hair and large, shiny eyes. Extremely black in complexion, he was given to histrionics and eloquence at all gatherings; never would he compromise his views on issues once he was convinced that they were right. Ordinarily, he was quiet and unassuming. His flat, long upper incisor teeth poked slantwise out of his thin lips, pointing roughly to the right of his narrow chin. This gave his face, with its narrow forehead and protruding cheekbones, a look that was at once severe and voluptuous. In the village of Kuntaa, where he resided, he habitually sauntered about in a flamboyant gown, stopping here and there to greet Elders, Zoes and friends. The villagers would gaze at him with admiration and awe. With admiration, because there was dignity to his mien; furthermore, unlike most Chiefs who regimented their people so often for love of crude power and authority, he was not a snoop, neither did he bother anyone. They looked upon him with awe, because of his rippling build, especially the solid muscles in his broad shoulders which radiated immense strength and power.

In his days, Chief Dadie had fought and won many a battle, but the present one which he had virtually lost, caught him unawares. For one thing, he had thought that the new Chief of the Kpelle would spend at least the first year of his reign consolidating his power rather than engaging in warfare. Of course he was aware of the perennial conflict that existed between the Kpelle and the Gola people, a conflict that centred mainly around the road to the coast. Of late, there had been several ambushes and two or three Kpelle men had reportedly lost their goods and lives; but these were isolated incidents and did not warrant a full-scale war. And as these incidents occurred shortly before the death of Chief Gbolokai, Chief Dadie was convinced that everything was buried with the dead. Thus he and Gbolokai's successor would begin a new era of relationships, forgetting the past misunderstandings and conflicts.

But then he had heard rumours of war arising from Fuama Chiefdom when Kortuma mounted the stool. Chief Dadie refused to believe these rumours for at least two reasons. If the Kpelle Chief was preparing for war with his land, he would not have gone to a Gola village, of all places, for medical consultations. Upon closely investigating the purpose of Chief Kortuma's medical consultations in Kuntaa, he had been informed that the Kpelle Chief was merely searching for a child. In fact, Chief Dadie was reassured by the fact that no enemy could possibly enter that powerful Gola medical centre and leave it alive, for there were numerous medicines of various kinds planted around the village that took care of any visitor who either harboured hate against the people of Golaland or who was in a state of war with them. Secondly, Chief Dadie had dispatched several spies to Fuama Chiefdom, and they had all had the same impression: Kpelleland was not on a war footing, for people played from dusk to dawn in the many Kpelle villages they visited; people went hunting, fishing, and farming as usual in Kpelleland. But because the war rumours persisted unabated, he had dispatched a limited force to patrol the border with Kpelleland. And he had received no news of any confrontation until his entire domain was engulfed in a war for which he was not fully prepared. It appeared to him that the fate which he and his people had been made to suffer was actually caused by a Zoe whose charms were stronger than those of his own Zoes. He drew this conclusion from a bizarre dream which he once had when the war rumour first began invading his land: he was on a hunting expedition and had run into a herd of antelopes in an expansive glade. Instead of fleeing him, the animals stood all around him, sniffing the musty air with their small, black snouts, and driving jungle flies from their behinds with whisking tails. Stretching his left arm, Dadie almost touched the one which stood directly before him; the animal gazed at him with its large, animated eyes with their dilated pupils. Instantly, all the animals formed a long line before him as if to make the killing easy and orderly for him. Dadie quickly placed an arrow across his bow and shot the animal that stood at the end of the line on his left. Then he shot the second one in the line. Then the third. Surprisingly, the animials did not fall, even though the arrows had poison. Rather, they stood on the same spot, the arrow heads that were made of iron buried in their flanks. When he had shot all the arrows in the large arrow bag which hung on his left shoulder, Dadie had not hit even half the animals. He pulled out the arrows from those he had shot and shot them again, but none of them fell. After going through this ordeal many times, Dadie grew desperate: he threw both bow and arrow bag away, repeatedly pounded his head with his fists and then pounced upon one of the antelopes, but he failed to subdue it, though the animal did not put up a struggle. Suddenly he woke up; a chill ran through his body, making him numb. He lay quietly in bed, trying to unravel the mysterious dream. He could not determine any plausible explanation for it. Thus he decided not to tell it to anyone until he had managed to find an explanation. Now he saw the clue in the daily reports of Kpelle atrocities in his land. Every day one or two of the men who had fled Kuntaa and who knew the location of his den, brought him tales of mass destruction of villages in the east. As far as the western region was concerned, only Kuntaa and a handful of villages and farms were destroyed. But the east had been laid desolate.

What piqued the Gola Chief most was the death of Bahla, his Kulubah and personal friend, during the siege of Kuntaa. After a month with no report from the limited force which his Chief had dispatched to the border, Bahla had volunteered to command the guards who took positions around Kuntaa, for it became increasingly clear that danger was near. Chief Dadie had agreed to this arrangement with the utmost reluctance. He had preferred that a lesser man command the guards and his Kulubah stay by his side because he had not yet decided on what action to take in the crisis and he was deeply troubled in spirit.

"Well, you may command the guards," Chief Dadie had said. "In the event of an attack, two things should be done immediately; don't waste time trying to think of doing something else: let there be a musket blast, and let a man run to my house as fast as his legs can carry him, announcing that Kuntaa is attacked. This will give the people a chance to flee the village."

For two weeks there was calm. And suddenly that fateful night came, when, for the first time in living memory, hostilities of untold proportions were unleashed on the historic citadel of the Gola. At

116

the sound of the musket, Chief Dadie and his wives and children managed to escape into the bush on the eastern outskirts.

For three weeks he and his troops of wives and children defied the hostile forest, managing to eke out an existence as best they could. During the day, his entire family stayed in the den while he wandered about the forest in search of game and foodstuffs. Of course the forest teemed with herds of antelopes, wild boars, and numerous species of rat. Each week he killed at least an animal or two and gathered what remained of cassava, eddoes, and potatoes on the ruined farms of Golaland to feed his family, all the while thinking of how to surrender to Chief Kortuma.

In an effort to do this, Chief Dadie had sent several men with white chickens to Chief Kortuma, but none of them ever returned.

"Ah," the Gola Chief thought with despair as he sat on a log in an open spot in the lonely forest during one of his hunting expeditions, his face buried in both hands, "If only Bahla were alive!" Bahla's death had had an unsettling effect on him. Bahla was believed to be the most powerful warrior that ever lived in Golaland. He was not only brave and wise, but had the most powerful war charm imaginable. This charm supposedly enabled him to turn himself into a tree, a leaf, a rock, or a creek whenever he was cornered, and he could materialise at will anywhere he wished. As he saw the situation now, Dadie believed that the only real alternative he had was to go to Chief Kortuma himself and plead for peace.

After contemplating his dilemma awhile, the Gola Chief composed himself, moved his hands from his face and tried to raise his face to the sky, but the blood suddenly froze in his veins and he grew heavy like a rock. There, before him, in broad daylight, stood the Master, the tip of whose spear was placed at his throat. The Gola Chief grew speechless and apprehensive, his beady eyes poked out, his lips agape. *Why?* the word flashed in his mind. A bearded man with bushy hair, dressed in medical clothes, pushing the tip of a spear into his neck was a vision he had never had during wartime. Usually, when at war, his dreams and visions involved farming, hunting, fishing, and other peacetime activities. But this vision of a strange-looking man attacking him with a spear in broad daylight was incomprehensible. The only plausible explanation of this was that the war was over and peace was at hand. He tried to shake himself as he often did when he dreamed a confusing dream so as to wake up and cast it out of his mind. But then the strange, unreal man thrust the spear deep in his neck and all he saw was total darkness.

II

For two consecutive days Korlu was having birth pains. Much to her own joy and surprise, she saw the time at hand when she would deliver her first child and be free from the stigma of barrenness. Though the pains grew increasingly severe with each passing moment, she relished it and never bothered to report it to Kona who continued to plague her with innumerable instructions on what not to eat and how to conduct herself. Kona had virtually forbidden her to eat meat, for Korlu could not imagine what animal she was permitted to eat: Kona had told her not to eat monkey, leopard, wild boar, antelope, rat, or elk. Monkey would make her baby ugly. Leopard would make the baby wild, irascible, and haughty. Wild boar would give her baby a long nose, and antelope would make the baby bony. Rat would give the baby a bloody nose and elk would cause miscarriage. Kona gave her herb water to drink each morning, noon, and night. Additionally, she gave her roots to chew, leaves to eat with kola nuts — taught her how to walk, how to lie in bed, how to sit down, and how to stand up. Korlu had strictly observed these harsh rules, if only she and her baby would live.

It dawned on her that the poor one's advice to her husband in the dream which Kekula confirmed, was largely responsible for her being pregnant, for it was after that dream that Kortuma again accepted her as a woman. Many years before then, he had given her up for barren, and refused to touch her in bed, making her wonder if she were still a woman. A full-fledged member of the Sande, Korlu was not that concerned about the pleasure which she missed, but the fact that Kortuma no longer gave her a fair chance to become pregnant, even though he maintained a facade of interest in saving her from barrenness. Everyone knew that no woman, under any circumstances, would ever conceive without a man, and some women started having children when they were well advanced in years. Perhaps she was the innocent victim of a wicked plot, the most probable culprits of which were her sonang who could have

118

ruined her good relationship with their husband through a love potion so that they might have him exclusively to themselves.

But Korlu took pride in the fact that, in all her troubles, she had a pure heart and a clear conscience, depending only on God and the Ancestors to save her from her undeserved disgrace and shame.

After years of unbearable suffering, her relatives, friends, and her own heart had tempted her to find a lover.

"You can't go on like this!" they had said. "As a full-grown woman, you have the right to a man. Your sanity, happiness and self-respect demand it. What are you afraid of? Baby? As long as you are married to Kortuma, any child you get belongs to him. So don't let that bother you. Maybe Kortuma's blood does not agree with yours. That's possibly why you can't conceive . . . a lover might give you a child . . ."

Korlu had resented this easy solution because she feared the pain and pressure of secret love and the possibility of permanent ruin to the individuals who engaged in it once it was discovered. Now the huge belly which bulged before her and rested on her lap when she sat down, defended her abiding faith in God and the Ancestors who never forsook the persecuted and the helpless. Often she caressed it and joyfully absorbed the pains caused by the twitching creature inside. So this was the beginning of motherhood, she often thought.

On the third day of pains, Korlu grew unusually heavy and could not leave her bed. Kona, Lorpu and a few elderly women that had had children spent the day with her. Towards evening they took her to an unfinished house on the western outskirts to deliver. The house had a roof and its undaubed walls of sticks were roughly plaited with bamboo. Termites had eaten many of the sticks and bamboo; wild grass and potato vines had crept in and wrapped themselves on the walls. Polang, who was given the task of preparing the house for Korlu, spent the entire afternoon hoeing the grass and pulling away the potato vines. She placed mats on the floor in the largest room and hung thick country cloth sheets on the walls of the room. Shortly after she had finished her job, the midwife and her assistant tied a large sheet of cloth around Korlu's waist, held her by both arms and led her to the house.

Chief Kortuma, utterly helpless, sat praying on the porch, a look of concern and apprehension on his face, and watched Korlu and her attendants walk with difficulty towards the outskirts. It soon grew dark and Lorpu came to him for the hurricane lantern. On this occasion, as on numerous others when she brought him reports of Korlu's progress, Lorpu maintained a bright face, however

119

strained it might have been, telling the Chief in a mild voice that all was well with Korlu. After all, a powerful midwife and herbalist was seeing after her. And so it was only a matter of giving nature time to do its work. At this, the Chief forced a smile, gave her a few coins and kola nuts, as well as all best wishes for Korlu's well-being, praying that the Ancestors would direct Kona's hands in her efforts. Until he heard a rooster crow, the Chief never knew that he had spent the entire night outdoors. Korlu must be having difficulties, he thought. He no longer believed Lorpu's optimistic reports, because if all was well as she claimed, Korlu should have delivered long before daybreak. On an impulse, he walked vehemently towards the 'midwifery bush', but stopped short of entering the house — bravely turned around as becoming a full-fledged member of the Poro Society, and went back to the porch. Scarcely had he sat down than he was up again, pacing in the yard with a bowed head.

Sumo who was on his way to his wine tree, saw the Chief and grew curious. He watched him awhile, wondering what was up, until he remembered that Korlu was carried 'behind the house' the evening before. Walking over to him, he said:

"I just heard that Korlu is behind the house."

"Yes," the Chief admitted. "Since last night."

Sumo observed his long, worried face and said, "This is her first time, as you know. It has to take some time. An innocent young girl like Korlu should have no problem."

"I hope so."

"Believe me!" Sumo bobbed his head emphatically.

"Lorpu said everything is going on all right, but I don't know why it's taking so long."

"Why expect a woman to have her very first baby at the twinkling of an eye? Korlu will have a nice, healthy baby. All you need is to be patient."

"Thank you, Sumo," the Chief said as Sumo walked away. "I hope you are right. I'll see you in the evening."

Seething with intolerable suspense and agitation, the Chief continued pacing up and down until he heard the excited, loud cry of the women:

"Baaaaaaaaaaa!!!"

Chief Kortuma rushed into the house for kola nuts and came to the porch where he sat and waited for the women. It was clear to him that all was over and that nothing had gone amiss, but his heart still surged with painful suspense: what child was it? The assurance that Korlu had pulled through without unusual complications,

120

however, gave him a ray of joy which overshadowed all other considerations.

Eventually the women emerged from the outskirts in the sultry heat of the overhead sun, dancing, clapping their hands to the rhythm of the motherhood song: *Is this a child-bearing stomach I have?*

When they reached the Chief's house, Kona, with her stooping gait, came forward with firm steps, waving her shrivelled arms like a bird in flight. At this sign the women became quiet.

"Lorpu, tell the Chief that we have done the big job which he gave us to do," she declared. "Let him wipe the sweat!" She spoke in a throaty voice as she stood, arms akimbo, looking sideways in a preoccupied fashion.

"Chief, that's it," Lorpu said, bouncing forward with a smile on her face. She stood below the porch, bent slightly forward and gently shook her body, both arms hanging on her sides like a monkey about to leap from one tree to the other. She swung her head sideways to the rhythm of her own movement. "You gave the women a job to do," she continued. "Now they have done it. Wipe the sweat!"

"Thank you," the Chief said, rising and adjusting his white robe. "What stranger is this?" he smiled, his eyes brightened as he came down the dirt stairs and stood before the women.

"Someone like you," Lorpu said, standing still, a serious expression on her face like the other women. Bowing her head with its colourful headtie, she said, "They were two. The one that looks like you drove away the one that did not look like you."

The Chief's face darkened, but he tried to look cheerful. After a moment of silence, he took out four of the kola nuts he had kept in his side pocket and gave them to Lorpu, the gown flowing down to his wrist.

"Here is the white thing," he said, rolling the gown back to his shoulder. "My hand is under what you women have done. May he live to be the next Chief of Fuama Chiefdom."

"Let it be so," the women clapped their hands and resumed singing and dancing, heading to the bush.

Chief Kortuma returned to the porch, both happy and sad. He could not celebrate the birth of his first son as he was inclined to do for fear of arousing the hate and envy of witches. And why should the Ancestors grant his request with a slap in the face? However, he was grateful that Korlu's life had been spared. He prudently concealed his grief in an effort to avert a greater disaster. As this was the first time that such a tragedy had happened to Korlu, to grieve over it openly would be an invitation to others of its kind.

After the sun had gone down and the evening shadow had fallen on the village, the women brought Korlu and her baby out of the bush. The baby was wrapped carefully in a piece of old blanket that had several holes, but was very clean. Lorpu carried the baby in her arms and walked beside Korlu whom Kona held by the left arm. She warned Korlu not to exert herself unduly even if she could afford it. Polang had already swept the house clean and made up Korlu's bed with dry palm thatch and banana leaves wrapped in blankets. She had also brought enough firewood and water into the house.

Lorpu took the baby to the Chief who was pacing up and down in the yard. Chief Kortuma held the baby gently in his arms and watched its tiny body and its large head scantily covered with dark, curly hair. The baby was a trifle too light, it looked pale and weak. On removing the blanket from its body down to the waist, the Chief saw that it was little more than mere bones roughly covered with wrinkled flesh. Now and then it shook one of its weak limbs or turned its head from one side to the other, wrinkling its narrow face with its tightly closed eyelids. After taking one last, critical look at his son, Chief Kortuma gave him back to Lorpu who carried him to Korlu. Later the Chief gave Lorpu a few coins and more kola nuts for the midwife and her associates.

In the evening, Sumo brought a gourd of palm wine for Chief Kortuma who sat quietly on his porch.

"I heard that you have a stranger!" Sumo exclaimed as he climbed onto the porch, carefully placing one foot before the other.

"You are quite correct!" replied the Chief. "A man stranger, too! Have a seat."

"I just got the news," Sumo said as he placed the gourd of wine beside the Chief and sat in a chair opposite him. "I told you," Sumo continued, growing a trifle uneasy when he saw an unexpected cold and sullen expression on the Chief's face. But he continued, "I thought of bringing you some wine to express my congratulations. Where is he?" Sumo yawned, exposing his dark-brown teeth shamelessly.

"With Korlu," the Chief said. "Let's go there."

They met Korlu lying by the baby on a mat that was spread near the fireplace. She lay on her right side and the nipple of her right breast was in the baby's mouth. The baby sucked it greedily, kicking its legs and arms in the air delightfully. Bending down, Sumo looked at him briefly.

"Thank you," he told Korlu, watching her loose hair and swollen belly; then he stared at Polang who sat on a low stool near the fireplace above Korlu's head.

"Hnn," Korlu answered.

Returning to the Chief's porch, the two men drank the wine which foamed down the rolled bamboo thatch at the mouth of the gourd.

"You always make good wine," the Chief flattered Sumo as he poured a cupful. "I don't know what I'll do if you ever stop making wine."

Sumo chuckled, his pot-belly shook.

"Nothing will stop me," he said. "Except death."

"Old age can stop you," the Chief said, placing the white enamelled cup to his lips. He took a long drink, belched, and placed the cup near the gourd. "You will be surprised when the day comes when you won't be able to climb a wine tree," he told Sumo.

"Well," Sumo remarked, "when I come to that bridge, I will cross it." He poured half a cupful of wine and took a quick drink. "I simply want to taste it for courtesy's sake, but I'm already full." He shook the cup upside down by his feet to dispose of the wine dregs.

"I can tell," the Chief said, clearing his throat.

"Now you have a son. Your dream has come true," Sumo changed the subject.

"Well, let's first see him stand on his feet." The Chief spoke gravely and looked meditatively into the distance.

"Will you give him the poor one's name?"

"I haven't thought of a name for him yet." The Chief drank another cup of wine. His eyelids fell slightly. "You know one thing, Sumo," he said seriously, becoming suddenly alive. "I believe that the Master has died."

. Sumo grew sober and uneasy. He looked at the Chief with a fixed and puzzled gaze.

"Why do you think so?" he asked.

"I get the feeling now and then," the Chief said. "It's not easy to beat an Upriver Zoe. But since he has never fought a war before, he might have lost all his men and got killed himself."

"Then why is it the war has not come to Fuama Chiefdom? If the Gola were so victorious, they would be tempted to take our land."

"Not while Kortuma is still alive. The wise man does not push his luck too far. And I don't think the Gola are fools."

"The Master, as you know, is a proud man. Perhaps he wants to get total victory before coming home, or sending you a message. He is ambitious, too. Maybe he might have decided to take Kuntaa, or even cut down Dadie — these impossible missions! However, let's wait and see."

"I often feel that we over-reacted by going to war with the Gola. If their real intention was to fight us, they would have been prepared for us and the war would have been over long before now."

"There's nothing we can do or say for sure at this time. What we should do is what you are already doing: go on living as if nothing has happened. If the dead animal gets rotten, everyone will smell it."

"I don't regret anything. The most important thing is that I have shown the Gola that I won't tolerate nonsense from them as long as I rule this land. The poor one used to joke with them by using persuasion, often at his own expense, in order to make peace. I am determined to prove to them that they have a different man to deal with. And they must fully understand the risk they would be running if they make trouble for me."

The Chief who was now drinking one cup of wine after the other, soon became tipsy, the light faded in his eyes. Sumo was getting sleepy.

"You need rest," he told the Chief.

"I have something good to tell you," the Chief tried to smile. Sumo watched his face with curiosity. "If the Master dies, you will be the next Zoe of Fuama Chiefdom."

"The Master again!" Sumo exclaimed. "Let's rest on this happy day. Don't worry about the Master. Our lives are in the hands of God and the Ancestors."

"Don't you want to be our Zoe?"

"I don't know — why me?"

"I have full confidence in you. Sumo, I know you can do it."

"You are giving me more credit than I deserve. I like the honour . . ."

"Look, Sumo," the Chief cut in, "nobody is born a Zoe. It's courage, it's sacrifice, it's intelligence that does the job. You already know a lot about medicines. You can start with what you know . . ."

Sumo grinned and nodded, not so much because he agreed with the Chief, but in order to be polite.

"Words don't bother you," he declared. "Do you really mean what you are saying?"

"Of course, I know it's risky," the Chief continued without answering his question. "But life is a risk, and to be a man is to take great risks. Once you are willing to risk everything at all times, including your own life, you have become a man."

"As far as I am concerned, the risk does not mean a thing. Why should someone like me, with one foot in the grave, be afraid of death? But in order to be a Zoe — and this is what most people overlook — you must have the talent. It's a gift! You see a certain kind of sickness and you are led by instinct to the special leaf that cures it . . ."

"Sumo, go and rest. I simply wanted to broach the subject and get your reaction. I am not worried about the death of the Master at all, because the death of one Zoe is not the death of all Zoes."

Sumo took one last drink and rose to go, obviously feeling relieved.

"Well, take good care of — I don't know whom — the stranger."

"Thank you, Sumo. I surely will, and when we take him out of the house, he will have a name of his own." The Chief drew the gourd of wine close to his feet and filled his cup again.

For the next three days the Chief and Korlu could not agree on a name for the child. In fact, Korlu said initially that it was too early to give him a name as it wasn't certain if he came to stay. But the Chief said if the naming should be delayed, people would simply call his son, 'Boy', or 'Old Man'. Korlu then suggested the name, 'Dog'. This would tell death that nobody cared that much about him, since death usually struck down only that which was precious. Death would not bother with a worthless dog. Chief Kortuma thought her argument was quite convincing. He had thought of the same name, but he later turned it down because it was too far-fetched. Death would think that they were trying to hide something. On the morning of the fourth day after the child's birth, just before he was 'taken out of the house', Kortuma suggested the name, 'Yorfii', an ordinary name with no special meaning. Korlu accepted it.

Early in the morning on that day Kona came, beaming with a smile, to perform the happy task of taking Yorfii 'out of the house' and initiate him into the world, to life, make him a part of the land. She wore a new lapa of a blue colour, which she had apparently kept for many a season. Tied roughly on her head was also a new white headtie. In her hands she carried a green pan filled with water and green leaves. Korlu sat on a low stool near the doorway. On her lap was the baby which was wrapped in a new lapa that had narrow, black and white striped colours. Chief Kortuma sat in an old rattan chair on the porch. Kona entered the house and placed the pan of medicine near Korlu, absently wiped her hands dry on her new clothes, took the baby from Korlu, removed the lapa, and gave it to

Korlu. Rising, Korlu gave her a stool, tied the lapa on her waist, went out to the porch and stood by the Chief. Kona raised the baby directly before her smiling face, her head thrown backwards.

"He's going to be a notorious man," she said teasingly. The Chief laughed. Korlu blushed. "He looks like the poor one," Kona told the Chief.

"Are you sure?" the Chief asked.

"Very sure! This is your father who has come back."

"I hope not."

"Why not?"

"I want that boy to be himself."

"It's strange. Have you people decided on his name?"

The naked baby writhed, kicked the air with his tiny legs, boxed Kona's breasts with his fists and sucked his lips.

"Yorfii," the Chief said.

"A good name. It's interesting how you people could decide on a name so soon. Some people never give a name to a woman's first child until after its initiation." Sitting down, Kona placed the baby on her lap.

"Such things don't bother me, Kona," the Chief said.

Kona scooped some herb water with her right hand and poured it into her mouth. Holding the baby up deftly with her hands, she sprayed him with it. The baby jerked and squealed. She handed him to Korlu outside and Korlu handed him back to her. This rite was repeated three more times.

"Never mind," the Chief told Yorfii who continued to cry frantically. "That's being a man."

Everything over, Kona laid the baby on her lap and told him:

"From now on, you are a part of us, part of the living. You no longer have the right to leave us. Understand! You are here to stay. And we want you to stay. Understand! We don't know anything about sickness or death here. People don't get sick here. Nobody dies here! If you exaggerate matters of sickness, we'll put you in an old basket, tie a rope on it and drag it about the village. Understand! Come for him, Korlu," she said as Yorfii continued jerking and crying. "He wants milk." Korlu took him and put a nipple in his mouth. "Bathe him this evening with the rest of the herb water," Kona gave the last instruction and got up to go.

"Thank you, Kona," the Chief said, rising and coming to the door. He gave her a few coins.

"Don't bother to spend money yet until we see him stand on his feet," she said, taking the coins.

"That's just your cold water," the Chief said.

For many days Chief Kortuma thought of his son. He was not so pleased with his emaciated look, but was hopeful that Yorfii would overcome that. He had seen many babies born poor and weak but grew up to be strong and plump. Chief Kortuma planned to train Yorfii to be a farmer above everything else. When his umbilical cord dropped off, he buried it with a kola nut in his bath fence, hoping that the kola nut would grow into a tree to establish his right to the land as a full citizen; he also hoped that his flesh would mingle with the earth, making him a lover of farming. Of course, he would train him to be a powerful warrior and instruct him in the traditions of the tribe. The Chief knew that the Poro would take care of these and many other responsibilites connected with Yorfii's upbringing. But the responsibility he could not delegate to anyone else was to train him to become a good Chief.

But Yorfii's feeble condition persisted through the first month after his birth. His limbs grew cold and weak, he could not drink enough rice water, and when he was 'stuffed' with it, he vomited every bit. Kona first considered this to be normal and she rubbed seybeh chalk on his body to make him warm. She said it would take time for him to get used to the food 'on this side'. But Yorfii grew worse in his second month. He turned extremely pale and weak and refused Korlu's breasts. This was the end of all hope. Kona was seized by a disorderly rush: she made all the child medicines she knew — some she rubbed all over the baby's body; some she squeezed into the baby's eyes and nostrils.

Meanwhile, she advised Korlu to keep the baby well wrapped in a blanket and refrain from being nervous with him. For the thousandth time, she recounted to her the numerous unpleasant experiences she had had with sick children:

"When I had my first child," Kona would say, "it was raintime, and famine was raging. I did everything a mother could do: hunted all over for rice, uprooted stumps of cassava trees, used every herb I knew! All in vain! The child died." She would slap her thighs with her hands and turn her small, wrinkled palms up. "I had two others," she would continue, becoming more absorbed in her own stories rather than the problem before her. "They died of mere headache and cough. You know, an Ancestor sometimes comes to you as a baby in order to make you a mother and go back. Let Kortuma have a powerful Zoe look into this matter." As Kona spoke, Korlu would bow her head in distress, fighting back the tears as it would be dangerous if any should drop on her sick baby. Kona would then take the baby gently from her and cuddle it. "Don't deceive Korlu," she would reprimand the child. "You are here to stay. I told you this before. Nobody dies here . . . give him some of his medicine," she would give the baby back to Korlu. The baby would stir weakly, crane its neck, turning its face from Kona as if in protest at her reprimand.

Korlu would force Yorfii's mouth open and pour in some of the brackish water of a concoction of herbs in an old clay pot Kona had prepared. The baby would spit out most of it and manage to swallow some. ·

When they had done the chores and cooking for the day, Lorpu and Polang would spend some time with Korlu, helping her to bathe and feed the baby. Now and then Chief Kortuma, speechless, would come by, look at his son with a heavy face, and leave the house, crestfallen. Many villagers called on Korlu during this crisis in order to console her.

Before she went to bed each night, Lorpu would tell Korlu, "Don't be nervous with him. Take care. Keep clothes wrapped about him, and if something happens, call me." To Polang: "Stay awake and help her."

Early one morning Yorfii shook and gasped violently. Korlu knew that the end had come. She rose up quickly, shaking all over, and laid him in her lap, piled more wood on the fire, and watched him. Polang was asleep. The baby grew calm and stiff. "Ao! Ao!" Korlu shouted tearfully. The baby jerked fitfully again, gave a shrill cry, and lay quietly in her lap. She placed the back of her right hand on his belly, she did not feel the belly rise and fall. Nervously she wrapped him in a blanket, laid him on the bed, and rushed out of the house, crying hysterically and running to Chief Kortuma's house.

Unable to climb the stairs, she simply collapsed below them, and writhed violently. Polang came running and crying, her hands clasped on her head. Chief Kortuma, dressed in short brown pants, a sheet of white country cloth slung over his shoulder, came to the porch and looked at the women in a confused and embarrassed fashion and then went back into the house. Lorpu ran out, fell on the ground by Korlu and Polang who were already rolling all over the yard, crying fitfully. Chief Kortuma came out to the porch again, went back into the house, returned to the porch, came down to the yard and walked vigorously to Korlu's house. But just before he entered the yard, a group of men who were all members of the Poro rushed upon him, grabbed him, and forced him back. The

Chief who looked dazed and perplexed as if he were drunk, put up a brief struggle and then submitted to the men. They took him to a house near the square where they guarded him. A large group of women and children had joined the Chief's wives in the yard, crying and rolling all over.

Kona came to the Chief's house at a trot, slapping her thighs, raising her hands to the sky, looking alarmed and desperate, and crying, "What has happened! What has happened! Oh, my people, what!"

Sumo who had just come from his wine tree, stood in his yard, a gourd of wine in his hand, and cast a puzzled stare at the weeping crowds in the Chief's yard. He instantly understood. Extremely shocked, however, the gourd fell from his hand and broke to pieces; the white wine flowed several feet in the sandy soil which sucked it in almost immediately. Hoping that Korlu and the Chief had done nothing rash and harmful to themselves, he walked pensively to the Chief's house.

Gbada walked bravely to Korlu's yard where several men had already gathered, looking at each other in confusion.

"Let's bury it at once," he told them as he entered the house, the men following him. "This is the first time that this kind of thing has happened to Chief Kortuma and Korlu. It would be bad luck for them if the corpse should linger here."

Soon they emerged from the house. The baby was wrapped in a blanket with a piece of mat in his hand. Gbada walked with firm steps before the group of men who were quiet and solemn as they walked with calculation behind him to the cemetery.

The villagers did their best to console Chief Kortuma and Korlu throughout the day. Korlu spent the day in Lorpu's house, where nearly all the village women were. Korlu wept a great deal and stopped only after an old woman gave her this advice:

"You should be grateful because the Ancestors have taken away bad luck from your path. When a woman's first child dies, it means that she will have many others, and that they will be strong and healthy until they become adults and grow old. But if you weep excessively, the Ancestors will feel that you do not appreciate their goodness. Thus you will have to face more of this kind of trouble."

Chief Kortuma who was expected to harm himself, surprisingly proved courageous. He sat in the dark, stifled room for a long time, the men surrounding him, and then suddenly stood up resolutely.

"Don't worry about me," he told the men. "A man has to pass through such things."

But the men did not allow him to be alone. They accompanied him as he walked about the village, on the river bank, and in the surrounding forests. Some of the men took his gun, spear and sword out of his bedroom and hid them. They advised Lorpu to take away her cooking knife and any tool or weapon that might be in his house.

Battered and exceedingly dispirited, Chief Kortuma and Korlu sat on his porch in the evening, the village Elders around them. Some of them sat on the porch, while others stood in the yard.

"We ought to look into it," Chief Kortuma remarked.

"As for me," Korlu put in, "I believe that it is God who gives babies and it is God who takes them away. I don't want you to get yourself into lots of trouble."

"I don't care what I get into!" the Chief snapped. "Fortunately, we have a man here who can hunt the witch for us. Where's Flomo?"

"Here I am," Flomo replied outside, climbed to the porch, and stood before the Chief.

"Get ready," the Chief told him. "I want you to bring the witch who has killed my child into the open. I'm tired of seeing babies dying here." Tucking his hand into his pocket, Chief Kortuma took out a white coin and gave it to him. "This is my word," he said. Flomo respectfully accepted the coin and left.

Though they had ideas of their own about the problem, the Elders made no comment because they realised that the Chief was in no mood to entertain argument or discussion.

"You women know what to do," Chief Kortuma told his wives. "Go and get everything ready for Flomo." He and the Elders went to the yard where they sat in their chairs to watch the ceremony.

After some time, Flomo brought his bag of blacksmith's tools that also contained a bushcow horn and a cowtail and placed it several paces from the crowd and squatted by it. Lorpu and Polang stood near him. Lorpu had a red rooster in her hand and Polang had a bottle of palm oil and some kola nuts. Several men brought some firewood and made a bonfire.

Flomo took out the tools which were no longer ordinary tools but supernatural forces, and laid them in a straight row near the bonfire. They comprised an anvil, a hammer, several pairs of tongs, a carving knife, and a short piece of iron that was sharpened at one end.

"I want palm oil now," he said. Polang handed him the bottle of oil.

Flomo sucked out a mouthful of oil and blew it on the fire. The fire glowed. He gave the bottle back to Polang and asked for kola nuts and clean rice. Polang gave him two kola nuts and Lorpu ran into her house and brought a small basket with clean rice.

Flomo contorted his face, bobbed his head sideways, his bright, piercing eyes rolling fiercely in their sockets. He parted his lips, showing his tobacco-stained teeth.

"Chief," he said, "do you want me to find the witch?"

"Even if it is I," the Chief said.

The night was murky and chilly. A huge crowd had now gathered in the Chief's yard, watching Flomo.

"You are a powerful Zoe," the Chief told Flomo. "There's no point in further talks. Whatever you do, you are saving us from witches. If anyone near or far, if anyone here in our midst is bewitching our children, point out that person." The Chief tucked his hand into his pocket and took out a piece of kola nut. Giving it to Flomo, he added, "I mean what I said."

"Thank you," Flomo said, laying the kola nut beside the charms.

Then he took the bushcow horn out of the tool bag. It was plaited with black thread, stained with smears of kola nut and blood. He planted it two feet from the fire. Rising, he took a brown cowtail from the tool bag and began walking with wide strides around the fire, swaggering, howling, raising his voice in praise of the power which he was invoking. After expending a great deal of energy in the process, he squatted beside the charms.

"I want four woman singers," he said. The Chief sent for four of the best singers in the village. Soon they came with keeh in their hands, the eldest sat on a stool beside Flomo. Her lips were parted with a smile, her white teeth showing. She held her keeh, plaited with strings of bead, loose threads tied in a knot at the end, and began joggling it, raising a nostalgic song, *I am going home.* The others responded in sharp and crisp voices.

As they sang, Flomo took two kola nuts from Polang and split them in four halves with his coarse fingernails. He joggled them in his hands and threw them to the ground, snapping his right hand fingers. Two sat up and two bent down. Usually success took a long time to come, but the witch he was hunting seemed vulnerable. He smiled and scanned the crowd with pride.

Then he took the chicken from Lorpu, twisted its neck, and cut it with a sharp razor. The blood gushed out. He sprinkled the charms with it, muttering incantations. At length he dropped the chicken to the ground; it wobbled for a moment and then lay still.

Everyone was silent, the singers huddled together behind Flomo

131

and trained their eyes rigidly on him. He was now tinkering with his charms intently. He laid them down, stood up and looked around. The crowd grew more apprehensive.

Suddenly a woman with tight country cloth panties, a piece of cloth tied around her waist, hair tousled, reeled through the crowd. The crowd cowered and withdrew. She seemed to be in a trance.

Flomo told the crowd, "Don't run away. Don't be afraid. She's not the witch. The horn called her to go and find the witch." He took the bushcow horn and told it, "Don't let her hurt herself."

The woman calmed down, and sat with her legs stretched before her, her hands clasped between her thighs, her head bowed, and her eyes shut. All of a sudden she began to groan.

Flomo tucked the horn in her clasped hands. "Take her to whatever place the witch is hiding. Anywhere. In the cemetery, under the river, into the trees, everywhere."

The singers resumed singing. As they sang, the woman held the horn tight and danced all over the yard and suddenly ran into the darkness.

Flomo resumed his roistering walk about the blazing fire, swishing the air with his cowtail. He did this for a long time until the woman, clenching the horn, rammed through the crowd and sat beside the fire, trembling. She swung her head from side to side. The air reeked with a strong, unpleasant odour.

"Everything is over," Flomo declared proudly. "I smell a witch! She has been fighting a witch in the cemetery."

He rubbed some chalk on the woman's ankles, in her armpits, on her forehead and breasts. She quietened down.

"What did you see?" he asked her in a loud voice.

"I . . . I . . .I . . ."

"Let her speak, I implore you, Oh, Gaiyomo! You are every man's father. Have pity on us. Let the secret of darkness be revealed. What did you see?"

"A . . . a . . . a . . . witch."

Flomo laughed.

"Do you want the name of the witch revealed?" he asked the Chief.

"Even if it is I," the Chief said.

The woman dropped the horn and fell flat on her back. Flomo rushed to her. She was dead. The villagers fled in terror. Flomo stood with dejection beside the body.

Chief Kortuma held his head in his hands and cried bitterly, "Why should the solution to one problem be another problem?"

12

When he spied distant darts of firelight, apparently issuing out of four different houses that stood wide apart, the man halted abruptly in the grim darkness as if he had encountered a mamba. Worn out, exhausted, and sore — his head and limbs heavy — pain shot through his entire body. His eyes, which had been accustomed to the night as he ran like a deer on the hideous jungle path, grew completely blind. Unexpectedly, he saw stars. The man collapsed on the gravelled knoll, unconscious.

Coming to before dawn, he sat up with a start and grunted. He rubbed his sore eyes lightly, squinted in the dark, seeing nothing. Strange! A cock crowed in the distance. Pepper birds chirped in the surrounding bushes. Almost dawn! Could it be that he was on the outskirts of a Gola village! The thought had a sobering effect on him. Unarmed and in possible danger, he felt extremely terrified and vulnerable. Once again he fell prostrate on his belly as if taking cover from a spearshot.

Unable to recall an unpleasant dream which roused him out of sleep soon after he retired to bed, Chief Kortuma was restless through the night. Usually he offered a peace sacrifice to the gods after an ominous, restless night, but as he had given up on them, he elected to take a bath early in the morning at the small rapids, in order to cool his tired nerves. But when he stepped outside in a country cloth toga, he found the misty morning cold and comfortable, though the sunrise rapidly drove the mist away. He resolved to take a stroll in the fresh morning breeze which he thought would be just as refreshing as a cold bath in the river. For some unknown reason, he began to feel a dislike for the river as if his aversion to the river gods had spilled over to the river itself.

His legs took him to the grassy road that lead to Mauwa, and when he reached the little gravelled knoll on the outskirts, his vision

133

caught sight of the wretched figure of a man lying on the path, arms stretched above his head, both legs bent like those of a frog. The Chief took cautious steps towards the body, observing it with curious eyes. The man's face was pinned to the ground, his bushy hair and beard riddled with splinters, chips and pieces of dry leaves. Except for a pair of tattered black short pants that left his private parts exposed, and a ragged singlet that comprised mere black strings, he was virtually naked. The Chief jabbed him with his hand in the ribs. The man blabbered, took quick and bewildered looks around him, sat up and gazed at the Chief with fearful eyes.

"Kolleh!" the Chief exclaimed, standing still and holding his toga more firmly. "This is Kortuma! Are you from the war? Are you alright?"

No reply.

The man watched him with uncertain eyes, crouched and stood up. Chief Kortuma observed his skeletal and ghoulish figure with pity. Upon discovering a thick scar that commenced at the top of the man's right shoulder and wended its way to the small of his back, the Chief's face darkened.

"That's war," he thought. "Don't be afraid," he said aloud. "If you have a message for me, let's go to the Kpaan."

Still speechless, the man followed him into the tangled bushes that were sodden with dew. They managed to make their way to the Kpaan, by-passing the village.

When they sat on one of the long bamboo benches, now termite-ridden and falling apart, Kolleh began to speak in a frantic, incoherent voice.

"The heroes will be here this evening," he said breathlessly, bobbing his head for emphasis, both hands gripping his knees. Slightly bending forward, he looked at Chief Kortuma in the face with a fixed gaze. "I came ahead to alert you so that you may prepare to meet them. We won the war three days ago. It was a long and hard struggle, but we did not want to betray your trust. The Master especially was determined to fight to the last man if need be, so long as he brought back victory. He was a strong man, an inspiring leader, a mighty Zoe, and a true hero . . ."

"So Gayflor died!" the Chief started and twisted briefly in his seat. His voice cracked, tears forming in his eyes, he said, "Tell me how he died." He wiped his face and assumed a brave and positive look.

"The surprise attack was a success," Kolleh said. "The Gola were not really prepared for war. We used a simple tactic on them and it worked beautifully. The Master divided the whole army into three divisions. I was part of the first division which was led by the Master himself. The third division stayed behind to guard the border, while the other two went deep inside Golaland and destroyed one village after the other. We . . . we lost men, of course. We certainly lost men. But . . . but . . . you see . . ." Kolleh paused for breath, hung his head sadly and reflected.

"I want to know how the Master died," the Chief maintained.

"He died near Kuntaa," Kolleh said, raising his head and looking aside. "You know, we didn't want to destroy that sacred village. But we had to, because that was the only way to strike down Dadie and Bahla . . ."

"Sure!" the Chief agreed. "You people got them?"

"Certainly!" Kolleh answered, looking at the Chief with inflamed eyes. He related the circumstances surrounding Bahla's death, and how he and others of his division took care of the Master after he was fatally wounded. When Kolleh came to the portion of his story which dealt with the Master's last command, Chief Kortuma rose up instinctively, took a few steps in the tall grasses until he almost ran into a palm tree with suspended dead limbs and fresh fronds that swayed in the gentle breeze. Returning to his seat, the Chief said:

"Why did he go after Dadie, alone?"

"Well," Kolleh clapped his hands once and rested them on his thighs, "as you know, if Dadie were not killed, the war would have continued forever, and the Master wanted to end it once and for all. Of course, we couldn't afford to let him venture into the deep forest, alone, especially as he was in such a bad shape. Well, we followed him at a distance for a while. When we suspected that he was about to notice us, we elected Digula to follow him while the rest of us waited all day under a huge beleh tree on the Haindi-Mauwa road. Towards evening — yes, it was almost sundown — we heard a rattling noise several yards from where we sat. Thinking that it was a Gola warrior, we took cover. But, surprisingly, it was the Master and Digula who emerged out of the bushes. The Master was hardly able to stand on his feet . . . yes, actually . . . he actually died the time he gave his last command and left Tinkayan . . . but he defied death because he was strong and because he was prepared to die with dignity, for there was no visible expression on his face — he looked calm and collected. When we converged upon him after he collapsed in the dry jungle leaves, we saw nothing about him that told of fear or pain or suffering, even when he expelled the last breath, only an atmosphere of peace and satisfaction prevailed, for the hero had laid down his weapons . . . so I decided to carry out his last command, or at least my part of it, which was to come and inform you that the Master had won the war . . ."

"I knew that Gayflor would die," the Chief wept. "He was too sure of himself. After his charms failed him once, he thought only courage and strength mattered. But I told him that death has no cure . . . Ahh Gayflor!" Looking at Kolleh gravely in the face, he asked, "How many of our men really died?"

Bending a finger as he called out each name, Kolleh counted: "Korfaa died. Bhenda died, Yaseer died. Bharsee died. Kpenkpa died. Loryii died. Seward died. Yakpalo died. Guladia died . . ."

"I'm not interested in their names. I simply want to know the number of men who died."

Lost in thoughts, Kolleh continued, "Kolimiling died. Fahn died. Kwesee died . . ." When he ran out of fingers, he started pointing directly at his toes one by one.

Chief Kortuma said in a loud, harsh voice, "Can't you simply tell me the number of men we lost? How many were they?"

Roused to attention, Kolleh looked at the Chief with an agitated expression on his face.

"Fifty men," he said.

"Are you sure?" the Chief said.

"Well," Kolleh said, scratching his head briefly. "You see . . . we . . . yes, Kuntaa was the last village we destroyed. Right after we destroyed it, we were supposed to meet on Tinkayan and celebrate victory; I mean celebrate victory in a small way until we returned home. But Gayflor fell . . . that was most unfortunate . . ."

"That's enough," the Chief said, rising. Shaking his head in frustration and disappointment, he adjusted his toga, held a knot of the country cloth before him with his left hand and began to walk slowly along the bushy path that led to the village.

Kolleh followed him to the outskirts, but suddenly ran towards Golaland like a man possessed. Chickens flew out of his way and dogs barked behind his back.

Chief Kortuma went into his bedroom, closed the door and window, lay down, and moaned for Gayflor. His wives, not knowing that he was moaning, thought he was simply resting after strolling so long in the hot sun. But they grew suspicious when he did not leave the room all day, nor touch the food they had prepared for him.

He was in his bedroom when the 'heroes' arrived in the evening, singing in unusually loud, shrill voices. Realising that this was a victory march, women and children ran about in a frenzy and rushed into their houses for refuge. The Chief wanted to go outside to meet the heroes, but his legs were heavy, for he had mixed emotions — the joy of victory was tarnished by Gayflor's death. As his wives had gone to their houses and he had forgotten to light the lantern, the house was dark and lonely. Rising from the bed, he put on a gown and went to the porch where he sat in a rattan chair and crossed his legs. The shadowy group of men approached him slowly in the bright moonlight, beating the dusty earth with their feet, singing and cheering.

Upon reaching the Chief's yard, they knelt down, except four men of equal height on whose shoulders was a makeshift bamboo bed bearing Gayflor's body. The body was wrapped up in a sheet of white country cloth. Gayflor's belly was swollen out of proportion. Coming down from the porch, the Chief stood before the heroes who cheered him and then gathered closely around him. A whiff of putrid flesh blew in his face. Not knowing where to begin, he commanded them with swinging arms to rise. They followed him to the Kpaan where they laid Gayflor in a clearing and genuflected once again before the Chief.

Speaking in a strong, loud voice, Chief Kortuma said, "Thank you, men of the Poro! No tribe can beat Fuama Chiefdom as long as I, Kortuma, am living!" A cheer. He wiped his face with his right hand, and suddenly it occurred to him that he had forgotten the cowtail, but it made no difference to him because he wasn't in a ceremonial mood — he did not even wear his medical clothes. "I came here simply to thank you and to bury Gayflor," he continued, holding his gown with both hands. "I knew that you would win because you are brave men. To be a man is not a matter of merely having something hanging between your legs, but to be brave. I know what it meant to be in the Gola forest, days and nights, for one long year living on wild fruits and deer, or rice and palm oil you managed to filch from farms . . . I know what it meant to be away from home, knowing that you could be killed at any time and might never return home again. To those of our warriors who did not return, Kortuma says, goodbye.

"Gayflor fell, or at least he has gone to look for herbs — for a Zoe never dies! The mighty Zoe has now joined the ranks of ordinary mortals. Now we are at liberty to address him by his own name — real equality is found only in death. I knew that Gayflor would bring back victory, though I did not know that he would bring it lying on a bamboo bed and wrapped up in a sheet of white cloth. Yet, Gayflor will be with us in spirit forever, and will be remembered for his great courage. May he cross the river in peace and sunshine."

"Let it be so," the men responded solemnly.

Chief Kortuma commanded four heroes to keep watch over Gayflor, while the rest were ordered to dig a grave for him by the river and storm the village in celebration of victory.

Immediately four heroes stood to attention at each corner of the bed while the others gathered shrubs and twigs, and ran wild into the village, killing animals and chickens; uprooting vegetables in gardens around the village; beating thatched roofs with sticks.

It seemed as though the village was besieged, but everyone knew that the war had ended, and all its bad memories and losses were being chased away.

A rooster that managed to escape the heroes' clubs, announced the dawn. The storming suddenly stopped and the heroes scattered the shrubs and twigs before the houses of those families that sustained losses in the war. Then they fetched hoes and shovels and went to the river bank to dig a grave for their fallen Kulubah.

The overhead sun laid bare the torn earth, dead chickens and animals, clusters of loose thatch, shrubs, and twigs that littered up the entire village. As the inhabitants of each house stepped out, they would look apprehensively in their yard. Those who saw bunches of shrubs and twigs before their houses either fell down in agony or screamed and ran into the bush.

When Yata, Gayflor's widow, stepped out and saw the shrubs in her yard, she sat on the porch, cold sweat pouring profusely out of her body. She scratched her head awhile, and went back inside. Her daughter, Kulah, still wrapped up in bedclothes, was fast asleep in her bed by the fireside. She shook her briskly and said:

"Wake up, Kulah! Kulah, wake up! Your father did not come back from the war, alive." Yata began to cry most piteously.

The girl twisted herself, stretched, and said with annoyance, "What?"

"Your father died in the war!" Yata told her bluntly. Then quietly, "But don't cry about it. A child doesn't cry for a dead person." She burst into tears.

"What!" Kulah cried out with alarm, jumping out of the bed, screaming. Yata pressed her against her breast, whispering in her ears.

Meanwhile, Chief Kortuma entered the house and called out, "Yata!" He walked into the bedroom when he heard Kulah's weeping voice and stood before mother and child who were engaged in a desperate embrace, shuddering with sobs. "It's Kortuma," he said. "Don't cry."

Yata pushed her daughter gently until they disengaged; rising, she opened the square bamboo window and light poured into the room.

"He meant much more to me than to anyone else," Chief Kortuma continued. Yata held Kulah by the hand. The two of them went to the bed and sat down. "He did not die in vain," the Chief said. "He saved us from slavery. He did not leave you alone. I will take good care of you." He touched Yata's left arm. She and her daughter started crying again. "Let's hurry to the grave," the Chief urged them. "It's a war death. We can't keep it long."

Yata grew calm, rose up and tied her lapa firmly on her waist. She tied her head with a headtie and took another one out of a black wooden box which she pulled from under the bed and tied Kulah's head with it.

The Chief led them to the grave. Yata bowed her head as they approached it. Her daughter held her right hand tight and looked at the body on the bamboo bed placed on top of the red dirt dug from the grave. Yata raised her head with an effort and stared at the body. Kulah stood beside her, still holding her hand.

"That's your father over there," Yata told her, looking down at her and pointing at Gayflor.

"Don't do that to the child," a voice protested.

But it did not bother Kulah. She wasn't yet convinced, however, that it was her father — bloated — lying under the coarse country cloth.

Crying voices raged back in the village.

The Chief took off his gown and handed it to one of the men who stood around the grave. From his side pocket he took out a long piece of black thread and tied it on Yata's left wrist and then tied the other end on Gayflor's left wrist which he pulled from under the cloth. Kulah winced, though the dark and swollen hand which the Chief pulled out had no resemblance to her father's own normal hand. She only wondered why it was connected to her mother's hand with a black thread. After tying the thread to the left wrists of the living and the dead, the Chief asked Yata to confess any unusual or sacred dealings she had with Gayflor.

"Don't be afraid," a voice said. Yata loosed her headtie, not paying much attention to the advice.

"She's brave," another voice said.

Yata looked down as she held the headtie with her right hand. With no hand to hold, Kulah who looked perplexed, stood still and watched her mother. Yata wiped her own sweating face with the headtie. Her roughly plaited dark hair stood stiff on her head.

"What we're trying to do," the Chief told her, "is bury Gayflor with love and honour." He touched her by the shoulder, looking at her with sympathy. "We want him to have a watchful eye on you and your child while he lives in the place of truth. What you must do now is tell us any unusual connection you had with him concerning such things as totem, medicine, vows, and so on."

"Yata, don't cry," a voice said.

She wiped her face again.

"Don't think that anything you happen to say here will be divulged . . . we're all members of the Poro," another voice remarked.

"Thank you," Yata said coldly. "Gayflor and I were married. We lived together, farmed together, slept together — and had a child. He used to do medicine work for me and for many people. However, if I tell you that I know something about his medical affairs, I would be lying. He was a different person, different in the sense that he came from another tribe, another land. I had only the faintest idea about his background. And so I have no unusual connection with him, whether natural or supernatural. I know only a few herbs: herbs for my head when it hurts me, herbs for my stomach when it pains me. As he goes to the place of truth, all I can say is goodbye, wishing him sunshine on his way. Let his good eye be on those of us remaining behind, especially on the child . . ." She stopped talking suddenly and burst into tears. Several men held her by the arms.

"Thank you," said the Chief. "We cannot afford to burden ourselves with tears and grief because Gayflor has died!" he said forcefully. "Life and death do not matter to a hero. And Gayflor was a brave man, a great hero, who gave his life that we may be free. Yes, he set us free with his blood. Now we can live in peace. Now we can go to the coast without menace and sell our produce and buy goods . . . goodbye, my dear friend and brother," he looked at the dead man with a sorrowful face. "May the Ancestors receive you in peace. Keep a good eye on your only child, on Yata. Don't disturb them in dreams or darkness." From his side pocket he took out a small knife, a spearlike blade stuck on a wooden handle, and cut the thread. "You're now in a different world," he said. "And Yata and Kulah are in a different one. You're no more related to them as before, and if there used to be a relationship between you and them, I now cut it altogether . . . men, let's give honour to Gayflor."

Two grave diggers jumped into the grave, stood at each end of the deep trough of earth, holding up their hands; the others laid strong vines across the trough, took Gayflor gently and laid him on the vines, each end of which was held by a man; then they lowered him to the bottom of the grave — the two grave diggers in the grave held him by the head and the feet, the vines were pulled away; and the two grave diggers settled him and climbed out. Kulah watched her mother sobbing. She, too, began to sob.

The wind blew gently, rustling the fronded palms and the thick foliage of kola trees. Wrens and pepper birds chirped and squeaked in the bushes. In the background the river rolled on as usual. All of a sudden, a man came forward with a cocked musket, stood at the head of the grave and fired. The Chief bent over the grave and pushed some red dirt into it with his left elbow and then his right elbow. Another musket blast. He stood up, looking into the grave with controlled passion. The men shovelled the red dirt into the grave until it was full, and they danced over the dirt, and shovelled in some more, making a mound. It was over.

Kulah ran to the grave and stood on top of it, her feet sinking into the loose earth. First, she clasped her hands over her breast, staring about in dismay and wonder. Then she placed her hands on her head, the fingers interlocked, looking up and down.

"Yata, come for the child," the Chief said, holding Kulah by the arm. Kulah walked reluctantly with the Chief to her mother, repeatedly glancing at the grave over her shoulder. Yata placed her by her side and walked quietly to the village. The Chief went with the men to the river to wash the bad omens from their bodies before entering the village.

The whispering leaves of the forest, the roaring of the river, and the songs of the birds made one great melody in the hot, bright sunshine.

As he walked to the village by himself, the men already gone ahead, Chief Kortuma was startled at a sudden change in the weather. It was slightly past noon, and the sky which had been clear, bristling with sunshine just a moment ago, turned completely dark. It began to drizzle. For a time he was uneasy until he understood that the darkness meant that the Ancestors were honouring him for the victory, and the drizzle was the tears of his men who fell in the war. He could not feel proud or sad. It seemed to him that the war was still in progress, and that this was just the end of the beginning. Thus, he must be extremely vigilant.

He tried to cast away the cloud that began to gather in his mind by thinking of some happy moments which he had spent with the Master and the lore about life beyond. For some unknown reason, the lore of life beyond enthralled him so that he began to feel that all was well with the Master; for, according to the lore, life was far better on the other side. One version of this lore declared that death was only a dream, an escape from this disastrous world to another world where there was no pain, disappointment, frustration, or sorrow. There life was free from the trappings of old age, decay, and death. Or one simply disengaged oneself from one's battered and frail body and went to a different land where one would take on a new body that was young, and lead a new life, free from the tragic memories of the previous life . . .

The village was strewn with dead chickens, dogs, sheep, cows, and goats — the ravages of the victory celebration. Chief Kortuma walked through the debris and went to his house. He sat in the rattan chair on the porch, held his chin with both hands, his elbows resting on his thighs. After some moments, he raised his head and stared blandly at the drizzle which suddenly turned into a rainstorm and lashed Kola and palm trees around the village, rustled thatched roofs violently, and whipped the mud walls of houses with rain. There was no-one outside; only leaves swirled in the rainstorm, the village reverberating with wailing voices. Soon the dusk would come, and soon the entire village would be buried in a terrible, black night.

13

Although the heavy losses which his army reportedly suffered troubled Chief Kortuma a great deal, he was relieved because the war was over and he had won the victory. Now and then a warrior that was presumed dead or missing, suddenly materialised in the village. In several months, some twenty-five warriors returned home. Some of them claimed to have got lost after leaving their divisions to hunt or find food on Gola farms. Others admitted that they were taken prisoner in the heat of battles, but managed to escape. Much to his satisfaction, Chief Kortuma discovered that only a quarter of his forces were lost in the war. But he was not carried away by the joy of victory, for he believed that the Gola could take revenge at any time. Thus he maintained a limited force to patrol the border and to carry out regular spy missions deep inside Golaland. For many months he only received reports of the slow recovery which the Gola people were making after their humiliating defeat. Occasionally, a spy would openly travel to the coast with a kenja of produce and return with a bundle of cargo without incident. Indeed, the road to the coast was now safe.

Fuama Chiefdom was returning to normal, too. The various households began making new farms for the year. Members of those households which the war had rendered fatherless, joined their closest relatives to farm. Kuu were organised throughout the land.

Chief Kortuma took charge of the Master's widow and daughter until they could cope with life without the Master, and Yata had managed to find a step-father for Kulah. The Chief's wives warmly welcomed them into their household, and tried their very best to comfort them. Lorpu lodged them in her house, expressing gratitude for their company. Fortunately, the farming season was at a peak; thus farm work kept them so busy that they found very little time to mourn over their irreparable loss.

That year, Chief Kortuma made an exceptionally large farm in Bodua forest, a dense, luxuriant forest beyond the river, north of

Haindi. His wives initially opposed the idea of making a farm in that forest because it was 'too far away, and it is risky to cross the river twice a day.' The women further warned him about the danger of 'human elephants' which abounded in Bodua forest. Besides the strong possibility that they would kill anyone who attempted to make a farm in that forest, they would certainly eat up any rice that happened to be planted there.

Like the average tribesman or woman, Chief Kortuma knew all about the lore of human doubles: the belief that real human beings could turn themselves into elephants, leopards, baboons, snakes, and panthers, among other things, to menace or kill other human beings and village animals, or ruin crops. However, he dismissed the women's fears with the casual remark:

"Don't worry about human elephants. I know what to do with them."

With the help of a number of expert elephant hunters, he fought the elephants in Bodua forest with all available weapons: guns, spears, traps, charms, and so forth. After they had killed four of them, it was virtually impossible to see their tracks in the forest again.

The rice did very well in the fallow, forest soil. In fact, the harvest was abundant throughout the entire Chiefdom. By the year's end, when the harvest was complete, scores of kitchen sheds were full to overflowing with rice. The Chief especially bubbled with joy and satisfaction because he was now convinced that the graduation festival of the Sande, which was scheduled to take place in the second month of the new year, would be a success. The road to the coast was travelled a great deal without incident, and parents sold bags of clean rice and bought clothes, beads, rum, cooking utensils, farming tools, salt, perfume, and so on, for their wives, children, and themselves. Chief Kortuma accompanied his own wives a number of times to the coast to trade. He bought clothes, tins of powder, perfume, hair lotion, and jewellery for them and his daughter.

Lorpu was especially impressed by the many beautiful things which her husband bought for her daughter and she said so to the Chief on one occasion.

"Well," the Chief told her mildly, "had I listened to you women and made a farm in the young bushes on this side of the river, we would have been in trouble — we wouldn't have got that much rice and we would have been compelled to buy these things for our child because we couldn't afford to leave her at the waterside."

Before he could make half the preparations he wanted to make for his daughter's graduation, time had already run out on the Chief. New Year's Day had come and gone and the first month of the year was almost over. Chief Kortuma was scarcely aware of this incredible flight of time until the head Zoe of the Sande, Lorlehn, and her assistant, Lorwo, called on him one evening to report that the current session of the Sande was at an end.

"Where there is peace," the Chief laughed as he received the Zoes on his porch in the moonlit night, "time flies. I never imagined that we were so close to that bridge . . . well, we must cross it."

Lorlehn was tall, flamboyant, and masculine — characteristics which detracted from her feminine charms, but made her a good Zoe. Her assistant was short, with a full bust, and looked grave. Both of them were dressed in short, medical shirts with two leopard teeth fastened to each shirt just above the midriff.

Chief Kortuma offered seats to the Zoes and repeatedly glanced at the rousing crowd of women which followed them in the distance. The women's masked dancer, Zoebai, short and agile, ran before the crowd in her black, loose raffia skirt and with her netted black face. She carried a switch in her left hand, which she wielded on anyone who stood in her way as she danced and ran towards the Chief's house. The women sang behind her, clapping their hands most vigorously. Just before they reached the house, Zoebai ran with tremendous speed and perched below the porch.

The village Elders had already gathered around the Chief and his Zoes on the porch.

When the women reached the Chief's yard, Lorlehn silenced them with a shout, raising both arms in the air. Taking three pieces of white kola nut from her Zoe bag that hung on her left shoulder, she handed them to Chief Kortuma.

"I salute you in the name of Zelei!" she declared. "You gave me a job to do and I have done it! The matter has reached you, Chief." As she spoke, she would bend forward slightly and then stand erect, her left arm akimbo.

The Chief received the kola nuts with a broad smile, watched them briefly and put them into his pocket.

"My hand is under what you have said," he told Lorlehn who had returned to her seat and was looking meditatively into the distance. Tucking his hand into the pocket of his flowing robe, the Chief took out a few white coins and gave them to Lorlehn. "Let this be my white heart," he said, "and may the Ancestors bless your work."

"Let it be so," the women responded, clapping their hands once.

Handing the coins to her assistant, Lorlehn said: "Here's what the Chief has given."

"Thank you, Chief," Lorwo said quickly. "May you get many more wives from among the new women."

"Let it be so," the Chief said with hesitation, laughing. Everyone joined in the laughter.

The women resumed dancing, singing, and clapping hands. Zoebai led them about the village, stopping here and there before houses to receive white things from families whose children would soon graduate from the Sande. They got coins, kola nuts, headties, rum, salt, and many thanks.

Obsessed with thoughts about the concluding ceremonies which he would soon perform, Chief Kortuma went to bed rather early that evening. He had witnessed many sessions of both the Poro and the Sande societies come to their painful ends, but this one moved him in a way he had never experienced before. It seemed to him that it would be his own burial ceremonies he would perform. He did not know exactly why he felt this way, because an occasion of this nature usually gave him a new spirit — as if he had been born again and everything had become new. He listened to the women's hooting and clapping, and thought that they were moving towards the road to Malamu. Soon the refrain of their song faded in his ears, and his wives rushed into his house, chattering, laughing, and giggling. He thought they were straining themselves to appear happy in spite of all that had happened. He hoped this festival would help Korlu overcome her difficulty, though what she had gone through left an indelible scar on her. Perhaps the only way she could manage to live with it was to become pregnant again. He could not understand why he thought of Korlu in this context at this time, for she was already holding her own very well. Since her trouble, Polang and Lorpu had taken care of her, not even permitting her to do household chores. Yata! How was she faring! He strained his ears but did not hear her voice.

"Well, this is their day," he said under his breath. "They must be happy."

He thought of the many Poro and Sande graduation festivals in which he had participated when he was a young man — how he and other young men would dance away for days, getting drunk and making love to scores of women. And no husband dared ask his wife to confess the name of a lover, for a graduation festival of either the Poro or the Sande was one occasion on which women might carry on affairs as they pleased, and were not obligated to their husbands.

146

Chief Kortuma thought that this was fair enough, for he saw no reason why men should enjoy so much freedom while women were kept under rigid control. He hoped that his own wives would enjoy the festival so that they would bring happiness to his household.

The birds were singing at dawn, and the Chief who was already awake, jumped out of bed and opened the window. It was dark outside; the songs of the birds were reinforced now with the frenzied crowing of roosters. It is certainly day, he thought. Most surprisingly, the Chief's thought flashed back to the kola nut which he had planted with Yorfii's umbilical cord in the bath fence behind his house. It would grow up as a salient but false witness to the fact that he had had a son. Perhaps it was an Ancestral spirit that had come to tantalise him. The trials might have been unbearable had Yorfii lived to call him father.

It was Polang who had slept with him that night. She was still wrapped up in bedclothes.

"Don't you know that we must be in Malamu before sunrise?" he told her as he shook her vigorously. She grunted and twisted herself uneasily. "Get up!" the Chief said.

Polang got out of bed and asked the Chief, "Will you bathe before going?"

"No," the Chief replied crisply.

She took a bucket of cold water to the bath fence. In a moment, she was back, her body wet all over.

"I can't travel with you without taking a bath," she said apologetically.

"Get dressed quickly and let's go," the Chief said. He was already dressed in a large flowing gown and a red fez with a black tassel, a leather bag hanging on his left shoulder.

Polang opened a wooden box at the foot of the bed and took out her new lapa which the Chief had bought for her. It was stiff with starch and smelled fresh. She gathered it fondly to her breast like an only child and inhaled its sweet scent. Doubtless, the boys would cast lustful glances at her, admire her beauty and fine clothes — or maybe they would go after the new girls whose coming out of the Sande often brought confusion in marriages . . . With an effort, Polang put the foolish thought out of her mind and tried to dress quickly, for Chief Kortuma was out on the porch, ready for the journey, and the first rays of the sun were now visible through the window. She took off the old, dirty lapa she wore, flung it to the bed, and tied on the new one. Then she put on a dress and a headtie that matched the lapa.

"Polang, are you coming?" the Chief called from the porch.

"Yes," she replied. "I am coming!"

In a moment, she was standing beside the Chief who cast an approving glance at her and said, "The clothes fit you?"

"Yes," she said, smiling.

"I thought they would." The Chief thought of Lorpu who was already in Malamu.

He walked down from the porch — Polang following him — stood in the yard for a moment, and stared at the heavy cloud that rolled slowly in the sky. The morning sunshine shimmered delicately behind the cloud. Chief Kortuma looked about the quiet village. Many of the people of Haindi had already gone to Malamu. With wide strides, he walked towards the road to Malamu, which was the same road that led to Mauwa. Polang, whose legs were quite short, followed him with quickened steps.

They walked in silence until they reached the outskirts of Malamu, where they were greeted by rumbling drums and voices. Chief Kortuma slackened his pace, Polang catching up with him. The players accompanied them to the village as they walked with poise and dignity. Another group of players spied them in the distance and began drifting towards them. Soon the royal couple were completely surrounded with players, all of whom were dressed in new clothes of brilliant colours. Many of the young men wore rolled-up headties around their heads. When they reached the square in the centre of which stood a cotton-wood tree that was studded with nests of sorya birds, the Chief raised his right hand forcefully, waving his cowtail with authority. A posia blew a whistle and there was complete silence. His eyes gleaming, the Chief smiled broadly, the thick flesh on his face wrinkled.

"Thank you, thank you," he said, bringing his arm down. Then, gesturing with his right arm that held the cowtail most forcefully: "Today marks the end of another session of the Sande. I am happy that you people are playing your part very well. As you have begun the day so well, may you continue to the end." In response, the drums rolled briefly and the players danced jubilantly. Tucking his hand into his bag, the Chief took out three white coins. The playing ceased instantly. A young man with large eyeballs, a brass whistle held between his lips, came forward and stood before him. The fellow was obviously the posia. "This is the white thing," the Chief said, giving him the money.

The fellow displayed the coins on his palm proudly, smiling.

"This is what the Chief has given," he said, swaying his open palm before the crowd. The drums rolled briefly, and the players began to shake their bodies. "No song!" the posia cried.

A song leader raised a song and the crowd began to sing and dance.

Chief Kortuma walked proudly through the village of Malamu which comprised only a few houses one could count on the fingers. Palm fronds decorated the main, large palaver house that would seat the new girls. It stood on the western edge of the square. The Chief headed for the Sande fence which was located on the southern outskirts of the village. The fence, which was old now, comprised bunches of bamboo thatch deftly tied with rattan and other wild ropes. It was flanked by kola trees. Chief Kortuma walked directly into the fence; the players turned around and drifted towards the square.

Behind the fence was a small palaver house in which Lorlehn, Lorwo, and a group of elderly women sat on a soft mat. Chief Kortuma entered the palaver house and sat in a rattan chair before them. Far behind the palaver house, in a large clearing, the new initiates were busy getting dressed with the help of their mothers.

Lorlehn stood up and adjusted her lapa, looking at the Chief. A little bell which was attached to her lapa jingled. Her face looked grim, and it was covered with beads of sweat. She loosened her headtie and wiped her face with it, and tied it on again. Then she spoke in a powerful voice:

"All you gbolokpolo-nga, hear my voice. Chief Kortuma gave me a job to do and I have done it to the best of my ability. I am glad to have lived to see this day. Except for a few initiates who remained to scratch the Big One's belly, I brought back all the daughters of Fuama Chiefdom whom he entrusted to my care. I now present them to him with my white heart and with the blessings of our Ancestors. May they live long and multiply."

"Let it be so," everyone replied.

Heaving a sigh, Lorlehn took a little black raffia bag from the loft of the palaver house and, giving it to the Chief, said, "This is the land which you gave me."

"Shake my hand," the Chief said, rising. He shook her hand and shook hands with the other women who cheered the Sande Zoe. "Thank you," the Chief said in a loud voice. "This is a great thing which you have done," he gestured with authority. "There are no hands more trustworthy than yours to handle with honour and grace this our sacred tradition. The Sande, like the Poro, came into being by the will of God and our forefathers ovserved it with great respect and reverence. Nothing under the sun can abolish it. It is our duty to maintain it. It is our duty to protect what the Ancestors defended with their blood and sweat. We cannot afford to let it pass away through sloth or folly. May such never happen!"

"Never!" came the rousing reply.

"I salute you for your good work. You used your strength, imagination and power without compromise so that our children might live. For three round years you have been on your feet, day and night, seeing to it that this session of the Sande came to a graceful end. Lorlehn, words cannot adequately express my thanks and appreciation for your good work and great sacrifice." He took three white kola nuts out of his bag and gave them to Lorlehn. "Let this be my white heart," he said. Lorlehn and the elderly women shook his hand and cheered him. The Chief sat down and put the little black bag into his own bag. It was slightly past noon, and the sun was very hot.

One of the women raised a song and all responded to it with vigour, clapping their hands. Lorlehn and Lorwo led them victoriously away from the fence. Chief Kortuma walked behind them. A horn sounded in the village and the new girls emerged gracefully from the fence and marched slowly with bowed heads, white linen sheets spread over them, towards the palaver house which was specially prepared for them.

Lorlehn and her assistant led them into the palaver house and saw to it that they bowed their heads at all times and sat shyly on the soft mats. Crowds of players surrounded the palaver house.

Chief Kortuma entered and stood on a central spot, watching the new initiates sitting on the mats, their legs stretched before them, their heads bowed, their arms folded, and their bulky, black hairdos shining in the bright sunlight. They wore a variety of clothes: some had on country clothes with black and white stripes or colourful fanti. Some wore sandals. Three old women, bowls of clean, white rice in their hands, rushed into the palaver house all of a sudden and sprinkled the new girls with the rice. Chief Kortuma wiped his face with a big, green towel which Polang presently handed him. His face beamed with joy and pride when he saw Lorlehn walking to him in her ceremonial gown that equated her with men. Very few female Zoes ever reached that stage. A bag of medicines hung on her left shoulder, a cowtail was held loosely in her right hand. She swayed it gently as she walked to the centre of the palaver house towards the Chief.

Blasts of musket echoed throughout the village.

150

"These are your daughters," Lorlehn said to Chief Kortuma when she reached him.

The Chief took three pieces of white kola nut out of his bag and gave them to her, saying, "And may this mysterious event, assigned to us by God and our Ancestors, continue forever."

"Let it be so," the people replied outside.

"Anyone who bewitches any of these innocent ones and tries to spoil the good work which you have done — may that person perish for us to walk over his grave."

"Let it be so," the people replied again.

The Chief adjusted his robe and looked around. He caught sight of his daughter and almost embraced her, but he bravely controlled himself and decided to wait for the proper time.

"Let all parents draw near," he announced. Immediately, all the parents gathered around the palaver house.

The heat haze danced over the village, but a cold, gentle breeze was blowing, making the heat somehow tolerable.

The Chief walked past the initiates under review, glancing at his daughter all the while. He observed their sleepy eyes, their hanging heads, their oily bodies. At length he took a little gourd from his pocket, opened it, poured some of its brown, powdery content in his left palm, and blew it over the girls. That would give them good luck. He looked around and bowed his head, lifted his head again and walked to a little girl and grasped her left arm. The little girl looked with puzzled eyes at the crowd, and then at the Chief. The Chief carried her to the centre of the palaver house and called her parents who danced as they came forward. Three musket blasts sounded outside.

Lorlehn whispered in the Chief's ear. Then the Chief said, "Here is your daughter, Miata, who used to be called Zongai."

The little girl's parents clapped their hands repeatedly and took her away, dancing gracefully as they went. In like manner the ceremony continued all afternoon and the Chief turned more than two hundred girls over to their parents. Those people who had received their children took them home to cook all the dry meat and fish they had preserved in oil, all the chickens and goats and sheep that they kept for the occasion — and dress them in the best clothes they could find.

Chief Kortuma suddenly stopped the ceremony and glanced sadly at the crowd. Taking a piece of white kola nut from his pocket, he called out, "Where is Korfaa?" After a few moments, Korfaa began to walk with difficulty into the palaver house, his wife holding him by the arm. Korfaa wiped his face with the tip of his shirt. The Chief watched him pitifully for a long time and finally managed to say bluntly, "Your daughter did not come back." Everyone watched Korfaa sorrowfully, making pitiful remarks. He buried his face in his hands. "She stayed to scratch the Big One's belly," the Chief continued. "The Big One sent you this white kola nut that you may not weep or grieve. Don't disobey the orders of the Mighty One!"

Korfaa shook his head frantically as he staggered in his wife's arms through the crowd. She, too, suddenly broke down and cried hysterically. Friends gathered around them, holding them by the arms, and trying to console them.

Meanwhile, Chief Kortuma's voice blared out grimly through the palaver house. He held his daughter, Yembele, now Paa, by her left arm while Lorpu stepped forward.

14

A bundle under his right arm, Sengbe stood anxiously in the sombre night, watching Paa through a crack in the bamboo door. Wearing only a wide towel around her waist, she was sitting on her new bamboo bed in her newly built zorba, examining her new clothes, beads, tins of powder, headties, dresses, mirrors, and jewellery, among other things, a slight smile on her face. About two yards from the head of her bed stood a small wooden table on which sat a crudely made lamp that comprised a cup of palm oil containing a large wick made of home-spun, white thread. A saffron flame flickered at the end of the wick. Paa would take one article at a time, look at it briefly in the lamp light, and lay it one side. Sengbe watched her lovely hair that had grown a lot more, and her round, fully developed breasts that were beginning to fall. He felt that she was more beautiful than she had been before her initiation. Her every movement pierced his heart most painfully like an arrowshot. The pain would first jolt his heart violently and then spread like poison through his entire body. Sengbe began to grow weak, but he resolved to fight the weakness until his aim was accomplished: to present his gifts to Paa with his own hands. He thought she had shown interest in him the night they played boa and other games in the square. She had pretended not to be aware of his fumbling fingers in her waist beads and her breasts touching his arms and chest. These were signs of welcome, but she had been spirited away too soon so that he had had no opportunity to declare his love to her. And memories of that night were supposed to remain buried in the past, for she was now completely transformed into a new person. All incidents before her initiation, such as debts, engagements, and promises, had no more claims on her. Thus, there wouldn't be much to talk about if they met, yet he wanted to spend the whole night just talking to her. Mustering the courage, he knocked on her door three times.

Paa looked to the door for a moment, a bottle of hair lotion in her right hand; her left hand which was empty, raised in the air. Hearing no more knocks, she laid the bottle carefully among the articles which she had already examined.

When she attempted to take another article for examination, Sengbe knocked on the door three more times, saying:

"Kpor! Kpor! Kpor!"

Standing up and looking at the door with a curious expression on her face, Paa said, "Who's that?"

Sengbe felt as if he had broken a sacred law of the tribe. His mouth watered with a metallic taste.

"Don't be afraid," he managed to say. "It's I, Sengbe."

Opening the door, Paa heaved a sigh and said, "I thought it was somebody else. Come in."

Sengbe stepped in haltingly and sat on the edge of the bed with its palm thatch mattress, his bundle still tucked under his right arm. Paa eased the door closed and sat near him, her back turned towards him. She watched the black wall with listless eyes and began to dig the floor with her toes. Sengbe knew that she was embarrassed. Any virgin in her place would behave exactly the same way, he thought.

"I brought this for you," he said quietly, giving her the bundle of presents with a smile. Accepting it with a grin, Paa laid it by her side and thanked him.

"My father told me that no boys may come here," she warned him in a polite, but serious, tone of voice.

"I know," Sengbe admitted. "I should have sent it by my sister or one of your friends . . . but, Paa, I wanted to give it to you myself! To see you, talk to you, hear you . . ." He spoke in a soft, tender voice.

"Are you asking for marriage?" Paa cut in sharply.

Sengbe knew that it would be self-defeating to admit that he was. However, he felt that Paa should know about his intentions.

"I love you, Paa," he said bluntly. "Please marry me." His heart pounded furiously. He wondered what Paa would say. If she should reject his proposal, perhaps all the girls of Fuama Chiefdom, if not the whole world, would reject him, too. Was his proposal timely? "Paa, don't be embarrassed," he broke the long silence. "I know that it takes time for a girl to make up her mind about marriage. You may think about it through this week if you like . . ."

"But if I say yes my father will say that I'm giving myself to a man!" Paa declared.

"I'll tell my sister about it, and she'll make a formal proposal to

154

you as though nothing has happened between us. Nobody will have anything bad to say about your name."

"It's time for you to go! My father won't be pleased to see you here!"

"But Paa . . ."

"Go!" She faced him presently, looking desperate. Dumb-founded, Sengbe simply watched her round, springy breasts; her smooth, beautiful skin; her plaited hair — a charm in her eyes despite the frown she wore in her face. "I'll think about it," she said with remorse when she observed his dismal look. Growing slightly relaxed, she said, "I'm afraid of my father."

Sengbe ran his hands down his blue denim short pants, adjusted his colourful shirt, and walked to the door.

"Goodnight," he said and disappeared into the darkness.

The meeting to which he had looked forward for so long, for which he had anxiously collected presents, had proved disappointing. The more Sengbe thought of it, the more it pained him. He remembered his father telling him once that first love was uncertain. But he thought Paa loved him, or else she would have rejected his presents. He walked hastily into his zorba and went to bed at once.

It was not long before Nyama, his sister, noticed that he was depressed. A short, good-natured girl, Nyama was always concerned about his welfare. Sengbe became unusually irascible and moody. He kept to himself, spending most of his time in his zorba.

One evening Nyama told their mother, Bhilika, "I think brother is worried about something."

Bhilika, who was a sensitive woman, answered her curtly, "He's your brother. Why not talk to him!"

"I thought, perhaps, he has told you about his trouble. I believe that he is love-sick."

"Has he told you that he wants to marry?"

"No. You know that Sengbe never tells us about his troubles."

"You go and talk to him."

She went to his room one evening. The moon was up and children were playing in the square. She knocked on his door. Sengbe opened the door and when he saw his sister, he turned away quickly in embarrassment and hurried to his bed, lay down, and watched the flickering flame of his own palm oil lamp that sat on a wooden table in the centre of the room.

"Brother, are you sick?" she said as she stood in the doorway.

"No," Sengbe replied.

"If something is bothering you, tell me. I'm your sister!" Sengbe was mute as ever. "If you want a wife, tell me whom you want and I'll try my best. Have you talked to any girl?"

"Yes."

"Who?"

"Paa."

"You mean Lorpu's daughter?"

"Yes."

"It's no problem. Lorpu — even Chief Kortuma — is our relative, so to speak. I don't think the Chief will refuse to give his daughter to us. All I need to do is talk to Paa herself. You said that you have already talked to her?"

"We didn't say anything much. She told me to go out."

"So you went to her room by yourself? She's right to be afraid. All the new girls are under a law — not to be alone with men for two weeks. Did you see the white thread on her neck?"

"I didn't look for that."

"That's the problem. After two weeks, they'll be permitted to take the thread off their necks and then they'll be free to do as they please. This is the Chief's only daughter and child. He might have high hopes in mind for her. All this can make any girl afraid. But I'll see Paa."

"I told her something. She said she'd reply later."

"Don't worry about that. I'll take care of everything. If you depend on her, she won't tell you a thing. She's a little girl, brother. Inexperienced. You might be the first boy telling her such a thing and she doesn't know what to say. Maybe she's afraid of men . . . I'm going to her now and don't think too much about it. Even if she refuses you, there are many other girls. We'll get you a wife. Did you give her anything?"

"A lapa, a headtie, and other things."

"There you made the mistake. You should have given me those things. And that's too much to start with. Anyway, I'll see about it. Don't worry."

Outside the children had formed a ring, holding each other's hands, singing, swinging around. A few older boys and girls stood around them, watching their performance with interest. Nyama walked about them for a while, and finally stood by a group of girls to chat.

"Nyama, what have you been doing this evening?" a girl asked.

"Talking with Sengbe," she said.

"Your brother?"

"Yes, my brother."

"You've been carrying on an affair; now you want to hide the secret by talking about your brother," the girl maintained, shaking all over with laughter.

"Quite frankly, I'm sick . . . the new moon . . ." Nyama pointed at the moon.

"Nyama, don't lie to us!" a girl said.

"Look, we've been thinking of playing — a gourd play — but we're so few . . . join us," another girl told Nyama.

"Well, I'm already here . . . I don't see you girls with gourds!"

"We'll soon get some."

"Do you think we'll have enough time? It's almost bedtime . . . Paa, I want to talk with you."

Paa walked slowly to her and asked, "Is it I?"

"Yes. It's nothing important." Nyama sounded as casual as she could be within the limits of her discretion. If she sounded serious, the other girls might detect the issue, and if she sounded trifling, Paa might feel insulted.

Several girls ran to their houses for gourds.

"I've been wishing to tell you something," Nyama told Paa, almost in a whisper. "But I wanted to wait until the stir of the society business was over. My brother, Sengbe, said that he loves you . . ." Nyama made a sudden break in her words and looked away, tinkering with her neckbeads. Her face looked slightly sullen as if she were preparing for the worse. Paa, too, fidgeted with her hands and dug the sandy soil with her toes.

"But why, why . . . but he saw me before and I told him I would think about it," she muttered. "Why didn't he see me again before telling you about it?"

"It doesn't matter," Nyama said. "Just let me know what you feel about it."

"I wanted to see my mother first."

"It's better for your parents to know about it through us, Sengbe's relatives. Otherwise, they might think you're going after men. Besides, they might ply Sengbe with many questions and he might abandon the whole affair in fear. Perhaps you love him."

"But . . . but . . ." Paa faltered.

Nyama glanced at her once again and said, "Don't be embarrassed to talk to me, a girl like you."

Her head still bowed, Paa dug into the sand with her toes.

"So what do you have to say?" Nyama asked her again. "We can't stand here all night! It's getting cold!"

The girls were now singing and dancing in the square.

"My hand is under it," Paa said. She looked and felt alarmed as if she had unexpectedly fallen into a deep river filled with ferocious crocodiles.

"Thank you," Nyama said, giving her a coin which she dug out of her plaited hair.

"But I'm still small!" Paa cried in a shrill voice.

"That's not for you to say," Nyama retorted. "And don't worry about it! Now let me tell you what to do. Take what I gave you to your mother and say, 'Nyama says that she loves me for her brother.' Before the end of this week, your father will have known about it and he'll be waiting for us to make a formal proposal."

Paa took the coin to her mother right away and told her what Nyama had said.

"Well, you are a full-grown girl now," Lorpu said. "I see no point in putting off your marriage. But do you really love Sengbe?"

"Yes, mother," Paa said.

It was difficult to tell the Chief about it, for his reaction could not be determined. He had not yet implied in any way that Paa was now permitted to marry. However, he must be informed without delay for Sengbe began to visit Paa regularly. There were other visitors, both boys and girls. One evening Lorpu told the Chief about the proposal and he immediately called Paa. Paa sat with diffidence beside her mother on the porch before him.

"Do you love Sengbe?" the Chief asked her. She could not say a word. Lorpu became uneasy.

"Tell him yes," she said.

"Don't put words in her mouth," the Chief said. "She's old enough . . . do you love Sengbe?" he asked again.

"Yes," Paa muttered.

"All right," the Chief sighed. "That's all I wanted to know. The matter is now in my hands. Go about your business."

At the end of the week, Sengbe's parents and his sister came to make the formal proposal. It was a bright, beautiful, starlit evening. As in other things, the Chief was moved when the moment came for him to accept the proposal. But he accepted it in good spirits. Sengbe's parents expressed gratitude to him, Paa, and Lorpu for the favourable reply, promising to advise their son to be a good husband. It was decided that the marriage should take place the next New Year's Day, which was about six months away.

After their engagement, Sengbe felt free to visit Paa as often as he wished. All her other boy friends ceased visiting her. The first night after their engagement, he went to her zorba when he had drunk plenty of palm wine. He sat by her on the bed. She turned her back to him as she did on his first visit, looking at the wall bashfully. Sengbe patted her back, quickly thrust his right hand before her, and grasped her right breast. That was his first real advance and he felt so good. Paa instinctively pushed his hand away, saying with a chuckle:

"Leave me!"

"Does it tickle you?" said Sengbe, laughing.

Paa nodded a reply, still chuckling. "What do you think?" she managed to ask.

"A girl's breasts are not made for her," Sengbe said. "They're for boys."

"Can someone tell you that a part of your own body is not for you?"

"I'm talking about girls." He tugged her by the hands. With her arms protecting her breasts, she lay on his lap. Sengbe stroked her loins, feeling excited.

Unexpectedly she declared, "Sengbe, why do you love me? You left all the beautiful girls and . . ."

"Nonsense. You are the most beautiful girl in the world," Sengbe interrupted. Paa sat up, Sengbe still holding her hands. "I don't know why I love you . . . I never thought I'd marry a beautiful girl like you — and a Chief's daughter . . ."

"Women are the same. Remember that! But I want to know what kind of wife you want."

"One like you."

"I mean the one in your mind. You don't know what I'll turn out to be."

"That's why I don't talk about what I want, but what I have. What you want can be only in your mind and you get something else, or something like it." He let go of her hands, proud of himself for saying exactly what he felt.

"I mean, what do you want your wife to be like, if you had a choice? I know all men's minds: she must wake up early in the morning before the first rooster crows, heat his bath water, hunt vegetables and cook, wash his clothes, take care of his baby — and all that."

"First of all she must be pretty," Sengbe said.

"Pretty!" Paa said sharply. "And she could be rude and cruel and lazy!"

"No, that's the first thing."

"But one person cannot be everything."

"I said *pretty* because I want to be proud of her. And I'll do all I can to make her look pretty."

"You can be proud of a good and kind girl, too. And besides, you won't have to spend all your money on clothes and hair lotion."

"She has to be pretty for me to love her. And then she has to be a true friend . . ."

"You hope," Paa cut in.

"I must go home. I'm tired and sleepy. I want to go home now."

"Do you remember the story of the marriage of beauty? Well, I see that you are bored and tired out. You've been drinking. I don't want my husband to drink. Remember that! Good night. Tell Nyama goodnight for me."

Sengbe spent the rest of the year almost exclusively with the Kortuma family, working with them on the farm and using the opportunity to talk and flirt with Paa. Sometimes they went fishing or hunting. It was all fun and pleasure. New Year's Day seemed to linger in the distant future and he thought he would die before it ever came around. The harvest was abundant, and he personally made several trips to the coast. What he earned from the rice he sold he spent entirely on clothes, hair lotion and jewellery for Paa. The many months of anxious waiting cost him many a sleepless night. He grew lean and always carried a strained expression on his face like an uninitiated child expecting to join a society. What made matters worse was the fact that many of his playmates avoided his company and talked unkindly about him behind his back.

His father and Chief Kortuma tried to help him relax by telling him often that the great day was just around the corner. They told him all they knew about love and marriage. Sengbe began to feel that he was becoming a man. He stopped playing in the moonlight. Now he spent his evenings talking with Paa about their future. Paa too put aside most of her childish ways and reasoned with him seriously. Sengbe detected that she was not oppressed by thoughts of the coming great day as he was. She expected it with delight; her cheerful disposition had not deserted her.

On New Year's Eve, Chief Kortuma summoned them to his porch and gave them a long lecture on the adventure on which they would soon launch. He spoke impressively with extreme conviction; they began wondering if he would be around to guide them at the beginning of their marital life. He sounded as though he was bidding them a kind of farewell. When he was through talking, Sengbe went into his zorba, where he preferred to be alone until the next day. He tossed in bed all night.

It was his father who shot the new year in the morning. He slaughtered four white sheep and sponsored several new year plays in honour of the groom and bride. The cooking was so elaborate that it took nearly all day. Towards evening, Chief Kortuma told Lorpu to get her daughter ready for the marriage ceremonies, and he sent word to Sengbe's father to inform him that he wanted the marriage to take place without further delay.

But Paa was already getting ready. She was bathing in the river. Upon her return, Lorpu told her it was time. The evening shadows were fast approaching. Lorpu told Polang and Korlu to sweep the yard of Chief Kortuma's house while she helped Paa to dress.

When they entered her zorba, Paa became rigid and quiet. A wave of depression fell upon her for the first time, but she fought it bravely so that it did not show.

"Don't let it bother you," Lorpu kept telling her. "What do you want to wear?"

"The clothes he gave me," she said. She opened her box and took out the right clothes and beads and hair lotion, rubbed a little of the lotion in her hair, watching her hair in a mirror. Her face looked bright as if it were radiating light of its own.

She put on a dress, tied on a lapa and a silk headtie; then she put on a large bunch of neckbeads. Before she stepped out, she remembered her earrings. She put on a pair of white earrings and took a last look in the mirror.

"Let's go now," Lorpu said.

As soon as they stepped into the Chief's yard, now crowded with players, a musket sounded behind the house. Dressed in a black and white striped gown, Chief Kortuma sat in a rattan chair in the yard, a soft mat neatly spread before him. He spied his daughter absently, and looking over his shoulder, glanced at the Elders and other townspeople that flanked him. The players began singing and dancing, forming a semi-circle around the mat. An old lady ran through the crowd with a pan of clean rice seeds, and sprinkled the rice all over the mat, walking around the mat with wide strides and chanting blessings. Lorpu eased her daughter to the mat. A blast of musket! Paa bowed her head shyly, her hands clasped between her thighs. People threw coins at her.

The Chief stood up slowly, stretched out his right hand which held the cowtail. The playing resumed, but soon died down.

"Thank you," he said. He scanned the crowd and continued: "This is no time for long talks. Today the house of Kortuma and the house of Dogbakollie will become one. I've looked forward to this

161

day for a long time. I, Kortuma, am my word. When I say something, I mean it!" A cheer. "And this one great house which we're about to build, may it prosper in peace."

"Let it be so," the crowd responded.

"May the spirits of our fathers approve whatever we do or say here."

"Let it be so."

"Well, I'm not an old man; so my store of blessings is limited . . . where's the uncle of Sengbe?" An elderly man stepped forward. Sengbe who stood behind the crowd ran to his zorba at a fast pace. No one took any notice of him as everyone was watching the Chief.

The Chief tucked his left hand into his pocket again, took out three cowries and handed them to the elderly man.

"Here is my daughter," he said. "She is my heart string. I hope you will take care of her like your eyes." The elderly man shook his hand, the crowd flooded upon him, shaking his hand, congratulating him.

The Chief took a kola nut from his pocket and broke it in two. He gave one piece to Paa and told her to eat it. Paa ate the kola nut quickly and took a swallow.

"Give it back to me," he said.

"I can't give it back to you," she said.

"Then it means that you will always be in the house of Dogbakollie as a wife of his son, Sengbe. Where is Sengbe?" he asked, looking around.

But Sengbe was nowhere around. His sister ran to his zorba where he usually hid himself in times of crisis. She saw him lying in bed.

"Brother, let's go," she pleaded. "Everything is about over." He rose and followed her with reluctance.

Chief Kortuma gave Sengbe the other piece of kola nut and told him to eat it. He chewed it roughly and took a swallow.

"Give it back to me," the Chief said.

"I can't . . . can't . . . give it to you," he stuttered.

"Then it means that you will always be a husband for my daughter, Paa, and you will take good care of her. Is there a log for you to cut?"

"No," Sengbe said with innocence. The crowd shouted with joy, for it was an honourable thing that there was innocence between the newly wed.

Chief Kortuma laughed. "When I train a child, it is trained," he said. He went to his porch and sat down.

Sengbe's uncle brought him a big, flowing robe. Chief Kortuma laid it on his lap and glanced at his daughter who still sat on the mat bashfully. Lorpu held her by the arm and led her to Senge's zorba.

The crowd resumed playing.

A few Elders sat by the Chief. Sengbe's father brought them a large gourd of palm wine. Korlu brought them a big, drinking cup.

"She is a beautiful girl," Gbada opened the conversation, taking a sip. "I wish I were Sengbe." Everyone laughed.

"If she gets a son, he'll be like you, Chief," Bhenda said, looking at the Chief. More laughter.

"If they get troubles, they'll be small ones," Mulbah said.

"The eyes of witches will never see them," Fahn said.

"If they make a farm, it'll be productive," Dakena said.

"If they sleep, they'll dream only pleasant dreams," Gbada said.

Chief Kortuma was not listening to the torrents of best wishes; neither did he drink. All of a sudden he rose up and placed the robe that was on his lap in the chair. He looked surprisingly disconcerted.

"Well, fellow Elders," he said, "I must leave you. Enjoy yourselves. If you should need more to drink, ask Korlu. Thank you for your kind words and best wishes."

The Chief then walked down from the porch.

15

Chief Kortuma wanted to be alone until the crucial phase of the marriage ceremony was over. He had full confidence in his daughter who loved him, and believed that she would, under no circumstances, give him shame. Thus he believed Sengbe's admission, that there was no log to cut. However, everything depended on whatever report Lorpu would bring back.

The Elders who were very much aware of his situation, respectfuly returned to their own houses. Meanwhile, the Chief went to his dark bedroom, lay down awhile, and then decided to take a stroll on the river bank in the cold evening shadows.

Unexpectedly, he heard thundering drums and voices on the road to Golaland. Hurriedly making his way to the door, Chief Kortuma saw a strange creature lying below the porch. The Elders were nowhere around. Scrutinising the creature, he discovered that it was Landa, the huge but swift Gbande masked dancer. A large crowd, larger than ever seen in Haindi before, soon gathered in his yard. Four men, dressed in raffia skirts, ran to Landa, cheering him, jumping up and down. One of them fanned him with a bamboo fan. Landa suddenly jumped up, took a few steps towards the crowd and returned. He looked beautiful in his raffia attire that extended from the base of his mask down to his feet. He had long, bearded jaws; large, conical, red teeth filled his wide, red mouth. Feathers of all kinds of birds imaginable were at the back of his head.

Landa rose impulsively once again, ran to the outskirts, and returned to the players. Nearly everyone in Haindi had joined the strange players. The surging crowd stood before the Chief's house, singing happily for Landa as he danced gracefully in the semi-circle which they formed. After dancing for a while, Landa spun around for a long time, wriggling his body, bobbing his head, and suddenly flopped below the porch. A tall man, dressed in a royal robe, stepped forward and raised his right hand to get the attention of the crowd. Just then, Landa stood up and saluted Chief Kortuma with a

164

couple of nods. Before the tall man could speak, Landa told the fellow with the bamboo fan:

"Tell Chief Kortuma that during the dry-time, I sit under shades of trees, watch monkeys fall from bush to bush, scattering half-chewed nuts about. Antelopes and red deer move around me in large numbers, snorting the fresh ground and chewing nuts, sometimes running right into me. I kill some, feast on them for many weeks; then I sit on treetops and sing with birds — tell him that I came from the forest." As the interpreter said so, Landa spun around. Coming to a sudden stop, he declared again in his loud, melodic voice, "I often visit the rapids of the Deyn River. At times I sit on a cliff. A crocodile would splash out of the water and creep towards me, without seeing me. I would knock him against a boulder, crush his head, tear him to pieces, and feast on him for a week — tell him that I came from the river." Landa spun around again, and the drums rolled softly. "I sometimes embark on the wind and fly around the world," he cried. "At times it takes me to the sun and the stars, from where I watch all manner of men roving the earth . . ." He did not finish telling about his adventures in the wind when he cried out sharply:

Zio Landa ma-oo!
Landa ma-oo!
Fona kula lopoi ma-oo!
Landa ma-oo!
Eeyo! Eeyo! Eeyo!

The drum beats grew rapid and fiery and the crowd responded with one voice:

He came from the forest,
He came from the river,
He came from the sun and the stars,
To sing and dance for Chief Kortuma.

Extremely moved, Chief Kortuma swayed his arms to stop the play. Then he told the interpreter who ran to the porch:

"Tell Landa that he is welcome to my village. Tell him that I am only a man and he is a Bush Thing, but I will do all I can to make his stay here very pleasant." The interpreter said so. Landa responded by opening his mouth very wide. Chief Kortuma ran down quickly, threw some coins into it and returned to the porch. Landa clasped his mouth closed, opened it again, crying at the top of his voice and spinning around. When his energy was spent considerably, he flopped again below the porch to gather strength.

The tall man walked forward with calculated steps once again, rolled up the edges of his flowing robe to both shoulders, looked over his right shoulder and nodded. Immediately two middle-aged women escorted a beautiful, young girl forward. Holding the girl by both arms and stooping slightly, they walked at a slow pace to the tall man. A boy spread a soft mat before the girl, and, with the help of the women, she sat down very gently. The women left her arms and returned to their places in the crowd.

The girl stretched her legs forward and clasped her hands between her thighs. On her waist was a large bundle of black and white beads. A colourful headtie bedecked her head; red and black strips of yarn were placed across her shoulders like suspenders and tied to her waistbeads. She wore a country cloth bombor of black and white stripes. All eyes were trained on her in the bright moonlight that showed almost like daylight.

"Chief Kortuma," the tall man spoke in a mild voice, "Elders of Haindi, and all of you who are present here — first of all, let me introduce myself. I am Gbanja, the new Chief of Golaland . . ." The drums rolled briefly. Chief Kortuma rose and sat down, watching the man with an incredulous stare. "Perhaps I have taken you by surprise the same way your warriors took us by surprise . . . but I am happy if I have surprised you with joy, Chief Kortuma," Chief Gbanja continued. "I did not come to recount the tragic conflict which resulted in heavy losses on our side. We lost our Chief and our legendary hero; this means that we lost the war. As fortune would have it, the Council of Elders elected me to succeed Chief Dadie. I came in the name of all the people of Golaland to try to restore friendship between our two lands. Whatever happened in the past, whether good or bad, cannot be undone. Chief Kortuma, let us make a new beginning. When I learned several months ago that you would give your daughter and only child to a man on this New Year's Day, I decided to send for Landa and his players up in Gbandeland to come with me to add more merriment to the occasion . . . and may this day of joy be a consolation to all of us for the immeasurable suffering and losses which we have endured!"

"Let it be so!" everyone replied.

"May it bring us closer together."

"Let it be so."

"Without suffering there can be no lasting peace, joy, or real fulfilment . . . once there lived a poor man and his dog in the deep forest. The man always complained because he had no human

166

companion. He was even afraid that, one day, he wouldn't be able to talk again because he had nobody to talk to. One day, as he complained, the dog unexpectedly danced all around him, wagging its tail, and said, 'Don't worry. Henceforth, I'll keep you company.' At first, the man was afraid, but he managed to control his fear and talk to the dog. After many years, the man and his dog entered a large town as they wandered about the countryside one sunny day. The townspeople were shocked to see him conversing with the dog. They told their Chief right away that a certain man who could talk to his dog had come to the town. Arguing with extreme conviction, the Chief said that it was utterly impossible for a dog to speak. He promised to give the man half his Chiefdom if he should speak with the dog in public. But he added that he would kill the man if he spoke to the dog four times and the dog did not speak in return. Accepting the challenge, the man went to the Chief's house. Everyone in the town gathered before the house. The Chief's Kulubah stood ready with his sword to cut off the man's head if he failed to make the dog speak. When the man greeted his dog the first time, the dog did not reply. Again he greeted the dog the second time. No reply. The man looked apprehensive. Everyone watched him piteously and feared for his life. He spoke to the dog the third time. No reply. 'Well, my dear friend,' he addressed the dog the fourth time, looking extremely desperate, 'you promised to be my only companion in this world because I have no friend or relative. Two of us have lived together for many years, keeping good company. Now I need your company more than ever before. Are you going to let me die? Or don't you know that my life is in danger? Please, my dear friend, speak to me.' 'You can always rely on my friendship,' the dog said to the astonishment of the crowd. 'I could have spoken the first time you spoke to me, but I wanted to let you suffer before I spoke. Had I spoken the first time, you would have taken for granted all the riches which the Chief might give you today. But now if the Chief happens to give you any riches, you will always appreciate them because you almost died for them . . .' 'Well, my dear man,' the Chief interrupted, 'you may have half of my Chiefdom. Your dog has saved your life.'

"I told this story to show that there is always something good in suffering, Chief Kortuma. The only real peace there is comes after war. We relish the light of day because we know the terror of darkness. Only the hungry man knows the pleasure of a delicious meal . . . may our two peoples live together in peace and friendship forever!"

"Let it be so!" the crowd responded.

"Conflicts are usually the result of indiscretion, carelessness, or the irresponsible acts of foolish people . . . may our Ancestors show us wisdom so that we may use the right judgment on all occasions."

"Let it be so."

"To prove to you, Chief Kortuma, that I am in earnest, and to confirm my good intentions, here is your sala wife." He pointed at the girl on the mat.

The drums rolled loudly, and the crowd resumed singing and dancing. Landa stood up forcefully, but he did not dance. However, his followers surrounded him so that he could not run into the crowd or into the sala wife in case he decided to dance. He simply stood by Chief Gbanja as the Gola Chief continued to speak, gesturing with his hands.

"And now, Chief Kortuma, may we always be friends."

"Let it be so," Chief Kortuma replied, alone.

"Henceforth, may your people be my people, and my people your people."

"Let it be so," Chief Kortuma replied again.

"Henceforth, may the men of Golaland and the men of Kpelle-land be brothers-in-law."

"Let it be so."

Overwhelmed with joy and surprise, Chief Kortuma walked down from the porch and embraced the new Gola Chief. He thought he heard voices singing in the distance. In a moment, he saw a group of women singing gei, dancing, coming towards his house. Two of them carried an open, white country cloth sheet with blood smears all over it; Lorpu danced heartily before them. The crowd watched the approaching women curiously, and when they saw the white sheet, they understood what had happened: the crucial phase of the marriage ceremony was over, and Paa had proved to be a virgin. The marriage was now a success.

Chief Kortuma ran to his bedroom and returned with coins, looking very happy. He silenced the crowd and said:

"Thank you, my people. Thank you. Where's Lorpu?" Lorpu walked up to him, still shaking her body. "All the thanks really belong to you," he told her. "I know that everyone will heap praises, thanks, and gifts on me — but this would have never happened were you not a devoted mother for Paa. Girls are so difficult to rear — so I thank you for bringing up Paa to be a woman, and you have taken her to her husband's room and come back with a bloody bedsheet . . . let this be my white heart."

Lorpu received several white coins from the Chief with thanks and gave them to the women who held the bedsheet.

"Today is a very special day in my life," the Chief addressed the crowd, gesturing vigorously with his hands. "Chief Gbanja and all the people from Golaland, Elders of Haindi, and everyone present, I wish to extend hearty welcome to the new Chief of the Gola and his people to my village. Chief Gbanja, your speech was most overwhelming. The brave and positive step which you have taken to bring our peoples together is very timely and most important. And what is more is that you never bothered to bring your own players, but rather Gbande players. This shows that you consider all peoples to be the same. I am convinced that our predecessors fought one another because they did not know this. I myself blindly followed their bad example. But the fact that people are the same means that the welfare of one people depends on the welfare of all peoples. Progress for one people can come about, therefore, only as all tribes learn to live together in peace. Thus I can say with utmost conviction that this is the real beginning of my reign as Chief of my people, for it is today that I have become a man.

"The Chief is a source of inspiration and peace for his people. In order to serve in this capacity, he must forget about his own security and well-being. He should not be easily provoked and should go to war only as a last resort. He must make every effort to see all situations as they are and not as he wants them to be. Many of our troubles are a result of trying to make things work by force, and what you accomplish by force is never enduring. I have learned from you today, Chief Gbanja, that love is a powerful weapon which can be used to solve problems and conflicts. But we often rely on the use of force and power as the only solution to our troubles when all that is needed is love. If our gods or Ancestors turn deaf ears to us, or if many of our aims and goals are not accomplished, it is often due to our own impatience or desire to have our own way in everything . . .

"Today, I can say in earnest, Chief Gbanja, that you have conquered Kpelleland. It is useless for me to stand here and now and try to say all that your action has evoked in my heart. You have proved to be a great leader and a mighty conqueror. I am profoundly happy that all our conflicts have ended in a moonlight. May the future of our two lands be bright."

"Let it be so," Chief Gbanja replied, alone.

"May we live together as one people."

"Let it be so."

Chief Kortuma embraced Chief Gbanja once again and the

playing resumed. The two Chiefs sat on the porch and watched the rousing crowd. Chief Kortuma's headwife led her new sonang, the sala wife, to her house as the crowd sang and danced away. Landa, who seemed to have an unlimited store of energy, danced and spun around, leading the crowd about the village in the pale silvery moonlight. Now he sang like a pepper bird, now like a leopard bird; now he crowed like a rooster and his crowing would lapse into the song of the palm bird. Now he sang a nostalgic song in a loud voice to which the crowd would respond heartily; now he stood on one spot, dropped his head to the midriff and swung around, blowing the crowd with dust. Frequently he ran back to the porch and saluted the Chiefs, telling them his many, incredible stories of adventure.

"You did well to bring Landa here," Chief Kortuma told Chief Gbanja, tapping the earth floor with both feet and twitching in the creaking rattan chair.

"Oh well," Chief Gbanja said, sitting erect and clasping his hands on his lap. "As you know, the Gbande people are good players. I knew they'd win the day."

"I love Landa," Chief Kortuma remarked. "He's the best masked dancer I know. He doesn't look as threatening as many others, and he sings well."

"Landa can be merciless at times. He carries you away with his weird fancies. I remember a woman falling down in tears after she threw all her kola nuts and coins at Landa in appreciation for his sweet song. 'If she enjoys Landa's song, why should she cry?' I asked. I was a young man then. The strange thing was that Landa was singing an ordinary song which the maidens sing when a young boy joins the Poro. Now I know that Landa got her because his songs touch the heart."

"Landa sings well . . . I definitely resolved against taking another wife . . ."

"I know," Chief Gbanja interrupted. "News travel in the jungle like fire in dry thatched roofs. I heard that you even turned down Chief Gbolokai's widows. That struck me as strange. I knew that you wouldn't turn down a sala wife. Every Chief needs one. And you don't have any. That's why I brought you one. You'd better start looking for a travelling wife."

Chief Kortuma laughed. "I guess you're right," he said, growing serious. "But I'll first let the sala wife get adjusted to her new home before taking another wife."

"I said to myself, 'Kortuma cannot afford to refuse a sala wife.' "

"You brought her at a time and in a way I could not refuse . . . I've always tried to secure myself and my people. Now the sala wife will always remind me that we are secure. You know, I even neglected my own wives to the extent that my headwife fell in love with another man. Thinking, worrying all the time. And doing nothing. But all that is over now. We grow wiser as we grow older."

"I don't understand that. A headwife acting like that!"

"She's still young, as you can see, and she wants another child . . . I realised my own fault even though it doesn't give her an excuse to do what she did. I'll start all over again. I've forgiven her; forgotten all her wrongdoings. We'll live together as if nothing has happened."

"You can trust the sala wife. She comes from a good family. Furthermore, a sala wife, as you know, is taboo to other men."

The moonlight faded gradually while the thundering clamour of drums and voices increased in volume. The crowd continued to drift about the village.

"Haindi has never been this crowded before," Chief Kortuma said.

The Chiefs sat all night on the porch without taking a sip of rum to fight the cold night air. Yet they did not shiver with cold or think of going to bed. In the morning, they were fresh and lively as if they had had a good night's sleep. Chief Kortuma slaughtered a lamb to make a modest feast for his guests. His wives decided to do the cooking in his own house. While they were cooking, he took Chief Gbanja for a walk on the river bank, where they spent many hours, conversing. Chief Kortuma felt greatly relieved to spend some time away from the crowd. Towards noon, they returned to the porch, where they met the Gola Elders who accompanied Chief Gbanja. Chief Gbanja introduced them:

"This is Sei," he pointed to a lean man with a scraggy neck. Sei smiled and shook hands with Chief Kortuma. "This is Old Man Zopon," Chief Gbanja continued. Zopon had a bald head encircled with a ring of white hair. He shook Chief Kortuma's hand. "This is Amah, and this is Jamele." Amah and Jamele looked alike as if they were brothers. They looked boyish though a few wrinkles were on their faces. Chief Kortuma shook their hands.

"Welcome to Haindi," he told the Elders. "This is your home. I hope you'll enjoy your stay here."

Korlu brought rattan chairs for the Chiefs. They sat down and conversed with the Elders, watching the players in the square.

The cooking was almost over and the women rummaged about the central room in search of pans and bowls to dish out the food. The sala wife, a bucket of water balanced on her head, climbed up the dirt stairs and entered the house. For the first time Chief Kortuma saw her closely, and her beauty enthralled him. He watched every step of hers until she entered the house.

Her beauty was not the sort that aroused erotic emotion. She was dressed as if she had just graduated from the Sande. A girl of medium height, she was firmly built, pliable, and young. Her skin was dark and shiny. She had round hips neatly fitted into a country cloth bombor and her head was covered with a large tuft of black hair. Her big breasts shook slightly as she walked. There was a charm in her round face with small eyes almost concealed beneath bushy eyebrows. Her lips were thick and dark. Kortuma debated in his mind about the time he would initiate her into womanhood. But she looked so gentle, delicate, and strikingly beautiful that to tamper with her would amount to throwing stones at a mirror.

Soon the food was ready. The Chiefs and the Gola Elders ate the lamb dinner heartily.

In the afternoon, Chief Gbanja thanked Landa and his train of players for their excellent performance. He gave them coins and kola nuts and bade them goodbye, wishing them a safe journey back home. Then he and his Elders thanked Chief Kortuma for his friendship and hospitality and also bade him goodbye. Chief Kortuma walked with them part of the way to their home. When they passed Gargbelei, a village that was about a mile away from Haindi, the two Chiefs shook hands in a farewell gesture, watching each other's faces.

Chief Kortuma pressed Chief Gbanja's calloused hand gently, thinking that the events of the day had been too good to be true. Gbanja's hand was strong and warm. Chief Kortuma felt it send a delightful tremor through his body. He pressed it with all his might like a drowning man desperately gripping a floating log. Then the pressure of his grip diminished, but Chief Gbanja held onto his hand fondly, and seemed not to wish to let go. He allowed Gbanja's firm grip to penetrate to his bones. All of a sudden, they released each other's hands, bade each other farewell and departed.

As he walked back to Haindi, Chief Kortuma imagined the beautiful sala wife: her engrossing youth and charms. He resolved to find a wife for Chief Gbanja, too; not now but later, much later. Perhaps next New Year's Day. He would surprise him with the ideal Kpelle beauty, a girl whose body was well proportioned and very black like that of a well-carved goddess; a beauty that would radiate joy, peace and benediction.